C0026 01133

D1178947

SPECIAL MESSAGE TO READERS

This book is published under the auspices of

THE ULVERSCROFT FOUNDATION

(registered charity No. 264873 UK)

Established in 1972 to provide funds for research, diagnosis and treatment of eye diseases. Examples of contributions made are: —

A new Children's Assessment Unit at Moorfield's Hospital, London.

•

Twin operating theatres at the Western Ophthalmic Hospital, London.

•

A Chair of Ophthalmology at the University of Leicester.

•

The establishment of a Royal Australian College of Ophthalmologists "Fellowship".

You can help further the work of the Foundation by making a donation or leaving a legacy. Every contribution, no matter how small, is received with gratitude. Please write for details to:

THE ULVERSCROFT FOUNDATION,
The Green, Bradgate Road, Anstey,
Leicester LE7 7FU, England.
Telephone: (0116) 236 4325

In Australia write to:
THE ULVERSCROFT FOUNDATION,
c/o The Royal Australian College of
Ophthalmologists,
27, Commonwealth Street, Sydney,
N.S.W. 2010.

Fay Weldon was born in England and raised in New Zealand. Her work is translated into most world languages. She lives in London.

BIG WOMEN

This is the story of women when they were wimmin: of that blossoming in seventies England of hope, freedom, equality, and sisterhood. It is a feisty portrait of four women's attempts and failures to create a new life. There's the feminist publishing house, founded one balmy evening at sedate No. 103 Chalcot Crescent in a flurry of argument, peace-making and naked dancing. There's Layla: noisy, darlingish, high-profile. And Alice, the academic, the philosopher, the — eventually — Glastonbury witch. And boring, sensible Nancy, the only one with any business nous. And Stephanie — the one who leaves her husband and children to embrace politics, men, other women . . .

Books by Fay Weldon
Published by The House of Ulverscroft:

THE HEARTS AND LIVES OF MEN
WORST FEARS

FAY WELDON

◆

BIG WOMEN

Complete and Unabridged

CHARNWOOD
Leicester

First published in Great Britain in 1997 by
Flamingo
London

First Charnwood Edition
published 1998
by arrangement with
HarperCollins Publishers Limited
London

The right of Fay Weldon to be identified
as the author of this work has been asserted
by her in accordance with the
Copyright, Designs and Patents Act, 1988

Cover Artist: Max Schindler

Copyright © 1997 by Fay Weldon
All rights reserved

British Library CIP Data

Weldon, Fay
Big women.—Large print ed.—
Charnwood library series
1. Feminism—Fiction
2. Publishers and publishing—Fiction
3. Large type books
I. Title
823.9′14 [F]

ISBN 0–7089–9036–3

Published by
F. A. Thorpe (Publishing) Ltd.
Anstey, Leicestershire
Set by Words & Graphics Ltd.
Anstey, Leicestershire
Printed and bound in Great Britain by
T. J. International Ltd., Padstow, Cornwall

This book is printed on acid-free paper

The world envied them, derided them, adored, loathed and pitied them by turns — these women who were larger than life. Layla, Stephanie, Alice, Nancy and company — a small, vivid group of wild livers, free-thinkers, lusters after life, sex and experience, who in the last decades of the century turned the world inside out and upside down. Unable to change themselves, they turned their attention to society, and set about changing that, for good or bad.

If in achieving so much they all but destroyed themselves, who should be surprised? Being flawed, they were the stuff of tragedy as well as triumph. They walked amongst ordinary mortals like goddesses down from Mount Olympus, without so much as deigning to notice their own difference.
'Who, me?' they'd enquire, handed doctorate or writ.
'Little me?'

Others described them as feminists, but they were never quite in step; too far in front to notice what the rest were doing. Layla, Stephie, Alice, Nancy and company. Big Women, not Little Women, that was the point: and Medusa, their creation. Medusa the Gorgon, the one who turned men's hearts to stone.

GLASGOW CITY'S LIBRARIES & ARCHIVES

LIBRARY WLLr		PRICE £17·99
DATE RECEIVED	− 3 APR 2001	
CLASS 1	CLASS 2	SUPPLIER ULVERS,
STOCK		

Part One

Part One

Will You, Won't You?

Slap, slap, slurp: a hollow, juicy sound. Stephanie's pasting up posters on the dark green wall of a Victorian urinal. The year's 1971. This urinal still stands there at the bottom of Carnaby Street, alongside Liberty's of London. See it now, as then. Stephanie is clearly not an expert at what's called posting bills. Paste dribbles down all over the place: they go up crooked, they overlap. But up they go. The legend *Bill Posters Will Be Prosecuted* gets obscured, as another poster slips and slides. 'Poor Bill Posters,' says Layla.

Stephanie doesn't get the joke. This is her life problem. Her life asset is her beauty. In 1971 she is twenty-five; she has perfect features, a lanky body, abundant blonde straight hair, and rather large hands and feet. Layla is twenty-six, shorter, plumper, funnier; she has curly dark hair. One side of Layla's face does not line up with the other, so she is called sexy and attractive, but seldom beautiful. Layla does not regard this as a life problem. She has too much to think about.

The posters declare over and over, *A Woman Needs a Man like a Fish Needs a Bicycle*. People stare a moment and pass on. The message makes no sense. Obviously women need men.

3

Everyone needs men. Masculinity is all. Armies need men, and government and business and technology and high finance. And teaching and medicine and adventuring and fashion. And all the serious arts. Offices, except for the typing pool, which is female, need men. It's homes which need women, except for the lawn which is male. Women are for sex, motherhood and domesticity. Men are for status and action. Outside the home is high status, inside the home is low status. In popular myth men make decisions, women try on hats. The world is all id and precious little anima. Layla and Stephie, friends, mean to change all this. *A Woman Needs a Man like a Fish Needs a Bicycle.* Ho, ho, ho. Everyone knows women compete for male attention; isn't this how the problem of female bitchery arises? Catty? Felines are nothing compared with women. Perhaps this puzzle poster is advertising something?

A couple of tourists, Brian and Nancy from New Zealand, emerge from the crowds in Carnaby Street. They have been rendered punch-drunk by colour, fabric, and the smell of patchouli. These are still flower-power and drug days. See feather boas, silk caftans, crushed velvet hats; lots of mauve, flares, miniskirts, platform heels; good-looking guys with lots of hair, girls with doll faces drifting behind them; wide eyes, fake lashes, white faces. Brian and Nancy both wear white Aertex shirts and tennis shoes for ease and comfort. Both are in culture shock. They flew in today from Wellington. (It took thirty-six hours.) They are accustomed to mountains, plains and sheep farms. Brian is gloriously handsome and golden. Nancy is pleasing enough to look at, but lacks eroticism: she's tall, long-limbed, and manages to appear gawky rather than slender.

Brian is reading a newspaper headline. *Oz Trial Verdict — the Bear's Obscene*. He has taken the paper from its stand but seems to have no intention of paying for it. The man who owns the kiosk lifts eyes to heaven. He is a relic of the old days. He has no nose. Leprosy ate it away. People avert their eyes but buy more papers.
'Total filth,' says Brian.

5

Nancy is staring at the poster, trying to make out its meaning. She senses that there is something mysterious and powerful here. Layla and Stephanie have finished with their bill-posting and now advance towards Brian and Nancy. Layla has a plank tucked under her arm. Nancy nudges Brian.

'Is something the matter, Nancy?' asks Brian, who has a man's dislike of subtle hints.

'Shouldn't we get on to the Youth Hostel?' asks Nancy. 'They fill up early.' She tries to draw him to one side but he resists.

'Stop nagging,' he says.

'Sorry,' she says. Women would say this to men automatically, far more frequently then than they do now.

'Sex life of Rupert Bear,' he says. 'Getting school kids involved. Disgusting. And this Neville fellow is an antipodean. But this thing is worldwide, I reckon. A worldwide epidemic of permissiveness.' He likes the sound of this. He repeats it.

'Could we pass?' asks Layla, politely, since Brian and his unbought newspaper bar their way. The noseless man smiles thinly under hideous nostrils.

'Ladies say please,' says Brian. At which Layla simply turns and swipes him to one side with the end of the plank, turns back, and she and Stephanie move on. Brian, knocked against the wall momentarily, recovers quickly.

'Aggressive bitches,' he says.

'You were in their way, Brian,' remarks Nancy,

6

which makes Brian wonder exactly whose side she's on.

'They must be feminists,' he observes.

'How can you be sure?' she asks.

'They don't even walk like proper women,' he says.

And it's true. All around Brian and Nancy doe-eyed and adoring women drift along in the shadow of men, stumbling on platforms, trit-trotting in stiletto heels. Layla and Stephanie stride; they wear jeans and T-shirts. Their equivalents today would be muscular and well exercised. Layla and Stephanie, for all their health, strength and energy, are soft-limbed, smooth-shouldered. Men have muscles: women have defencelessness as their weapon. No wonder this world is so erotic, super-charged: composed of polarities as it is. He, she. Hard, soft. Think, feel. Yin, yang. Nancy stares down at her laced canvas sandshoes, with their flat heels which seem to sink you into soil, and is suddenly dissatisfied with all things practical and sensible. Brian shoves the newspaper, badly folded, back into the kiosk rack. The newspaper seller snarls, all red gum and broken teeth and no nose. Brian does not even notice. But on the way past, he too stops and stares at the posters.

'I don't understand that,' he says. 'Is it some kind of stupid ad for something?'

'I think it means women could exist without men,' says Nancy.

'But why would they want to?' asks Brian. He's genuinely puzzled. There will always be women waiting for Brian, with his powerful shoulders, bronzed skin and blue eyes gazing out at the white-topped, non-existent mountains. It is hard for any of us to get beyond our sample of one; namely, ourself.

Stephanie drives her little Mini home. Layla goes too. There is to be a consciousness-raising meeting at Stephanie's house at No. 103 Chalcot Crescent. The drive takes only ten minutes. Traffic flow is half what it is now, and there are lots of parking places, even down the pretty, narrow, Georgian street which curves between Regent's Park Road and Chalcot Square. In those days you could get a house in Chalcot Square for £30,000. Today, expect three-quarters of a million. So it goes. Everyone has a property story. Look right from the porched windows of No. 103 and see the green of Primrose Hill, look left to the double-fronted green and white curved house at the end of the Crescent, which was once a brothel. Ancient taxi drivers would report that years ago, in his youth, a royal scion would be wheeled by giggling girls up and down the Crescent in a pram, dressed in baby clothes. Whatever changed, except the status of certain roads in certain areas? Primrose Hill, now so salubrious, used to be known as the Coalblow, so much soot drifted over from the King's Cross marshalling yards; here was the highest bronchitis rate in the entire Western world. Not that a man in a pram would suffer much, in the time it took to get to the end of the street and back. It would be worse for the girls who lived and worked there, but they were two a penny, then as now.

At this time the Crescent was a home for artists and Bohemians: the academics were moving in: soon it would be the bankers' turn. Stephanie's husband Hamish lived in the Crescent and owned an antique shop around the corner in Regent's Park Road. He was an artist by talent and temperament, but made an allied living buying and selling the artefacts of the past. In those days few could tell a Victorian handsaw from an Edwardian fire-tong, oak from pine, or Roman glass from Woolworth's. Now everyone knows.

As Layla and Stephanie unpacked the Mini they saw Zoe approach, pushing little Saffron in a buggy. She was crying: Zoe, that is to say, not Saffron. Zoe had a degree in sociology, and staying at home to look after her child depressed her. She found the company of children boring and her husband difficult. He was an engineer and talked mostly of bridges, and occasionally slapped Zoe, which was not the sin it nowadays is. And which she could have prevented had she really tried, but she enjoyed occupying the moral high ground.
'Zoe,' asked Stephanie, 'what's the matter?'
'Bull wouldn't baby-sit,' said Zoe. 'I had to bring Saffron along. I hope you don't mind. You can't blame Bull, I suppose.'
Zoe's husband's name was Bullivant Meadows.
'Can't you?' asked Layla. 'Why not?' She had

10

the plank tucked under her arm again. Zoe stopped crying and looked at it warily.

'It seems a bit much,' said Zoe, 'excluding men from a meeting and then expecting them to baby-sit.'

'I don't see why,' said Layla. 'Men have babies too. And what is playing squash but a club from which women are excluded?' Bullivant played squash for his county.

Zoe looked baffled and Stephie observed, 'One day we will live in a world in which men aren't called Bull.' And they all went inside.

Now, inside there was all the generosity, jumble, untidiness, and the over-regard for the past and lack of regard for the future which typified those years. While only too anxious to do away with the social and domestic restraints of the present, everyone's ambition was to retrieve the junk of the past and live with it. Dusty old kelim carpets covered the floors; old oak chairs collapsed under you, too worm-eaten to function; cracked glass paintings covered the walls; ships in bottles and matchstick palaces collected dust on every available shelf. Newness in objects had no value: only what was old and craftsman-made was accorded respect. In this ambience Hamish, buying cheap from little old ladies and selling dear to young professionals, made a good enough living. It was Stephanie's misfortune to be earning her living in an advertising agency, which of all new trades was the newest, and the most ungentlemanly, being so concerned with commercial success. Hamish found Stephanie's job difficult to accept. He came from Glasgow where his mother worked in a betting shop, and should, as his wife observed, have been accustomed enough to women working, and to frivolous and anti-social ends at that: nevertheless, he was troubled. He had hoped for finer more artistic things. And as their two little boys, Roland and Rafe, played with their Victorian toys upon the dirty floor, who was there ever at hand to take out the wooden splinters which so frequently pierced their poor little fingers? Only the au pair girl, whose face and accent kept changing, and whose nature and skill with a needle was unpredictable, and who had left last week, anyway.

Hamish, who is in his mid-thirties, muscular, glowing from within with a tawny, sexy flame, black Zapata moustache as was the fashion of the day, hiding an over-sensitive — or was it cruel — upper lip, stands in the conservatory beating a refectory table with a length of chain. Bang, bang, crash, tinkle, over and over again. Zoe comes to see what's happening, dragging Saffron behind her in the pushchair. Saffron, disconcerted by the sight and sound of a man beating up furniture, sets up a wail.

'All Saffron ever does is bawl,' complains Zoe to Hamish, by way of conversation. 'She's so ungrateful. I'm doing this for her future not mine. She doesn't realise the risk I'm taking. Supposing Bull throws me out?'
'Bull, Bull, Bull,' says Hamish. Zoe comes round quite a lot, to talk about Bull and eye Hamish up. All women eye Hamish up. They seem unable to help it, and he doesn't even particularly encourage it. Hamish goes on banging.

Zoe goes on into the room where the meeting is to be held. It overlooks the street.

Stephanie and Layla put their pots of paint and paste and left-over posters with the other junk under the stairs. In this recess also find a Venetian glass goblet with a broken stem, an Etruscan vase in two pieces, half a Roman head with the nose eaten away, and other treasures. Two small dark boys with narrow faces and almond eyes sit impassively on the stairs and watch the grown-ups; Rafe and Roland. Both suck their thumbs and wear pyjamas.

'Go to bed, boys,' says Stephanie. They rise obediently and go.

'Are they frightened of you?' asks Layla.

'No,' says Stephanie. 'They just want a quiet life. They will do anything to avoid a conversation with me, even obey me.'

Layla's turn to go in and stare at Hamish. Bang, bang, bang.

'What the fuck are you doing, Hamish?'

He doesn't deign to reply. Stephie follows after to offer an explanation.

'He's giving it a bit of age. Antiquing it up. It's made from new wood, but in an hour you'd never know it. Old tables fetch more than new.'

'I'm surprised your principles allow you to tolerate this,' says Layla.

'Morality is a relative when it comes to antiques,' says Stephanie.

'A man has to make a living somehow,' says Hamish, banging away.

'He's not in a good mood,' says Stephanie. 'I got promotion at work today. Now I earn more than he does.'

14

'Women earning more than men upsets the natural order of things,' says Hamish. 'Anyone can make money in advertising.'

'You only make money in advertising or anywhere if you're shit hot, Hamish,' says Layla. And she enquired as to how the kids ever got to sleep in this house: she was sure she never could.

'God knows,' said Hamish, but he gave up banging with his chain and offered the two women the glimmer of a smile. He was not without politeness. He even enquired as to how the bill-posting had gone.

'We'd have got more up,' said Stephanie, 'but we had to get back for the meeting. For all I knew you'd refuse to open the front door. Men do that kind of thing.'

Hamish said he'd left the door on the latch so women could just walk in if they felt like it and he wouldn't have to stop work. *Open house for women* presumably meant just that. The point was to raise women's consciousness, forget what kind of woman, which was never specified. Delinquent or criminally insane notwithstanding, a woman was a woman was a woman, by inference. So welcome all comers: what need of locks. Hamish did not, incidentally, think that the slogan *A Woman Needs a Man like a Fish Needs a Bicycle* was particularly effective. It was obscure and surely Stephanie with her training in advertising understood the folly of the opaque.

'Besides,' added Hamish, 'people have more

15

to worry about than the oppression of the female.'

'Like what?' asked Layla.

'Paying their rent,' said Hamish. 'Saving for their funeral, their teeth falling out. Exploitation by the bosses. Hunger, penury, disease, and so forth.'

'Show me a man having a bad time,' said Layla, 'and I'll show you a woman having a worse one. I quote our mentor, Alice.'

Layla was nothing if not honourable when it came to quoting her sources. Layla had been brought up in Rhodesia. She'd run away to London when she was nineteen and gone to Cambridge for a year before being sent down for lack of application to her studies. She owned a vast house in Cheyne Walk which she filled with friends and lodgers. It was unmodernised and she complained of the cost. Layla worked in a publishing house, not because she needed the money but because, she explained, she liked to have objectives. She had to be nailed to the ground by other people's expectations or else she'd simply fly off the face of the earth. She said what she thought, and did as she felt, a privilege granted only to those who inherit money, and who care more what they think of other people than what other people think of them.

Hamish remarked that Alice had an elegant turn of phrase, and as a token of his appreciation he would bring the meeting coffee at half-time, and how many were expected?

16

'Five,' said Stephanie.
'It is not multitudes,' said Hamish.
'It is a beginning,' said Stephanie.
Hamish began hammering again. He was courteous to his wife but estranged from her. Their eyes looked past one another. They were not easy in each other's company. But neither spoke of it to the other: 'talking it out' was a concept not yet invented. Marriages were conducted in silence.

Two women now knocked upon the door, and, finding it open, simply pushed and came into the house.
'Like a public meeting hall,' said Hamish, with distaste, though who but he had left the door unlocked?

Daffy and Alice were the names of the newcomers. Daffy was in her late twenties. She wore a boiler suit and big boots, but the disguise merely accentuated her ravishing prettiness, the slender line from shoulder to buttock, the swell of the breasts, the slimness of ankle. Whatever she wore it was the same: she scarcely noticed any more. Alice was tiny, round-faced, dark-eyed, serious; only her eyes moved rapidly: the rest was slow: she had the gift of stillness. Alice was all mind and very little matter: she was an academic: asexual, as if too much thought had sucked her body dry.

Layla, Stephie, Daffy, Alice and Zoe. Five furies in the front room, sitting in a semicircle.

17

'Dorothy couldn't come,' said Stephanie. 'She had to cook the children's tea. And Maureen decided against it. She doesn't want to upset her father.'

'The man's lament,' said Layla. 'Where are you going, my darling? Stay home with me, wife, mother, daughter, whoever you be. Female to my male. Surely you love me? Don't I cherish you, protect your virtue, provide the roof over your head, keep your false friends and your mother at bay? Stay home, woman, as your love for me surely dictates. Warm my bed, perfect my table, iron my shirts.'

'Do you find that tempting?' asked Stephanie, for something melancholy in Layla's voice suggested that she did.

'Of course. I'm a weak sister. Aren't we all?'

'No,' said Stephie, and her accusing eyes drifted over to where Daffy sat, and her expression said, 'Weak, weak, weak.' And Daffy smirked.

Layla said, 'Since this is our third meeting could we all try to be honest with one another? Say what we really think and feel? Men have made us meek little creatures: it's to their advantage. But we weren't born like that.'

'There'll be trouble,' said Stephanie.

'Good,' said Layla.

18

At the same time as Daffy smirked in Primrose
Hill, so did a young reception clerk in the Youth
Hostel behind Tottenham Court Road. He
smirked because he saw that Brian, the simple
antipodean, was taken aback to discover that the
Youth Hostel no longer ruthlessly separated men
from women for their overnight stay. Brian and
Nancy would share a dormitory. What they did
or did not do in their bunks was no concern of
management. He smirked because he had what
nowadays would be called an 'attitude'. He was
tired of dealing with tourists: of working while
they had a good time: he was glad when they
were disconcerted.
'It's OK,' he said. 'We're half-empty. You'll be
on your own.' Nancy and Brian lugged their
iron-framed, canvas rucksacks up the stairs.
Then the old and rich travelled easily, with
porters attending every step of the way. The
young and poor had a heavier time of it. Now
at least their rucksacks are lighter, being made
of steel and nylon, and oppress them less.
'I told you there was no need to rush,' said
Brian.
'Half-empty', said Nancy, 'is the same as
half-full. We're here nice and early.'

Little events shake the world. If Brian hadn't
chosen to read a newspaper without paying

19

for it, if Nancy hadn't seen a poster saying *A Woman Needs a Man like a Fish Needs a Bicycle*, if the Youth Hostel had been full, and so on, and so forth. But more of this later.

In the front room of the narrow house in Primrose Hill, Layla, Stephie, Daffy and Zoe were grouped round Alice, who sat like the High Priestess in a high-back chair, straight, formal and composed. She spoke coolly and with conviction. Little Saffron drowsed, still strapped into her pushchair, in the space between her mother and the oracle.

'The Socialists claim', said Alice, 'that if you improve the condition of the working man, remove the injustices of capitalism, the 'women's problem' will automatically be resolved. To improve the lot of women first improve the lot of men. But do we anticipate that men will allow this to happen? We do not. Where did our association with the Marxists and the Trotskyists leave us, we the women who wanted to join with them to change the world? Where were we when the barricades in Paris fell?'

'Making the coffee,' said Stephanie.

'Addressing the envelopes,' said Zoe.

'Filling their beds,' said Layla.

'And when the State has withered away,' said Alice, 'when the rights of the workers are finally established, what's the betting that's where we still will be? Women cannot depend upon men to save them. We must depend upon ourselves. We must speak out with loud clear voices.'

At which Daffy stood up. Her skin was luminous: pale and fair. Her lips were full and so deeply pink it seemed she had lipstick on, but of course she hadn't.

'But if I stand up in a room full of men and speak, my voice goes high and squeaky. Like this,' she said, demonstrating.

'High and squeaky. I feel stupid and they all look at me.'

'I think Alice may have been speaking metaphorically,' said Stephanie.

Stephanie came from a Jewish family of high achievers. Her father ran a chain of toy-shops but had over-expanded too suddenly and lost his money. He and Stephanie's mother, who had been in politics and had helped engineer the National Health Service, had retreated to Ibiza where they lived in passionate love, above a friend's clothes shop. Stephanie was left to make her own life in London. She had met Layla at Cambridge in the days of her parents wealth, and even then had felt orphaned, as is ever the fate, as Tolstoy pointed out, of the children of lovers.

'What's metaphorically?' asked Daffy, whose mother worked part-time in a betting shop, and whose father was a railway engineer.

'Daffy,' said Stephie, 'you're such a fool it's hopeless telling you.'

'I didn't risk my marriage to come here to listen to ordinary female squabbling,' interrupted Zoe. 'I can hear that any day round the toddlers' sandpit.'

No one took any notice of Zoe. Daffy turned on Stephie.

'What right have you to call me a fool?' she asked. 'You're so pompous, Stephie. You think you own the universe. You're worse than a man. I'm tired of being patronised. And that goes for all of you. I do believe you're jealous.'

'What is there to be jealous of, you silly cow?' Layla summed up. 'Sit down everyone.'

So they did and tried again. Alice continued. 'The Marxists say that men are born free but everywhere are in chains — '

In the Youth Hostel Brian and Nancy found their way to their allocated dormitory. It was a large bleak room with a high ceiling, white walls and four bunks.

'Just think,' said Nancy, 'we can have it all to ourselves. Just you and me, Brian.'

They had been engaged for four years, and never, as the present so crudely puts it, had sex. All Brian said was — 'I wish you wouldn't wear your engagement ring so openly.'

'Why?' She was hurt. It was a diamond ring, and Brian and Brian's parents, apple-farmers, had clubbed together to buy it.

Nancy may not have had a wedding ring as most of her school friends now did — marriage in her early twenties being *de rigueur* for a girl: but at least she had an engagement ring. And all her own teeth, which was unusual for someone from New Zealand, whose soil was somehow inimical to the formation of good enamel. Nancy's mother on her seventeenth birthday was given the traditional gift to daughters from the father: a set of state-of-the-art false teeth: the originals taken out to make room for them. Nancy's mother, when asked by Nancy why she had divorced her father, would only ever reply, 'To save your teeth, my darling. Had you been a boy, I might have stayed.' Assiduously, ever

24

since, Nancy had cleaned her teeth and done her best to be ordinary and like everyone else; or, in the fashion of daughters, everyone else except her mother. But blood will out.

Had Nancy's grandfather given Nancy's mother a different present on her seventeenth birthday, had Nancy's mother given her daughter a different answer . . .

'It's not that I don't want the world to know we're engaged,' Brian said to Nancy, as he neatly unpacked his rucksack, shaking, airing and folding, using the top bunk for his purposes. 'It's just that this is so mean a city. People are quite mad. Someone crazed on drugs might steal it.'

Nancy was unpacking her things, less carefully than Brian, scrabbling for the blouse and skirt she wore in the evenings, putting them on the top bunk, planning to sleep on the bottom, within touching distance of Brian.

'If you put your stuff up there,' said Brian, 'you'll only have to move it all when we go to bed.' He assumed he'd be taking the top bunk, out of touching distance of Nancy.

Little things, little things, shake the world. Big things make the world heave and move, Titans stirring beneath the surface, turning over in their sleep.

'If man is born in chains,' says Alice in Primrose Hill that night, 'how much truer is it that every woman not financially independent finds herself chained to an individual man, husband or father, needing his goodwill for her very survival and that of her children. Conditioned by necessity to smile, to please, to wheedle and charm, to placate.'

'I try not to smile,' said Stephanie.

'She doesn't have to do much fucking trying,' whispered Daffy to Zoe.

'Even if she is financially independent within marriage,' said Alice, 'and women have always worked, in the fields, or as cleaners, servants, washerwomen, and in the factories, she is allowed no dignity for it. Her earnings are seen as pin money.'

'Wherever there's shit work to be done,' said Stephanie, 'that's where women are.'

'I don't think we should use swearwords,' said Zoe. 'It loses us credibility. Men don't like it.'

'Oh, for fuck's sake,' said Layla. 'Who cares what men like? Haven't you heard a word Alice has been saying?'

'I just want to establish', said Zoe, 'that Stephie had no right to call Daffy a fool at a consciousness-raising meeting. We are meant to be sisters.'

'It's my house,' said Stephie, feebly.

'Though sometimes,' said Zoe, 'I can't be sure whether or not I'm talking sense. Ever since I had a baby no one seems to hear me. Perhaps they're right. Perhaps motherhood has turned my brain to porridge. I have to pinch myself to remind myself I have a degree in sociology.'

Saffron had turned herself round in the pushchair in spite of all the straps and now faced her mother, not Alice. The pushchair was in danger of tipping backwards.

'My education has not equipped me for life,' said Zoe.

'Supposing I go home and Bull hits me for coming here when he specifically told me I wasn't to?'

'Then we do what a group of women did in Germany last week,' said Stephie. 'We go round to your house, heave Bull out, pull down his trousers, and march him up and down the street for all the neighbours to see, with a label round his neck saying 'wife-beater'. This is what they chanted: 'Any woman who sleeps with the same man for more than one night is a fool and a reactionary.' That is a translation. It may well have sounded better in German. But the point's the same. Women have to take responsibility for what happens to them.'

'I don't see why,' said Layla, 'when you can so easily blame men.'

'You're a mad woman, Stephie,' said Daffy, with confidence.

'Personally I'm going to go and make coffee,

since your husband has failed to bring us any.'
'You better had,' said Stephie, 'since it's all
you're fit for. Go back to the socialists, where
you met my husband. It's where you belong.'

At which Daffy slammed out and Alice
continued as if nothing had happened.
'We are on the verge of the greatest revolution
the world has ever known. The moment of
praxis approaches. Theory feeds through into
action, the stresses of oppression build up and
burst through, as burst they must . . . ' and
so on, while in the kitchen Daffy found mugs
amongst the chaos of a kitchen where food
was occasionally cooked, but often thought
about. Here were garlic presses for non-existent
garlic, saucepan lids for no longer existent pans,
a wooden butcher's block brought home by
Hamish but covered with children's painting
material, old bills, overlooked letters, postcards,
wooden spoons, a Victorian knife sharpener, a
dozen blunt and rusty knives, matches here,
cracked pottery lemon squeezers there; bread in
one place, butter in another, jam nowhere to be
found, a fridge you shuddered to look into.

Daffy found the instant coffee with no trouble,
and looking around, longed to bring order to
the chaos, cleanliness to the grime, care to the
uncared-for. Hamish came in as she knew he
would.
'I was just coming to do that,' said Hamish.
'She who earns most outside the home must be
obeyed inside the home.'

'But you can still make us wait,' observed Daffy.

'Oh, shrewd, shrewd,' said Hamish. 'Why are you wearing that ridiculous garment? I can't tell where your tits begin or your bum ends.'

'That's the reason why. To save us from lascivious looks and so we're all equal and don't compete for male favours. Why should we dress for men?'

'Perhaps I should wear a skirt,' said Hamish, 'to keep women in face.'

'That's silly.'

'No more silly than girls wearing trousers,' he said. The water boiled in the kettle. Neither switched it off, a task necessary in those days. It continued to purr steam into the room. Someone had removed the warning whistle.

'Women only want to wear trousers because it's the garb of the ruling elite, that is to say, men. Men don't want to wear skirts because that's what the servants wear.'

'Women want to wear trousers so men don't look up their skirts,' said Daffy.

'Why bother about any of it,' said Hamish, 'when a girl like you can get what she wants just by standing around.'

'I'd feel more like arguing only your wife Stephie keeps calling me a fool.'

'She only calls you a fool,' said Hamish, 'because she knows I like you.'

He undid the top of her dungaree straps. She made no move to stop him other than by leaning over to switch off the kettle, to show she did not really care, one way or the other. He undid the other strap. Underneath, her blouse, which was her little sister's, gaped open. The bare, rising, pale pink, translucent skin of her breasts could be clearly seen.

'I'm a traitor,' said Daffy.

'All women are traitors,' said Hamish. 'That's why feminism will never work.'

His hand slipped down to touch the breast, fingers stretched to find the nipple. The hand was none too clean, marked with furniture polish and rust from the iron chain. Daffy rather liked that kind of thing. Stephanie hated it: she washed frequently.

Stephanie, meanwhile, found herself not paying total attention to Alice. She wondered what was going on in the kitchen, while trying not to. Alice, in any case, was talking to Zoe, speaking to her as to a child.

'By Praxis,' said Alice, 'I mean the moment theory meets its response in everyday life: when the convergent dynamics of oppression and protest meet. Something happens.'

'I'll open some wine,' said Layla, 'since neither Hamish nor Daffy seem capable of bringing coffee.' And she went to Stephanie's cabinet, brought out four bottles of Bulgarian red, found a corkscrew on the windowsill between unkempt pot plants and opened all four. Stephanie still said not a word; her face was arranged into a careful, attentive and amiable mask.

'Praxis,' went on Alice, 'means culmination, breaking-point. Also, interestingly enough, it's a term used in Victorian pornography for orgasm, and a Victorian girl's name, though I don't suppose the parents who used it understood the double meaning: certainly not the fathers. Girls who enjoyed sex were known as nymphomaniacs, and the threat of the description still keeps many a girl out of a man's bed today.'

'I'm always being called a nymphomaniac,' said Layla, liberally pouring wine. 'And I've always taken it as flattery.'
'That's because you have your own money,' said Zoe, 'and don't have to worry about what men think of you.'

Stephanie drank a whole glass of her own bad red wine almost straight off, and then another. But she would not go into the kitchen: would not.

Hamish had Daffy's breasts uncovered, the corners of her blouse tucked under her armpits, and the top of her dungarees flapping down below her waist.

'Did you burn your bra?' asked Hamish.

'It fell to pieces in the wash,' said Daffy. 'I only have the one. I don't earn much. I can't afford another. And they support themselves well enough. I have good muscular tone.'

'Stephie's flop all over the place,' said Hamish.

'Some men like that kind of thing.'

'Comparisons are odious,' said Daffy, 'especially when it comes to women's tits. Men are always doing it, to make women feel bad. Do we women talk about your private parts? No; we are too polite: we understand your insecurities.' But she made no move to break away from his hands.

'Supposing Stephie comes in?' she asked all the same.

'All the more exciting,' said Hamish. 'I'm fed up with her. Anyway, she rations sex. She uses it as a controlling device. I doubted the wisdom of her fish and bicycle poster, so she'll have a headache for a week.'

'That's terrible,' said Daffy.

At which point Stephanie came into the kitchen. She would not, she would not, but then she did.

So go most of our resolutions. She found Daffy half-naked and Hamish's hands upon her.

'I came for some wineglasses,' said Stephanie by way of excuse, which she could not help feeling was needed.

Interrupting other's intimacies calls for immediate apology, although on reflection outrage rather than apology can be seen to be more appropriate. Pride suggests that the urge to scream and scratch should be controlled. Better for the self-esteem to imply that nothing profound or important has been lost.

'Actually, Hamish,' said Stephanie, 'this is last-straw time.'

Things had not been going too well between them. Hamish had what was called a wandering eye, though he would claim it was woman's eyes wandered to him. Mind you, according to the custom of the times there was no very great sin in turning visual delight into sexual delight. It got it out of the system.

But Stephanie took what Hamish took lightly very heavily indeed. While Hamish declared that Stephanie's 'career' — any woman with a career was still seen at best as a contradiction in terms, at worst as a description of a masculinised woman with a moustache and aggressive tendencies — was more to do with her desire to get out of the house and away from the children than any need to earn money.

In other words they were no longer 'in love' or all in all to each other, and not very happy living together, but the custom of the times also suggested that this was just the way things were; no reason on this account to leave home, break marriages, seek personal happiness by setting up another household with a different partner. The human right to veracity and authenticity in personal experience was not yet established. To be 'happy' was no one's quest, simply to get by was enough.

That the man-woman-child threesome was an innate bar to the perfectibility of family happiness was just another fact of life. People lived with angst, and saw nothing wrong with it.

When Stephanie said, 'This is the last straw, Hamish,' the world shook a little. The Georgian glasses jammed together on the dresser — any good housewife in those days knew that glasses, especially valuable old ones, should never touch: but this was Stephanie's house — trembled and clinked, and later, when the day of the dishwasher dawned, and they were subjected to yet more stress, broke almost at once. But the shaking of the house might of course have been the coincidental fall-out from an IRA bomb let off in Trafalgar Square. Who is to say? Or of course the bomb might have been the outer and visible sign of the internalised psycho-social praxis of that night's events in Primrose Hill. Synchronicity, as Jung might have observed.

Stephanie took the wineglasses and went back to the meeting, leaving her husband and her co-conspirator flesh to flesh. The objects on the dresser stopped trembling.

'Men control the means of production, capital and labour,' said Alice. 'They keep power to themselves. Thus the skill, the input, the energy of half the world's population is lost to humankind. Everywhere women are despised; seen as second-class citizens. Their inferiority is built into our language, our constitutions, our laws, our institutions. To undo the very structure of our societies is a momentous task, but it must be done, and can be done.'

'Men's greatest achievement', said Zoe, 'is war. Women's greatest? Babies. Perforce. You just lie there and pregnancy happens. Go on lying and you push it out. What sort of achievement is that?'

Little Saffron slept, soft arms drooping over the side of her pushchair, not yet called a buggy.

Layla opened another bottle of wine.

'Men have art, women have babies,' said Layla. 'That's what is said by men, if a woman takes up a brush or a pen. Ballet dancers are allowed, of course, because women have always danced before men, to entice them: and singers, because mothers sing lullabies.'

Nowadays few mothers sing to their children to lull them to sleep. Rather they read the little ones stories to develop their intellects. It's all uppers, not downers, for the growing child. When adulthood is reached, the opposite occurs. Soothe and lull, soothe and lull: more sleep less stress.

Stephie said nothing. She was pale.

'Of course great female artists exist,' said Alice. 'But they are hidden from history. They have always existed. Patriarchy denies them.'
'There's Austen and Brontë,' said Zoe, always one for an impartial truth.
'Dead,' said Layla. 'Only when women are dead do they enter the canon as honorary men. And what are those particular stories but schoolgirl fodder? Marry or starve with Austen: dive into masochism with the Brontës. Mad Mrs Rochester in the attic pays the price for sexual desire. How are you doing, Stephanie? How are Hamish and Daffy getting on with the coffee?'
'Just fine,' said Stephie. 'Just fine. Can we consider the double bind of the working wife? When I'm at home I have to pretend I don't go out to work. No tales of office life can be told. I certainly can't let on that I enjoy it. When I'm at work I have to pretend I don't have a home. No one there even knows I have children. I wouldn't get promotion if they did. Employees want your full attention, husbands want your full attention. What's a woman to do?' (Well, what changes? But that's another story.)
'What about the children?' asked Zoe primly. 'Don't they deserve your full attention? Otherwise,

why have them? I think it should be husbands first, children next, employers third.'

'Shut up, Zoe,' said Layla. 'Everyone knows you're miserable at home.'

'Life without any of them is possible,' said Alice. 'Spouseless, childless, self-employed — free.'

'But how do we compel men to let us in?' demanded Stephie. 'If I get a rise I'm accused by my colleagues of taking the bread out of the mouths of family men. I am meant to turn the offer down. If I come home and say 'goody-goody, I got a rise', my husband says I'm a castrating woman. My earning threatens his male dignity. He fears impotence. He has his revenge.'

'Well,' said Layla, 'If you didn't insist on calling him 'my husband' all the time and not 'fucking Hamish' he might be less inclined to role-play.'

'I am universalising', said Stephie, 'from my sample of one. I'm entitled.'

'Stephie's going to cry,' said Zoe. 'Where's Daffy?'

'What upsets me,' said Stephie, 'is that some women are just constitutionally incapable of sisterhood. What are we to do about that?'

Upstairs in the marital bedroom the bed began to squeak. The sound could be heard in the room below. Sexually open as all tried to be, and believed they were, embarrassment descended on those in the room below. Even Layla did not know what to say.

Meanwhile in the Youth Hostel, at the back of Tottenham Court Road, Brian asked Nancy to wash his socks.

'Better wash these now, Nancy,' he said. 'I'll need them tomorrow.'

Nancy took the socks as he peeled them off and handed them to her. They were warm, damp, too thick for the weather, and dirty white. It did not occur to her to say 'wash them yourself'. It was not customary, in those days, for women to say such things. It was a seller's market, men being a scarce commodity: men paid no piper but still called the tune.

These days the demographical tables have turned; there are more young men than young women in the world — medical care and life-friendly wars ensure their survival — and women have learned the art of the cartel. They know well enough that if they stare blankly and shake their head so will all the other women down the line. Socks get thrown away, not washed. Manufacturers ensure that washing machines lose them, or remove colours unevenly, and render them shapeless. The life expectancy of the sock falls and falls.

'OK,' said Nancy, cheerfully, years ago.

Myth had it that men were hopeless at domestic tasks. The logic was thereby sustained that men should do what they were good at — creating art, mending the car, contending with the outside world, bringing new ideas into the home, disciplining the children, earning, and so forth — and that women should do what they were good at — cooking, washing, having children, nurturing, soothing, consoling, and being flattered by male sexual attention, and so on. Step outside these roles and both were in trouble: women would be labelled shrill, aggressive, slut, nymphomaniac, and worst of all simply unfeminine: terms of opprobrium for men were in short supply. On the queer side, a bit of a pansy, was just about the best that could be done.

Anyway, here's Brian saying, 'And be sure to get all the soap out of them. If you don't they stay stiff. You know how I hate that,' and Nancy happily saying, 'I'll be careful,' as she potters off to the wash-room to do the socks in the washbasin.

She even sings 'Greensleeves' as she goes, so pleased she is to be in England's green and pleasant land, no matter how domestic tasks pursue her across the oceans.

Squeak, squeak, squeak. Layla wonders if Daffy has bothered to take her boots off, and if not, how Hamish will manage to find an entrance, because without first unlacing the boots how will he get the boiler suit off her, its legs being tapered.

Oh, happy days, when contraception first arrived, and no one thought of Aids, or other penalties of permissiveness, and sex was without ceremony and often instant. 'Why don't we do it in the street?' Why not, indeed?

Squeak, squeak, squeak. In the faces down below was puzzlement rather than shock. Something was bothering them, beyond an abuse of sisterhood, beyond the expected villainy of men. Before an earthquake air pressure falls: animals sense it, and babies, and Theseus the Hero is reputed to have had the gift of predicting the stirring of the Titans.

This evening, in this room in Primrose Hill, London, the assembled women sensed something not quite amiss, something momentous, not yet happening, but about to happen: earthquake-style. Squeak, squeak, squeak.

Alice moistened her lips with her fragile virginal pink tongue and continued.

'We must', said Alice, 'address the subject of women's low self-esteem. If a tutor hands an essay to a group of students, male and female both, and says that essay is by a woman, men down-mark it but women down-mark it more. Say it's by a man, and men up-mark it, but women up-mark it yet more. What further demonstration do we need that women can be their own worst enemy? So crushed that they collude in their own oppression, indeed, exacerbate it.'

'We need role models,' said Layla. 'Strong, proud, effective women. But where are they? Where are the women big enough in soul and nerve to win this battle, to carry this revolution through?'

'I see them here,' said Alice. 'In this room tonight.'

At that moment little Saffron woke and set up a wail. Squeal, squeal, squeal.

'Shut that child up, can't you?' said Layla.

Revolution, folk wisdom has it, costs the lives of a generation, while it settles down, only to become the established order. After the French, the Russian, the American revolution, millions died of hunger, disorder and the effects of sudden change, of too much attention to ideas and too little to the crops in the fields. Of course everyone dies anyway — and though it's more

43

soothing all round if we die at a ripe age, in our customary beds, the leaders of any revolution find the irritation a small price to pay for their principles. Why should the Women's Revolution be different? Perhaps little Saffron sensed this, which is why she woke up so suddenly, and in so bad a temper.

Over in the Youth Hostel it occurred to Nancy that it was a strange thing to do, thus to wash Brian's socks. They were not married, only engaged; he did not support her. Why was his convenience, his leisure, his rest, so much more important than hers? Was there not a great indignity in behaving as she did? What did she want Brian *for*, exactly? For the excitement and flattery when, as occasionally he did, he kissed her, some magic electricity passed from his lips to hers, and he focused on her central being, whatever that might be, and for once she had power over him. She wanted him for sex, in fact. Yet sexual fulfilment, in the interests of respectability, was what he denied her. The rinsing water finally ran clear and cold. Woollen garments should have a final rinse in cold water; then they dry softer. This is true, though hard on the hands.

In Primrose Hill the bed squeaks on; however Hamish found ingress to Daffy the results seem satisfactory. The squeaks stop for five minutes, then start again. Still Stephanie smiles on, though the others see the smile as fixed, not exactly happy.

'Women have to learn to rise above the personal,' says Alice, 'to ignore their samples of one; otherwise they fall into the trap of male expectation. We must all accept that the personal is the political.'

There is a silence while they consider this. Squeaking from above, albeit coincidentally, stops as well, thus underlining the importance of the utterance.

'The personal is the political,' repeats Layla. 'We need none of us be alone, ever again. That is amazing.'

'Alice says these things,' says Stephanie, 'and then they drift off into oblivion. It mustn't be allowed to happen. This brilliance must be recorded, printed, headlined. We need a newspaper.'

'We need a publishing house,' says Layla, 'and a successful one. The thing to do is specialise in women's classics. This way we will do

46

everything we want: we will reclaim female history, women's art, our self-esteem. We will record the ideas that shake the world. We will honour Alice. I work in publishing: it's what I know how to do. Running these places is child's play, so long as you don't have to bother with male status-seeking.'

'Let it be part newspaper, part publishing house,' said Stephanie. 'But for God's sake can't we forget about the past? Forget about art? We live in the present. We must find the women writers of today.'

'You can forget that lot,' said Layla. 'They're too busy being sensitive and pleasing men. Focus on the women writers of yesteryear. Anyone whose works are out of copyright, and you don't have to pay. A guaranteed readership — everyone reads classics — and pure profit. This is an amazing window of opportunity.'

The squeak, squeak, squeak had started again.

'What are you talking about, Layla?' demanded Stephanie. 'Window of opportunity! Profit! We're talking about feminism.'

The squeaking stopped so abruptly that everyone had to try to work out what was going on. Perhaps the lovers, and not before time, had run out of steam. Saffron slept again, soothed by the ambient feeling of relief.

'We can always talk about both,' said Layla.
'Talk all you like,' said Zoe. 'It's money you

need. Everything needs money. If I want a pair of shoes I have to ask Bull for the money, and he always says what's wrong with the ones you've got on, they don't let water, do they?'

'Money for small things is always difficult,' said Layla, 'money for projects less so. I've always found the bank manager won't lend you money for a crust of bread, but he will if you say you need a hat. I've got family money. I can call it in.'
'Well lucky old you,' said Zoe.

'So long as the funding doesn't come from men,' said Stephanie.
'Darling,' said Layla, 'I shall be careful to ask an aunt, not an uncle, if it keeps you happy. You are so fucking stuffy, Stephie. Stuffing fucky, Stephie. Here's to you, and your denial of the inconvenient!'

And she raised her glass of wine, perhaps her fifth, to Stephanie. They were on the fourth bottle. Stephie raised hers.

Upstairs coitus had resumed, but in a more languid position. Sideways in. Hamish went on complaining.

'Stephie has no time even to make the bed. I have to bring you in here to one that's unmade. The brutal fact is that she has no time for me, no time for the children. She has no heart. She holds 'let's-hate-men' meetings in my house.'
'I don't hate men,' said Daffy.
'I can tell that,' said Hamish.

'I hate living with my mother,' observed Daffy. 'It's such a horrid mean little house, and this is so lovely, or would be if it weren't a mess. You probably feel you can't bring clients home, when you want them to look at important pieces *in situ*.'
'The best I can do', said Hamish gloomily, 'is to use the place as a workshop. Why don't you leave home if you don't like it?'
'I'm only a typist,' she said. 'I can't afford to leave.'
'Then why don't you marry someone?' he asked.
'Men marry good girls,' said Daffy. 'I'm a bad girl. Everyone knows that.'
'Yes,' said Hamish, 'you certainly are.'

It became impossible to talk further, for all their developed expertise at talking and love-making at the same time; encapsulating life story, life problems within strokes, as it were. Shortage of breath in the end must triumph over even a frantic desire to communicate, apparently long denied to both of them. Thus in those heady days, the totality of the other could be assessed and judged within hours. Courtships and affairs which today take years were raced through within hours, days. And oddly, life itself seemed to go more slowly.

Rafe and Roland, those two dark, solemn, self-contained children, who seemed to both their parents like stolid cuckoos in a noisy and riotous nest — for which fact both blamed the other — sat and watched TV and ate crisps down the corridor. Salt and vinegar, nothing fancy.

Brian and Nancy lay in their matching bunks, bodies neatly and chastely arranged, in touching distance of one another. Nancy had contrived to end up in the lower bunk, in spite of Brian's instructions to the contrary. He was not yet ready for sleep, and spent the drowsy moments instructing his fiancée, as he so liked to do.

'It's called jet lag,' Brian said. 'Apparently it's to do with the body's internal clock mechanism. The body's organs have their own rhythm and take time to adapt to the time zone that the brain recognises.'
'I could have told them that,' said Nancy. 'Isn't it obvious?'
'Things have to be named,' said Brian, 'before they can be understood.'

Brian had a degree in philosophy from Canterbury University, though you would never have thought it. Five years of active non-reflection can weaken and slacken the muscles of the brain. If non-reflection goes on for too long the brain can appear to wither away altogether, except for those small sections of it devoted to practical matters, the absorption and passing on of information, and obsessive opinions. The awareness of this tendency, and the inability to do anything about it, was then, and is now, what drives graduate, stay-at-home mothers to distraction. You don't have to be a mother to suffer from it but it helps.

'You know so much, Brian,' said Nancy, out of the habit of and training in flattery. All women once used to be trained thus. Flatter the man, keep him happy, restrain your tongue, and never appear more clever than he. In those days men customarily married women younger than themselves, less well-educated, of lower social class, with a smaller income and a lesser intelligence. In the typical household it was observable to a growing child of either gender that the woman was the weaker and inferior sex, this being the fact of the matter, so far as anyone could see, and this everyone grew up to believe, and to mark accordingly such essays as turned up in research projects. Up for the men, down for the women.

Now that equals tend to marry their equals, in age, education, and earning capacity, the conviction of male superiority is less prevalent. And of course these days fatherhood, sapping will, ambition, energy, the way it must, does to men what once motherhood did to women.

'A girl has to have someone to explain things to her,' said Brian.
'I like jet lag,' said Nancy. 'It makes me feel kind of languid, kind of nice.' Sexy, she would have added, but it was not a word yet in general

use. There not being a word for it, the feeling stayed elusive, flitting.

Nancy stretched out her hand to touch Brian, where it dangled, rather like Saffron's from her pushchair, limp and soft. She stroked the back of his hand with her forefinger. 'You could move in here beside me, Brian,' she said. 'We could lock the door.'

Brian moved his hand gently away. He would have preferred to snatch it — she could tell from the tension in the muscles, but he managed not to. He was all control. She liked that. So much the better, she anticipated, when he lost it.

'People do these days,' said Nancy. 'Especially if they're engaged.'
'We'll wait for all that till after we're married,' said Brian. 'Quite a nymphomaniac you're turning out to be.'
He was joking, but only just.
'It's just everything's so kind of exciting, and abroad,' pleaded Nancy. 'I want something amazing to happen. Don't you feel it, everything buzzing out there? Colour and light and sound and change?'
'People take drugs,' said Brian, 'if that's what you mean. They get out of control.'

Nancy pushed down the blanket to expose naked breasts. 'My face may not be up to much,' she said, 'but I have beautiful breasts. My doctor

53

says I have the most perfect breasts he's ever seen. Please look.'

But he wouldn't; he merely hoped she'd change her doctor.

'Nancy,' he pointed out, 'the best way for a girl to keep a man is not to give him what he wants before marriage. And I suppose you do want to keep me?'

'Of course I do,' she said.

'Then cover yourself up,' he said, 'and go to sleep and don't tempt me.'

She covered herself up. He closed his eyes but she could tell he wasn't sleeping.

'You say 'what a man wants', ' she observed, 'but supposing the truth is he doesn't want it? What sort of marriage would it be then?'

'Marriage is about the begetting of children, not sex at every opportunity,' said Brian. 'And abstaining from sex before marriage is a sensible convention. Supposing you got pregnant?'

'For the last ten years,' said Nancy, 'there hasn't been a problem. The pill makes you fat, makes you sick, makes you die sometimes, but at least you don't get pregnant.'

'The pill's for bad girls,' said Brian, 'not good girls. Bad girls like sex. Good girls want babies. Can't you leave it alone, Nancy? A man likes to do the pursuing, not to be pursued. He's born to be the hunter, not the hunted.'

54

Nancy sat upright in bed, suddenly.
'I'm not going to marry you, Brian,' she said.

He opened his eyes.
'What did you say?'
'That's it,' said Nancy. 'I shan't repeat it. You heard well enough. I'm not going home either. I'm going to stay here, find a job, make my life here. A woman needs a man like a fish needs a bicycle.'

She lay down again.
'I'm tired now. I'll leave you in the morning.'

And she went to sleep dreaming of fish and bicycles. Brian dreamed he was on a ship, slipping further and further into cloud, waving to someone on the sunlit pier, who was Nancy.

Over in Primrose Hill, in the boy's room, the TV mouthed its way silently on. The boys had turned off the sound and climbed into their beds, still fully clothed. They sucked their thumbs, like babies, in their unwashed, unkempt, unfed sleep.

Downstairs music was playing. The night was hot. The window had been opened. Layla had taken off her T-shirt. She wore a white bra. Now she was taking off her jeans, sitting on the sofa, easing the fabric off one leg with the foot of the other.

'But the fact is,' said Zoe, 'there isn't any great female literature. All the best stuff is written by men.'
'Not if we define what's great and good,' said Layla. 'Not any more. I'm in charge round here. You're such a wet blanket, Zoe. I don't want you anywhere near our publishing house, ever.'
'I wouldn't dare join you,' said Zoe. 'I'd just like to be asked. I can feel Bull's anger. I can feel it. Male anger shakes the world.'

tors will become the oppressors. So man denies them for his own survival. Becoming romantics of female rage, he cries out rather, now. Becan hardly change his own nature.

And it certainly did if wishing made it so. Half a mile away, Bullivant, aware of his wife and child's absence, suspecting their whereabouts, left the marital home, a substantial house in then unfashionable Belsize Park. Bull was thin, tall, and personable; an angry ectomorph.

'Men use their anger as a way of controlling women,' said Alice. 'As they see us uniting, their rage seems to know no bounds, but in truth they are frightened, scared out of their wits. What we do seems to them unnatural, dangerous, powerful enough to put out the sun, stop the planets in their revolutions. Man has the race memory of Orpheus imprinted in his being, Orpheus the poet, pursued and torn to pieces by the Maenads, the mad women who in religious ecstasy hunted down and destroyed men. Orpheus looked back to see his love, to make sure that Eurydice followed him out of hell. In other words, in rescuing her, his lover, from the dark place, he tried to understand her — and thus he lost her. Not only that, the women had their revenge. Orpheus was destroyed. Women won't rest till they have victory; they want triumph. In their hearts they want not just equality but the death of man: they cry out for vengeance for past wrongs. This is what men fear. That the oppressed in turn will become the oppressor. So man fights now for his own survival. Becoming conscious of female anger, he ups the ante; now he can hardly endure his own rage.'

The music was loud: they weren't really listening; and Alice scarcely understood herself, as often happens to oracles, what she was saying. Meaning flows from the Maker through the minds and mouths of Prophet or Priestess, but has only an imperfect human vessel to work through. Listening to her own words Alice felt garish and vulgar as a seaside spiritualist, and downed some more wine.

'Maenad,' Layla was saying. 'We'll call our publishing house Maenad. Let men tremble.'
'We'll have the suffragette colours on the spine,' said Stephanie. 'Purple and green.'
'We'll have no such thing,' said Layla. 'Far too murky. You have no taste, Stephanie. Leave such things to those who have.'
'We can't possibly be called Maenad,' said Stephanie. 'It's far too threatening. We don't want to intimidate men before we even begin.'
'I don't see why not,' said Zoe.
'Because no one would take us seriously,' said Stephanie.

'Money makes everything serious,' said Layla. 'Even women. I want angry women to buy our books. You want victim women to read them. I want women to glow with confidence and be as glossy as men: you want their moans to get a hearing.'

'It is not so,' said Stephanie. 'I'm just saying I will not be involved with a publishing house called Maenad.'

'Then what?' asked Layla.

'Artemis,' said Alice. 'Let her be called Artemis. The hunter, not the hunted: Diana of the chase, cool and fair. Lucina is her other name.'

'Artemis is dull,' said Layla. 'If we can't have Maenad, I'll settle for Medusa. One look at her face and men turn to stone. You're such a fucking stuffy, Stephie.'

'And you're so foul-mouthed, Layla, and a bully,' said Stephanie.

'I hate confrontation,' said Zoe. 'And why have you taken off all your clothes?'

Stephanie, seeing Layla all but naked, was beginning to take off her own clothes. Remember it was a warm night, the music rocked, they had all been drinking and the spirit of the Muse was upon them, and the exhilaration which came with her.

'Because I'm a woman and not ashamed of it,' said Layla. 'And not afraid either. Nor should any woman be. Naked, free, unashamed. For God's sake, Zoe, take off some clothes. Let me see what you're made of. Is your nakedness meant for Bull alone, is that your problem?

59

Throw off the shackles of clothing and with it the shackles of wifedom. Alice, I need to know you have a physical existence and you're not mind alone. I have to see you before I can believe you. And let's have Saffron naked too. Don't you want her to grow up proud, free and female? Isn't it for her that we do all this? I can almost see the point of having children. Daughters, anyway.'

She alarmed them, but the music was loud, and she danced, and soon they were all naked and dancing about the room, regardless of who could see their cavortings, that is to say a little cluster of neighbours and passers-by, outside, gazing in, growing every minute, whom Bull sent flying as he strode by them and up to Hamish's front door. He too saw, and expecting no better was a little mollified to have his worst fears realised. Being right can work wonders for anyone. Outrage justified is outrage halved. Nevertheless, how he banged upon the door.

Upstairs in the bedroom Daffy and Hamish contemplated a new relationship. The lesson of the sixties was that on average one in ten of the one-night stands (or compacted relationships) so prevalent at the time would result in something that *lasted*. If only the humiliations inherent in a ninety per cent rejection rate, for this was what it amounted to, could be endured, true love would in the end be found, and claimed.

'Stephie will never forgive me,' said Daffy. 'Because what I have done is unforgivable.'

'My plan is', confessed Hamish, 'to behave so badly that Stephie will finally get the message and go. In giving her cause to hate me, I am doing her a kindness.'
'I'm not sure it works like that, Hamish,' said Daffy, 'but I admire you for trying. And I never liked her anyway.'

They stopped to listen to the music down below. The base notes seemed to travel through the very fabric of the house. Thump, thump, thump — and now an extra banging noise, Bull striking the front door again and again.

And now Alice turns up the music. In the front room they do not at first realise that Bull is at the door, though they are aware of the watchers, and careless of their existence.

'Let everyone see,' cries Layla. 'Tits, bum, teeth, in the privacy of our own home. Do we ask for an audience? No, we don't. Is prurience in our hearts? No, it is not. Is it in theirs? Yes, it is. Too bad!'

Zoe danced, but with one hand over her crotch and the other arm clasping Saffron, so her breasts didn't show. 'What are you ashamed of, Zoe?' demanded Layla.

'Nothing,' said Zoe, bravely, lying.

Bull had once casually told Zoe her breasts hung too low. For *breast* read *essay*. The man downgrades but the woman downgrades more. And the insecure man of the sixties free to talk about such things, as his forebears forbore, made a habit of publicly complaining about the form, shape and size of the bosom which bobbed along with such docility by his side. As a criticism it was unanswerable, there being no set standard of excellence, no norm, and nothing a woman could do about it anyway.

'We're going ahead with this, Stuffy Stephie,' said Layla, 'and Academic Alice. We're going ahead with Medusa.'

'We are,' said Stephanie, 'but who's in charge?'

Stephanie's bosom was generous and bounced. Layla's smaller, neater, higher. Alice had almost no breasts at all.

'All are in charge,' said Alice, as she lumbered by, little white arms stretching, curvy as a leaping salmon.

'*Hierarchical is male*,' she chanted.

'*Former structures stale*
Women are not fools
So group decision rules.'

'Supposing we make money?' Layla enquired. 'Who takes it?'

'*Sisters care, so sisters share*,' came back the answer.

'*Plough profits in, and reap the wind.*'

'What an uphill struggle this is going to be,' said Layla, but she acquiesced. 'Mount Medusa like Mount Ararat, towering above the floods of Babel.'

Layla too spoke with tongues. Saffron babbled for all of them, now wandering naked in search of her clothes. Saffron preferred to be clothed; it felt safer. There seemed to her to be at least a dozen unclothed dancing women in the room. The bang, bang, bang of male wrath was upon the door, so loud now they had to take notice. Zoe looks out of the window and shrieks.

'It's Bull, I told you so!'

'Too late!' cries Stephie.

'Too late!' cries Layla.

'The moment of Praxis,' cries Alice. 'Dance on. What happens will. The fates are here amongst us.'

And such was the nature of the dance, indeed, it seemed to be true. The muses danced gracefully in their languid threesome, the Maenads wailed, the furies shrieked.

Hamish meanwhile, an ethnic gown flung on for modesty, was at the door to let Bull in. Daffy wandered down, wrapped in a towel. Rafe and Roland, woken, dishevelled, sat on the landing to watch whatever drama was about to unfold. If sometimes they could not tell TV from real life, who could blame them?

'Where's my wife?' yelled Bull. 'Where's my child?'

'In the front room with the others, I daresay,' said Hamish.

'It's a woman's meeting. Go on in. Be my guest.'

Bull charges past Hamish and slams open the door of the front room: he is met by a waft of wine, a blast of music, overheated breath. The room, which for the first instant seemed crowded, contains his naked wife, already searching in a pile of discarded clothes for hers, and his child, Saffron, in vest and pants, pulling on her socks. She's a competent little creature. Hamish walks in and takes off the music.

'Nice dancing, Daddy?' asks Saffron, anxiously. 'Mummy, put your clothes on.'
'Disgusting dancing, darling,' says Bull.

'Sorry, Bull,' says Zoe, but she seems oddly unmoved, merely placatory. It occurs to the others she had expected him to come after her, is not sorry to be caught.
'What the fuck are you sorry for?' enquires Layla. 'What's to apologise?'
'Foul-mouthed bitch,' says Bull to Layla. 'Leave my wife alone. If you come near her again, if she speaks to you harpies ever, it's the end of our marriage. I keep the house, I keep the child, she's out on the streets.'
'That's going a bit far, Bull,' says Stephie. 'That's a little Victorian.'
'It may be Victorian,' says Bull. 'But it's the law.

65

She's a lesbian, she's an unfit mother. She has already exposed my daughter to moral danger.' He turns on Layla, fist raised.

'Don't be cross with Layla,' says Zoe, in a voice which has turned soft and wheedling, and which they haven't heard before. She has jeans and T-shirt back on by now. She strokes Bull's raised arm. He lowers it. 'It's just Layla's way. We weren't doing anything wrong. It's just so hot and we felt like dancing. We're not lesbians, honestly.'

Alice is already zipped back into her boiler suit. Layla's all but clothed again. Someone shuts the window, pulls the curtain. The crowd of watchers dissolves.

'Moment of choice, Zoe,' says Layla. 'Go with him or stay with us. Be a man's woman or join Medusa.'
'I have to go home,' says Zoe. 'Bull needs me. And Saffron starts nursery school tomorrow.'

Bull's hand holds hers, and she holds Saffron's.
'Sweet,' says Hamish.
'Yuk,' says Stephie.

'Let her go,' says Alice, 'it's fated.' But whether she's talking to the women or the husband, who's to say?
'You wouldn't have been any use to us, Zoe,' says Layla. 'No backbone, no stamina, self-absorbed, your brain's turned to porridge; go

66

your own way. Some women are incapable of sisterhood and you're one of them.'

Zoe gives a little cry of distress, but Bull is already hustling wife, child and pushchair out into the corridor. There he sees Daffy towel-wrapped on the stairs, and is mollified again, by the proof of his conviction that this is a house of disreputable and disgraceful goings-on.

'Medusa,' says Alice, to anyone who cares to listen. 'The time is ripe, the ceremony fits. But it is Artemis who is involved. Artemis who claims Zoe the fruitful as sacrifice: Persephone and Eurydice in the one form. After the sacrifice the new growth begins. I see blood upon the ground and sorrow. Artemis the hunter destroys what she brings forth.'

If you'd asked her afterwards what she'd said, she couldn't have told you. Sometimes her mouth opened and the words flowed, without any particular willing of her own. Usually such gifts are given to the simple, the garrulous, the gullible: Alice could at least render the outpourings graceful, and properly formulated, so their origins seemed to have some tenuous connection with wisdom and experience.

'Beware,' said Alice, suddenly, 'lest the wounded return to devour.'
'Shivery,' said Layla.

Out in the street Zoe kept step with the striding Bull.

'Now don't upset Saffron, Bull. She's very sensitive.'

'Naughty Mummy,' said Saffron.

Daffy retreated back to Stephie's bedroom. Hamish followed. Stephanie gave them a few moments and went on up, still unclothed.

'Remember,' called Layla after her, 'the personal is the political.'

'I will,' said Stephanie, all resolve.

In the bedroom Daffy had her boiler suit on again and was trying to lace her boots, knotting the laces where Hamish had scissored them. But once knotted, how to get the knots through the eyelets? She gave up and sprayed herself liberally and defiantly with Stephanie's big bottle of stale duty-free Chanel No. 5.

'Do you like this house?' Stephanie asked Daffy, when she'd finished with the scent.

'I do,' said Daffy. 'It's a mess, but it would clean up well.'

'Then have it,' said Stephanie. 'But the husband and the kids go with it.'

'OK,' said Daffy, after a little thought.

Hamish drew his naked wife out into the corridor, where Rafe and Roland overheard but were not seen.

'Are you out of your mind?' he demanded.

'I told you it was the last straw,' said his wife.

'But you are meant to throw me out, not leave,' he said.

69

'Too bad,' she said. 'I'm off.'

'But I'm the guilty party,' he said, 'and there are lots of witnesses.'

'I don't want anything,' she said. 'You can keep the lot: house, things, children. I want a new life.'

'You are an unnatural woman,' he said. Back then, that was a fairly ferocious insult. These days it meets with a ho-hum.

'So be it,' she said. 'Keep Daffy too, as the housemaid. Fuck her and she won't ask for payment. It will work out cheaper for you like that. As for me, I am to be reborn. Let my sisters take me.'

And she went downstairs again with a cry of 'Shall we go, Layla?' and Hamish pattered after her crying 'Is this all? Is this all the end of a marriage deserves?' with the two boys clutching at his African robe, for they could see he was all they now had in the world, until Daffy eased their clawing fingers free and soothed them. She had no children of her own but her instincts were good, if not, to date, her behaviour.

Stephie, mother naked, led Layla out into the street. All Stephanie took with her was her car-keys. Later she was to return to the house and claim a few documents — passport, driving licence, that kind of thing — but otherwise she kept to her resolution. Nothing from her past, nothing. Not even snapshots of herself as a child, her parents hand in hand in the Ibiza sun, her graduation ceremony, the boys as babies — nothing. To be without a past is to be free, or so she thought.

Layla got into the side door of the car. Stephie got into the driving seat, limbs gleaming under the streetlamp, in the wedge of light which poured from her front door, where Hamish stood silhouetted, and next to him, Daffy and her two children.

Stephie switched on the ignition and, peering ahead, bare boobs pressed into the steering-wheel, for she had not brought her driving glasses, they set off for Layla's house in Chelsea.

It was her finest hour, her finest gesture. The night Medusa was born.

Well now let us move on a year. Carnaby Street is still in full swing: the fashions have changed, but minimally. Many girls wear hot pants. Stretches of bare thigh between boots and mini are all the rage: the kind of thing that whores would wear, now acceptable, if still provocative. Female sexuality is the thing: passivity passé. Platform soles are the opposite of stiletto heels. Girls want to be looked at, marvelled at, but have lost interest in enticement. Carly Simon reproaches us from a dozen boutique entrances; street vendors sell mood-watches, which change colour according to your state of mind: the face is black when you're depressed, blue or green if you're cheerful.

Nancy, back in Carnaby Street again, finds she misses Brian. This astonishes her. She retreads the paths she took with him, on their one and only day in London together, if only to persuade herself she did the right thing. She wears a black skirt, a white blouse and sensible shoes, and looks like an office worker: it is her intention so to be. She has found herself a walk-up flat on the seventh floor of a gigantic house in Earl's Court. She has learned shorthand typing, made very few friends, and finally today feels herself equipped to look for a temping job. To this end she goes to a secretarial agency in Regent

Street and there encounters Marjorie Price, a neatly coiffed, pale woman in her late middle age — spinstery, as the description once went; a childless, unmarried woman, in those days an object of pity rather than envy, someone who has failed in life's task.

How fast things change; how fast things are made to change: all it takes is a handful of determined and energetic women; big women not little women.

'You must be the one who rang me,' says Marjorie. 'The one from New Zealand. A nice place, by all accounts. You should have stayed. You don't look the type to thrive in swinging London.'

'Am I dressed wrong?' asks Nancy, nervous.

'Not in my eyes,' says Marjorie Price, 'but hardly the height of fashion. You won't be looking for a receptionist's job, I take it. Back office, more like, where looks don't count.'

'I want a job with prospects,' says Nancy, overlooking the insult. 'Something that will take me up the ladder of success.' She used the phraseology current in the secretarial school where she had spent her savings. What one pays for, one values, at least temporarily.

'The ladder of success,' says Marjorie. 'That old thing. Better for a woman to stay on the bottom rungs.'

'Why do you say such a thing?' asked Nancy, startled.

'Because the truth of the matter is, if you can

look after yourself why should a man want to? Look at me.'

'I don't want to be looked after by a man,' said Nancy.

'A women's libber,' said Marjorie Price. 'I might have known. All you young girls come to me with these ideas. Ten years of the typing pool and it's another story.'

But she consents to give Nancy a shorthand and typing test to see what her speeds are. Nancy does well enough. She mentions her degree in English Literature and her accountancy qualifications, hoping to impress, but the news seems only to depress Marjorie Price the more.

'You are far too qualified for your own good,' she said. 'No employer will look at you for fear you'll take their job away, will bite the hand that feeds you. No man wants a girl cleverer than he, and quite right too. You will become sour and bitter. You will have expectations the world cannot meet. You're too picky already. A job with prospects! Too picky about jobs, too picky about men. You will end up with the habit of turning things down. You will end up like me. I had a double first in classics from Oxford; now I have nothing. No family, no children, just a card index to love, and not a word of Latin do I remember. What's a career once you're over fifty but a glorified job? I'll be frank with you. I have no time for women's libbers. They make someone like me feel I've wasted my life, following rules they now laugh at.'

'It's the married women with children flown the nest who feel that most,' said Nancy. It was hard to type her fastest and listen to what was being said.

'Eighty words a minute,' said Marjorie, 'but I'll give you ninety because I was talking. I have so few people to talk to I end up talking at strangers. What's your shorthand?'

'One fifty,' said Nancy.

'You seem like an honest girl, for all your strange ideas,' said she of the double first, forty years on. 'There's a job round the corner at Medusa Publishing. More women's libbers. They're everywhere. Terrible employers. Long hours. Low pay. They call themselves a co-operative. Nice for those who run it — hell for the employees. No one in charge, so no one to blame when you get things wrong. I don't recommend it.'

'Sounds wonderful to me,' said Nancy.

'It would,' said Marjorie Price sourly. 'What makes you think their typing pool is better than anyone else's? You swim round in the same old water, and not even a passing male to cheer you up.'

And she put the Medusa card away and fished out the one for Battersea Power Station.

'Don't let your chances slip by,' she said. 'Before you know it you'll end up like me. Now at Battersea you'll find some nice young technicians. Always go where the men go. Where there's power there's men. Where there's books

75

there's women. Not in the top jobs, of course, but doing all the work.'

Nancy said she'd have the Medusa job, thank you very much. Those were the days of full employment, when the employees picked and chose and employers were grateful for what they could get. Those were the days before it was customary for women to go out to work, to snatch the bread from the mouths of family men.

Those were the days when people used typewriters and slipped carbon between sheets of paper; and rolled them in together, trying not to smudge their fingers and everything else in sight. If a typist made a mistake she had to type the entire page again. So very few mistakes were made. Nancy left Marjorie Price, with her double first, picking the black carbon ink out of the letter 'o' with a pin kept especially for the purpose. Picking out the keys could be almost as pleasurable as squeezing blackheads.

Nancy went round the corner to a small narrow house in Wardour Street where Medusa had its offices. Wardour Street then as now was a place where US film companies run dour offices, sound studios proliferate, as do whores and their customers, pimps and their friends. At that time Medusa employed between ten and twenty people, on an ad hoc basis. Sometimes the Advisory Board, twelve strong, recruited by Stephanie and Layla, outnumbered the staff. The first revenues were beginning to come in. Some employees had a background in publishing; most made it up as they went along. The process seemed simple enough. You decided what books to print, what you wanted on the cover, found printers to print it, bookshops to stock it, newspapers to advocate it, and some method of collecting the money. One person could do all this, from first principles, but obviously as more books were published some division of labour would sensibly occur. What Medusa would try not to do was fall into hierarchical and bureaucratic mode, typical of male organisations. Men were status-seekers and empire-builders; they shuffled for power one over the other: at all-women Medusa, the ambition was to get the books out to readers, not to win applause.

That some qualities are simply human, not specific to one gender or the other, took time to learn. Put women in a situation where status is possible to achieve and power available, and they too make the most of it. But who at the time knew a thing like that?

Picture Nancy now as she sits demurely on a hard chair, while Layla sprawls behind a desk and Stephie sits upon it and dangles her legs. Such informality is new to Nancy. She is not sure if she likes it. She felt happier with Marjorie Price.

'I see the Acme Agency sent you,' observed Layla. 'It's our favourite. If you can survive Marjorie Price you can survive anything. She acts as a filter. You say on this form you saved for three years to come to London with your fiancé. Why should we be interested in your saving habits?'
'They loom large in my mind,' said Nancy. 'It just sort of slipped in.'
'Self-centred,' said Layla. 'And 'sort of' isn't a good sign.'
'Give the girl a chance,' said Stephanie.
'Girl?' enquired Layla.
'Oh, for God's sake,' said Stephanie.

'And then this fiancé, this person went home and you stayed on. Why does she want us to know she was once engaged to be married? Typical!'
'Well,' began Nancy, but Stephanie interjected. 'That's a remark, not a question. Why did he go home and you stay?'
'For personal reasons,' said Nancy, crossly. 'Why

don't you test me on my speeds?'

'We don't have a stopwatch,' said Layla. 'You have a degree in English Lit, qualifications in book-keeping — I don't understand all those initials — and secretarial skills. How boring and sensible.'

'Look,' said Nancy, 'I am a boring and sensible person. I have a tidy mind. I like things to be in order. You need me.'

'You think we're untidy in here?' asked Stephanie.

'Yes, I do,' said Nancy.

There seemed to be no clear spaces anywhere; it distressed her. Pot plants mingled with unwashed coffee mugs: letters were discarded where they were opened, papers and envelopes meant for the bin lay around on the floor: filing trays overflowed. Clearly anything problematic would sink to the bottom of files and stay there.

'I don't think you're right for us here at Medusa,' said Layla.

'But thanks for looking in.'

'Why won't I do?' asked Nancy.

'Frankly, darling,' said Layla, 'you're right. You're too fucking boring.'

Nancy stood up.

'I really don't like bad language,' she said. 'I find it most offensive.'

'It's meant to be,' observed Layla.

'It's a sign of an impoverished mind and an impoverished vocabulary,' said Nancy.

80

'That's better,' said Layla. 'We only pay twelve pounds a week. We all get the same.'

'I don't see how I'm expected to live on twelve pounds a week,' Nancy complained.

'We manage,' said Layla. 'We help one another out.'

'And if things get too bad,' said Stephanie, 'Layla pays out a bonus.'

'I hope they're tax-effective,' said Nancy. 'Bonuses can be tricky, tax-wise.'

'It's your job to make sure about boring things like that,' said Layla. 'In the meantime just remember you're the dogsbody, and it's last in first out.'

'I accept that,' said Nancy.

'You are privileged to work here at Medusa,' said Stephanie. 'I hope you're strong. You look strong. Books are a heavy trade.'

As indeed they are. Three months later see Nancy toiling up the steps of the British Museum. The muscles in the tops of her arms were well developed. Now she was broad-shouldered, as she hadn't been since her swimming days at school in Wellington. She carried a bag of books in each hand. She carried them for Alice.

Alice, like Karl Marx before her, was writing a book. She brought her own reference books into the library, which was not normally allowed, but the senior librarian, although male, accorded her this privilege. When Alice was seated in her chair beneath the dome, and Nancy had settled her in, Nancy would go back to the office and check through everyone's in-trays, to make sure nothing important had been neglected. She would empty the wastepaper baskets, wash up coffee mugs; send out invoices, check receipts, keep the card indexes up to date, do Layla's shopping, carry Alice's books, organise Stephie's divorce and access days, water pot plants, fire and hire employees, persuade bookstores to stock Medusa books, conduct market research on Charing Cross Station. She was tired. Sometimes she snapped at her colleagues.

Today, when she arrived back at the office and someone had spilt sugar into her typewriter and not bothered to clean it up, she said to Layla: 'This is absurd. I do all the work round here, and get none of the credit. I am chronically exhausted. Last night I nearly fainted in the tube on the way home. I had to sit with my head between my legs.'

'How inelegant,' said Layla. 'And how lucky you were to have a seat.'

But the next day she took Nancy to a used-car salesroom and bought her an ancient car, which chugged and sputtered around the block, and cost £120.

'Remember, it's the Medusa car,' she said, 'not yours, Nancy. But you can use it when no one else wants it, and park it outside your place. I'll deduct sixty pounds from your wages over the next year. That's very generous.'

'Oh, thanks a million, Layla,' said Nancy, with an irony which escaped Layla. 'But if I'm sixty pounds down over the year, how will I pay my rent?'

'Six pounds a week is far too much for a room,' said Layla.

'Why don't you go and be one of Alice's parents' lodgers? That's food as well for only five pounds.'

So Nancy took up lodgings in Enfield, where Alice lived with her parents Doreen and Arthur. Doreen was stout and wore an apron. Arthur was very thin and a pigeon fancier. Both were eccentric. Nancy's room was small but cosy, if not conducive to courtship. How could Nancy, so much under Doreen's nose, even bring men home, foster a relationship? Not that there was time or energy left over for such extravagances. The journey from Enfield was twice the length of the one to and from Earl's Court: but at least, as Layla pointed out, the car was not under-used. Nancy could drive Alice in to the office in the morning, dropping books off at relevant bookstores as she went.

When Nancy first presented herself to Doreen one Saturday morning, and Doreen looked her up and down and said she'd do, Nancy, feeling suddenly the lack of a mother, burst into tears. Doreen gave her cheese on toast and sweet tea, and soon Nancy felt better. Doreen took her up to the loft where Arthur sat amongst his pigeons, who strutted around the floor and eyed Nancy with beady looks but didn't scatter at her approach.

'She'll do,' said Arthur. 'The birds get on with her.'

Nancy smiled.

'She wants a rest and some looking after,' said Doreen.

Doreen tapped on Alice's door.

'She's here,' she said, 'and she'll do.'

'Come on in,' said Alice.

Alice had the best room in the house. It got the afternoon sun. It looked out on to a rectangle of back yard and beyond that a railway line, and trees. Alice sat cross-legged on her bed. On the shelves were weighty academic tomes, and respectable reference books: on her desk were crystal balls and tarot cards, astrological tables and the apparatus required for divination. A black cat with not a single white mark sat on the desk and occasionally stretched out a languid paw to tap the paper on the typewriter, as if reminding Alice there was work to be done. The walls were hung with silk, on which were embroidered pentacles here and the signs of the zodiac there. The coverlet of the bed on which Alice sat was embroidered with the Tree of Life. Alice was casting coins. The *I Ching* was open in front of her: also, in old brown bindings, a novel by Mrs Gaskell and one by Edith Wharton.

'All that education,' complained Doreen, 'and still she believes in magic.'

'It isn't magic, Mum,' said Alice, crossly. 'The *I Ching*, like all other methods of divination, simply helps focus the mind.'

'So long as you take it with a pinch of salt,' said Doreen.

'Believe it and don't believe it at the same time. Don't let it take over.'

'Mother's a one to talk,' said Alice, 'Mother's a faith-healer.'

'I was,' said Doreen. 'Till I got frightened. I got the idea the spirits took strength from the patients, not the patients from the spirit.'

'Never trust an after-lifer,' said Alice. 'That's Mum's philosophy.'

'Don't tell me,' said Nancy, alarmed, 'that you're casting coins and consulting the *I Ching* to make an editorial decision?'

'Fiction isn't my strong point,' said Alice. 'The coins merely echo the mood of the times. The Wharton looks too chancy: we'll go for Mrs Gaskell.'

It was, time would prove, the wrong decision, but perhaps Alice interpreted the oracle wrongly, as she herself was on occasion wrongly interpreted. Who is to say?

And so Nancy moved in with Alice and was to stay for three years, in a little room unconducive to courtship, a fact that suited everyone but her. So it goes.

Medusa was described in the press, rightly, as a shoestring operation, but received a lot of press coverage, much of it dismissive. The gossip columnists took pleasure in referring to the Harpies of Medusa, the bra-less harridans of the publishing world. Publishers themselves, though male, were helpful. It had become apparent that there was a woman's market out there. Let Medusa develop it.

Medusa paid its writers notoriously little. If the writers did well, they'd soon desert to the mainstream publishers, for mainstream contracts. If they didn't do well, forget them. But perhaps this is the cynicism of the eighties speaking: perhaps established publishers genuinely wished Medusa well. Good nature and self-interest can coexist. Stephanie was beautiful: Layla was described as the thinking man's popsy: both were an on-going source of scandal and entertainment in the gossip columns. Alice was considered a hopeless bluestocking: only those who couldn't get a man developed the life of the mind.

Meanwhile women read, thought, began to speak up in public, took strength from one another, learned to withstand mockery and required justice in the home and in the workplace:

mockery and derision aimed at the women of Medusa was a small price to pay. They could put up with it, and did. Men would walk out of rooms when they walked into them: so what?

The History and Nature of the Female Orgasm was not a filthy book, simply an honest one. *The Hidden Order of Female Art* by no means special pleading. The novel *Sisters* won a literary prize or so. *Gender Statistics* became a seminal book in the universities. *Women — Made or Born?* one year outsold the Bible, and was presently to enable Medusa to move to better offices and get itself organised.

Money and success, as Layla observed in the beginning, means you get taken seriously.

Let us look in at a meeting of the Advisory Board. Nancy is presenting the annual report. Round the big table are young, enthusiastic, eager, female faces, all without makeup, serviceably dressed. Time is on their side, and the future is theirs. Only Layla wears a skirt. Boiler suits are out: jeans and jumpers in. A couple of babies have been brought in; they're female. The boys, by common consent, are left at home. Proof copies of the next season's lists are on display. *The Inessential Gender — a History*, magazines from Stephanie's new newsprint division — *Liberation Review*, and *Multigender Dialectic: the Feminist Primer* rather badly printed. And down at Layla's end of the table a display of Medusa Classics, elegantly packaged, eloquently produced.

'Medusa is now a shareholding company,' says Nancy to the assembled women, 'minimally in profit. Our retail outlets are properly established, and male resistance to the idea of a separate literary market for women for the most part overcome. The 'women's market' no longer means romances and *Woman's Own*. It means serious books at serious prices. Nevertheless, problems remain. The company's undercapitalised. We live from hand to mouth. Profits from *Women — Made or Born?* paid back our starting-up costs, but sales are falling off.'

Nancy, out of delicacy, made no mention of Layla's occasional large injections of family cash into Medusa's coffers. These appeared in the books merely as *'Anonymous donations'*. 'Public demand', Nancy went on, 'can't always be predicted. If only it could. Thus *Made or Born* does startlingly well: *Multigender Dialectic* may have to be withdrawn for lack of forward orders. We can build up a core of faithful readers, women loyal to our imprint, of course we can, and will: but real profits always lie within the margins of guesswork, which is an uncomfortable place to be. As the women's courses in the universities proliferate, thanks to Alice, Medusa will of course provide the standard texts, there being no one else in the field — and we will find ourselves safer.'

'Why are we talking about profits?' protested one of the Board. 'Our main business is to reclaim women's artistic past. Commercial success isn't our aim: why even talk about it?'
'Fuck art,' said another. 'We exist to raise female consciousness.'
'In order to exist at all,' said Layla, 'we have to break even. I'm not going to go on digging into my own pocket for ever.'

Layla's hair was short and curly. She was said to have a new lover, whom the newspapers longed to identify, but couldn't, and her eyes were bright. There was a feeling around the table that she lacked the capacity for constructive self-criticism.

'There's certainly a case for breaking even,' someone said, 'if only so Layla doesn't always get her own way.'

'Money should be the last of our considerations,' said Stephanie, 'when it comes to choosing the list.' She was looking drawn, and had a spot on her normally perfect chin. She had trouble with her conscience, and her children, and still lived at the top of Layla's house. She made frequent attempts to move out, but would develop an allergy or flu or hurt her back if the attempts showed signs of success, and so stayed on. Her divorce from Hamish lingered on. Fine gestures create legal opportunity. Nakedness in public gets publicly discussed. Newspaper cartoonists revelled in the vision of a naked Stephanie, bosom pressed against a Mini steering-wheel. It was hard for her. Layla was patient.

'So what's for dinner today?' enquired Layla of the assembled Board. 'Oh, goodie, look! It's integrity.'

'We need to keep afloat, of course,' said someone piously.

'But not be a prey to crude commercialism. That's the male way.'

'I disagree,' said Layla. 'Since the male way keeps men so comfortable, I don't see why women shouldn't do the same.'

'I'm trying to speak,' said Nancy crossly. 'Can

we not have these interruptions.'

'They are not interruptions,' said someone. 'They are important contributions to a debate. And why are you standing up there at the end of the table, Nancy; spouting at us as if you saw yourself as apart and superior? Surely this is a co-operative in spirit as well as actuality. We were told Medusa would remain hierarchy-free, even though for technical reasons never fully explained to us we became a shareholding company. I see no evidence of that spirit here today.'

'Trouble at mill!' hissed Layla to Stephie. 'Told you there would be,' said Stephie.

'Be all that as it may,' said Nancy firmly and loudly, 'as I have been trying to explain to you, we have to raise further capital or Medusa will once again approach Standstill, as the *I Ching* describes it. Stasis. And I'm sure none of us would want that.'

Alice had converted Nancy to the *I Ching*: tactlessly, Nancy now referred to it. There was further uproar. Many of the Board members had backgrounds in Methodism and the old Adult Education movement, and were stern rationalists.

'You haven't been doing the *I Ching* again, have you!' cried one woman, in the exact tone of voice she'd use to rebuke a child — 'What, soiled your pants again!' Women had yet to learn the art of scolding without appearing either maternal

93

or shrewish: to develop the male knack of making reproach seem to come from some cosmic, a-personal source. Accused of nagging over centuries, they had developed the tendency. These days men nag, women reproach.
'Casting coins to tell our fortune? This is a responsible women's publishing house; these are the seventies, not the sixties.'

An innocent asked what the *I Ching* was, protesting that it wasn't fair to women to intimidate women by raising matters and using words which not everyone understood: it was a male trick.

Someone explained that the *I Ching* was a Confucian book of oracles: you asked questions, it answered them, like a wise old man, through the pattern the coins threw up.
'Man!' someone shrieked. Why was a feminist publishing house asking questions of a man?

Alice said in her soft voice, 'Don't be alarmed. The book has a foreword by Jung, whose concepts of the anima and the id have so informed the women's movement we can almost reckon him an honorary female. Publishing, as Nancy has pointed out, is a matter of prophecy. We merely use what is available.'
'Please, no one mention the *I Ching* outside these walls,' begged Layla, with an alarm unusual for her. 'If the press get hold of it, they'll have a fucking field day.'
'Language!' reproached Nancy.

94

'Oh, for fuck's sake, Nancy,' said Layla. 'You're the dogsbody, not the nanny.'

And so the meeting continued, as had many before, as did many after. There was to be a further share issue amongst such members of the Board as could bear to be tainted by commercialism. These included Layla, Stephie, Nancy and Alice. Big Women all. Of the initial share issue a year back, thirty per cent had gone to Layla's mystery backer, whom she claimed to be a member of her family, and was most assuredly female.

'I haven't seen her naked,' said Layla. 'I can hardly ask her to fucking strip, but she looks like a woman to me, and her children call her mother. OK?'

Nancy's hopes of romance, never quite stifled, were given encouragement by her encounter with the man known at Medusa as Layla's live-in lover. His name was Johnny; he was a writer and book-critic, charming, literate, impoverished, unmarried, and very English. Johnny was assumed to be cover for Layla's real lover. He was a man of no interest to the press, being neither a socialite nor a truck-driver. These days enough couples lived together without benefit of marriage ceremony to make 'living in sin' not much of an issue. It was still customary, of course, for cohabiting partners to be slept separately if ever they stayed over at a parental home.

The war of the generations flickered on, soon to be swamped by the gender war. Layla's secret lover was supposed to be royal, and rich; but no one knew for certain, and she wasn't saying. Or perhaps, some conjectured, he didn't exist at all: he was Layla's invention, a matter of innuendo, a method of turning away enquiry so she could get on with the real love of her life, that is to say, Medusa.

Nancy's mean little car — it had turned out to be a real goer, in spite of its looks — parked outside Layla's house in Cheyne Walk. Yes, even there, in those years, on that broad thoroughfare which runs alongside the Thames, before parking meters, before traffic wardens, parking was possible. She heaved Layla's shopping out of the car and up the steps to the big front door. She rang the bell. Johnny opened it, his face unshaven, pen in his hand. Nowadays when the doorbell rings people save, if they're sensible, before leaving the computer. Then, they just finished the sentence and took the pen with them. The clothes of the literate were dotted with ink stains.

'You'll be Nancy the dogsbody,' he said. 'Meet another.'

'I'm the accountant, really,' said Nancy. 'But it suits Layla to keep me in my place.'

She went into the large, neglected, inconvenient kitchen and spent some minutes wiping out the fridge before restocking it and then she began the task of putting the groceries away.

'I like a woman who's neat and tidy,' said Johnny, admiringly. 'You remind me of my sister.'

He talked of his upbringing in the shires, his inability to play cricket or do as expected: she talked of her precipitate leaving of her old life in New Zealand. Both were pleased to have found a confidant. People had become so interested in the present and the future, it was hard to find an audience for nostalgia.

She asked if he was fond of his sister.

He said he liked her very much; too much, according to his psychoanalyst. Nancy was encouraged, firstly because an unhealthy regard for a sister would be more than healthy if diverted to her, and secondly, because being in psychoanalysis still seemed to her exotic. Three or four days a week you visited a man of high intelligence, who was versed in the ways of another culture and used an obscure and elitist language. You lay on a couch for an hour and you talked and he listened and made notes, using this coded terminology to define the pattern of your thoughts. Occasionally he would say something wise. But mostly he took your mind out of your head and studied it like a thing; holding it this way and that way, peering at it, readjusted its tuning, and at the end of ten years or so you were more like other people: certainly more like your psychoanalyst.

It was a male thing, not a female thing. Women did not have the time; their minds were considered amorphous, flopping all over the place: if you took them out to examine them, they'd melt and dissolve like a blob of jelly under a tap. The female mind would give up with a weary sigh and not exist, carried away and dissolved in a flood of love which flowed like tap water, love for the analyst, the positive transference. Freud had tried psychoanalysis with women: it never really worked. They'd all been fucked by their fathers, anyway.

Or was it that they just said they had? Or were angry because they hadn't been? It was impossible to discover which. In the end one was just sorry for the fathers. That was psychoanalysis. Male and mysterious. Later it was to feed out into the population in its lite form, 'therapy'.

The gender switch operated; therapy turned out to be female, and about feelings, those little sisters to the major male passions, not at all the workings of the mind: therapy was thalamus-centred: brain-stem stuff, basic. And it was Jung, Freud's friend, gender-traitor, who helped throw the gender switch: anima this, anima that. See in therapy the flight from the frontal lobes, where the educated rationalities of doubt and conscience are located.

At the time Nancy just gaped at Johnny and said, 'Psychoanalysis! My God. Isn't it very expensive?'
'Massively so,' said Johnny. 'My sister, who married a clergyman, says such a degree of self-interest is a sin and I should give what I have to the poor. But there are so many poor, and only one of me.' He had a charming smile. She thought he was wonderful.
'Layla lets me live here free,' he said, 'so I can afford it. She's very generous.'

They agreed on Layla's essential kindness, and parted friends. Nancy went home to tea at Doreen's with ham, potato salad, and a side helping of grated cheese, not exactly dissatisfied with her life, but with the feeling that she had, from that day of decision when she'd joined Medusa, unnecessarily limited her life. There were whole worlds out there she knew nothing about. To live in big cities is to have to worry about this kind of thing, from time to time. Back home she'd just have worried about the kids, and the weather and the sheep. The more limited the horizon, the more tranquil the mind. But what is life without aspiration?

Stephanie was awarded 'access' to her children only one day a fortnight. Hamish had 'custody, care and control' because not only had she walked out on them, but walked out naked. Watch her now, one Friday afternoon. She asks Nancy to leave her desk and drive her to Primrose Hill. She does not want to go alone. Nancy obliges, but for once with not too good a grace. She is busy. She will have to return to the office, which means she will get home late and tired.

'It must be really wonderful to be an editor,' said Nancy, with a trace of old-fashioned cattiness, as she backed out of the alley behind Medusa where the staff, for a small fee, now parked their cars. The pavement outside the offices had been double-lined with yellow. To everyone's astonishment you could no longer park where you pleased.
'What do you mean?' demands Stephanie. She is wearing a Laura Ashley dress in a tiny flower print; she hopes it makes her look dowdy, sweet and maternal; all it does is make her look as if she's got out of bed in a hurry. When Nancy remarks on this, Stephanie replies, 'Well, that's what mothers *look like*: but what would you know, Nancy?' Stephanie's access days brought out the worst in everyone, for some reason.

But thirty, for many of them, was approaching: the bourn, the dread age from which no life traveller returns, or if she does will never be the same again: the age at which the twenty-year-old hopes to die, yet assumes she will never reach. After thirty, you were within spitting distance of death. Spit away if that's what you felt like, but it took courage. Thirty used to be the age after which motherhood seldom happened, and marriage almost never; and you were faced with the consequences of your courage.

'Editors make value judgements,' said Nancy. 'I don't call that work. It's just everyday life.' She ground the gears, unusually for her. 'In the sense that it's enjoyable and it's what you are and not what you do that counts. To say this is better than that and get paid for it, and accorded status because you do, and not even have to be in the office to do it, must be bliss.'
'But the responsibility of judgement is a burden,' said Stephanie, 'and when you get it wrong it's all your fault. You get the blame, so you get paid more, in recompense for that. I feel resentment in your driving, Nancy. I'm sorry I had to ask you to help me out. I do realise you're busy. But my hands shake so when I get near the house I'm not safe driving myself.'
'Oh, it's all right,' said Nancy. 'I'm pre-menstrual, I expect.'
'When you say that,' said Stephanie, 'you play into men's hands. Don't do it.'

'I forgot,' said Nancy, bleakly. There was a great deal to remember. At this time a good feminist denied the hormonal pull of the monthly cycle: strove to separate her womb and its behaviour from herself, even to the extent of denying any link whatsoever. 'Put it like this. I'm in a bad mood.'

'And on access days,' said Stephanie, 'I'm just miserable. Only once a fortnight! I never knew it would be so hard.'

'What I don't understand,' said Nancy, 'if you have all day with the children, why do you only turn up at tea-time?'

'I don't know,' said Stephanie desperately. 'There just always seems so much to do. Women work twice as hard as men. Hamish has everything and does nothing: he puts a few things in a shop, tells lies about them, marks up at a thousand per cent and people queue to buy and tell each other what a great guy he is. He has the house, the children, and a mistress to do all the work. And I came away with nothing.'

'But that's what you wanted,' said Nancy.

'I was manoeuvred into it,' said Stephanie.

'It was a noble thing to do,' said Nancy, 'all the same.'

Nancy had to search for a parking place in Chalcot Crescent. There were double yellow lines around the corner in Regent's Park Road. She had to park in someone's garage entrance, to let Stephanie out. The boys were coming home from the shops with Daffy, who wore elegant thigh boots and a long pink sweater. She looked older and braver than before. She carried a plastic shopping bag in each hand. The boys, who seemed to be thriving, ran free. They caught sight of Stephanie and went into a double act to which they were clearly accustomed.

'It's the witch!' cried Rafe.
'The nasty old witch!' cried Roland.
'Isn't she ugly,' shouted Rafe.
'Back of a bus, back of a bus,' shouted Roland.
'Be quiet, the pair of you,' commanded Daffy.
'How dare you speak to your mother like that.'
The boys made sick sounds and faces and ran into the house.

Daffy put down her bags and faced Stephie.
'I'm sorry,' she said, 'but they expected you this morning. We all did.'
'You poison them against me,' said Stephanie.
'I don't,' said Daffy. 'Honestly, I don't. I don't have to. They just hate you.'
She was helpless in the face of evident truth.

Children do not take kindly to being left, and that's that.

Stephanie looked at the closed front door of her erstwhile home and wept.

'My home, my home, my children.'

'You left it of your own free will,' said Daffy, kindly, but at a loss, and wanting to get on. There was so much to do in a house if it is to be clean, look tidy, be properly stocked, and those who live in it to be nurtured and feel confident. In fact one never stopped. And Hamish was sexually very lively, and though sex revitalises in one way, in another it can induce an untimely languor. If there was sex before breakfast, breakfast tended to see Daffy refilling the teapot with boiling water instead of emptying out the old and making fresh. Stephanie, in her time as mistress of No. 103, had ignored all domestic matters and concentrated on the life of the mind. It was as if the house itself had thrown Stephanie out, Daffy once confided in Hamish.

'Don't be so whimsical,' he replied. 'It was you who drove Stephie out, Daffy, you who deprived my children of their mother. Don't try and shift the responsibility.'

And indeed, in those days, it was generally accepted that in any quarrel over a man the women were to blame. The woman who lost him had 'failed to keep him'. The woman who won him had 'led him on'. The man stood centrally, smiling, erect, free from accusations. Daffy saw

105

nothing strange in what Hamish was saying. It was in a man's nature to part your blouse and put his hand on your breast: your female duty to politely dodge, or if you failed to for one reason or another, to accept responsibility for the consequences, including all the housework and childcare which might come your way thereafter. Man's sexual nature was women's responsibility. Now yet again the gender switch has operated. If in doubt, blame the man.

'You stole my children,' wept Stephanie on the pavement, while Nancy watched aghast from the car, and Daffy picked up both shopping bags in one hand — Stephanie did not help — and, with the other, led Stephanie, in her sprigged and forlorn Laura Ashley, into the house which had once been hers.

As Johnny said to Nancy when later that night she dropped off some books for Layla — she was unlikely to get home until ten, and toasted cheese late at night gave her indigestion — 'I suppose we must take a moral here from Brecht's *Caucasian Chalk Circle*. The land belongs to he who tills it. The child belongs to she who cares for it. What once was Stephie's is now Daffy's.'

That was in the mid-seventies: socialist days. Long ago. The notion of primal ownership has returned with a vengeance: and the profit therein. The rain that falls from heaven belongs not to God but to the Water Board, the forests nature grew are fenced off and belong to the Forestry Commission; your very corpse belongs to the state: its parts up for sale for research purposes. Money has won over human dithering. The natural mother owns the genes of the child she forgot and can claim that child back from the adoptive mother any time: the moral right of the one who toils is swept away in the tide of mine, mine: the country you claim is the one of your ancestors not the one which reared you. And no one goes to see Brecht any more, except out of curiosity about the strange view once commonly held of what was owed to whom, and why. And to partake of future, of course: a little sip at a diminishing stream. Drought time.

To Johnny, Nancy replied, that being then, 'I suppose you're right. But she's very upset.'
'So upset,' said Johnny, 'she goes on living here rent-free. Layla thought she'd stay for a month or so, but years later here she still is.'
'The house is large enough to swallow her up, I should have thought,' said Nancy. 'I have the tiniest room in a distant suburb.'
'Come in,' said Johnny, 'and have a drink and talk about it.'

But she wouldn't. Later that evening a friend of Layla's, a certain Humphrey, art dealer, came round and Johnny decided that he, Johnny, was definitely gay, he should stop fighting it: years of psychoanalysis to heal the tendency had failed. His hand stretched out to stroke the back of male necks, not female: preverted, sick: so be it. Nancy had seemed the nearest he could get to male in female form — the sinewy arms, the firm jaw line, the friendly eyes under heavy brows, and he had thought some compromise was possible: but Humphrey, young, soft, male, quirky lisp and all, was the one whose absence dimmed the light of being alive, who left a room most empty when he walked out of it, and that was that. He did not look for a father figure, as his analyst had suggested. If anything he, Johnny, was the father, albeit a soft and gentle and anima-ridden one, and Humphrey was the son, albeit precocious. Nor had Johnny's mother, cosseting and petting him, turned him gay by the intensity of her affection: her affection had been intense because of his gayness, which had been born into him: a simple matter of fellow feeling, rather than a damaging neurosis. A mutation was as far as he would go: a perversion, no. They could put you in prison for it, but all that proved was that the law was an ass.

If Nancy had not been nervous of getting home too late, and causing a flutter in Arthur's dovecotes, and of the cheese and toast lying so heavily on her stomach she couldn't sleep: had she not returned to Medusa to finish the work the adventures of Stephanie had interrupted, had she accepted the drink Johnny offered, if, if, if. If it's any consolation to those who feel their life has been changed by an unkind fate, it's seldom this particular incident or that which wreaks the damage. Nancy's nature and Johnny's nature, those immutables, led them to react in ways bound to have, in the end, predictable results. To waste time on the 'if onlys' is absurd. 'If only' I hadn't said I loved him he would still be with me. 'If only' I hadn't told my son he wasn't his father's natural child. 'If only' she'd stayed a minute longer at the party the car wouldn't have swung round the corner and killed her. One does what one does. Self-destruct, not event, is at work.

Part Two

Part Two

A Nest of Randy Vipers

Alice is not idle. Alice has decided to change the world. It is easier than to change herself. She has been awarded an honorary degree by her alma mater. She is a Doctor of Philosophy. See her now process through cloisters, a small figure in a black gown with a cerise hood lined with orange fur. The men who designed her gown have an idea of grandeur but no colour sense. The garments were designed before even the word stove came to Europe; when a learned man sat huddled in furs to keep the chill out and his brain was shrivelling in the cold: when the master and mistress lay lengthwise in the bed, and the servants slept at angles all around to keep them warm.

Gowned old men are all around. They whisper instructions in her ear with fetid, helpful breath: old lips touch the white lobe. Someone holds an elbow: withered bodies brush up against her. Oh, give us warmth, give us youth; all we have is dignity, and how cold it is; the brilliance of the mind casts shadows, and in the shadows our bodies are obliged to dwell.

Alice stands on a platform to receive her parchment roll, to be capped. The mortarboard, when finally it descends, is too big. It descends almost to her eyes. She is sashed in purple silk. The colour clash is horrendous.

'Alice Stepford,' says the Dean, 'Doctor of Philosophy of this university, in recognition of her most notable and praiseworthy works on the Philosophy of Gender — '

Behind the Dean, on the platform, are seated ranks of dons. Those who sit in the front stay awake, those who sit in the back, drowse and snore. The hall is hot, the ceremony long; they are old, old: few have thought a fresh thought for thirty years. Five years after a double first and the mind gives up, though the voice goes on droning. Academia to a man can be as motherhood is to a woman, intelligence-wise. Mention of the Philosophy of Gender makes a few minds click to attention.
'What new discipline is this?' Gender has not been a word much used in universities till now. The world is male: the greater male includes the lesser female, as it still does today in legal documents. Say 'mankind' and find it includes women, should the question arise. The female is an unfortunate mutation of the male: such mind as exists is clouded by emotion. Gender is of little interest.

Later that night Alice dines at High Table. There's game and roast potatoes, gravy, bread sauce and heavy claret: such menus were established before the days of central heating. Scandinavians eat lightly, fish and pickles on bread, because their Northern houses have to be warmed or else they die. Those in temperate climes fare worst: their diets are designed to

114

create heating from within. After dinner Alice is required to make a speech: she speaks easily, off the cuff, her voice soft but clear; the less loudly she speaks the more others are required to pay attention.

'Fifty-one per cent of us,' she is saying, 'the majority of the human species in fact, have lived for all time on the dark side of the moon; unseen, unknown, unstudied, without history. Like the animals, women are suspected of having no immortal souls; to be so rooted in their bodies, spirituality can barely find a foothold. How grudgingly the Christian Church allows them in, but someone has to arrange the altar flowers and sweep the floors. And as in the church, so in the universities. A woman is allowed a brain; open her skull and there it is, indistinguishable from its male equivalent: but as for the mind, that intangible province which hovers in the brain's vicinity, forget it. Don't you find this extraordinary? I do. Doesn't what is extraordinary merit our attention? Is it not disgraceful that no such discipline as Gender Studies exists within our universities?'

Down the table the Regius Professor of Chemistry woke up and said to a Senior Fellow in Economics, his neighbour, 'Who is that woman? What is she talking about?' He was so old he could scarcely see his own experiments. Wine and gravy mingled on his upper lip.

'It's All Fellows Day,' explained Young

Economics. 'We gave her a Doctorate.'

'Then why doesn't she just sit down and be grateful?' said Chemistry.

'Because we expect her to make a speech.'

'Can't hear a word she says,' remarked Chemistry. 'Thank God. Wake me when she's finished.' He closed his eyes again.

'Gentlemen,' said Alice, 'the times they are a-changing. You must bring your ideas up to date or perish. Your money is running out. To bring in the funding you require you must expand your intake. You must take in bright women or you will be flooded by not-so-bright men. You must take women in at all levels, from undergraduates up.'

'Is she talking money?' asked Chemistry, opening his eyes quite wide and alert.

'She is,' said Economics.

'Interesting point,' said Chemistry. 'The lesser of two evils. Which will do us more harm, stupid men or bright women?'

Along the table, if you counted the closed eyes, only two of them were female, and they belonged to a Fellow in English Literature, whose husband had once been a Professor, ennobled for his services to Shakespeare. The wife had been given tenure on his death: his wisdom and decision was seen to still reside in her, to speak through her, as if by magic. It happens in universities as it happens elsewhere. When a great national leader dies, the wife, sister or daughter takes over as the best that can be

116

achieved in the sorry circumstances of death. Mrs Gandhi and Mrs Bandaranaike; Yoko Ono speaks for John Lennon, and no one argues. Such is the power of seminal fluid or daughterly duty: Athena bursts from Zeus her father's head. How primitive we are. The Professor's widow slept, knowing she was wise so to do: she had forgotten nearly everything her husband ever said, and had never really been in the habit of thinking for herself. When she spoke others looked at her strangely.

'Gender Studies,' said Economics. 'Bizarre.'

It is observable at any executive meeting that the first time someone brings up a subject so far unheard of, the one who voices the idea is considered mad and the matter is swiftly dropped. The second time it is mentioned the matter is seriously discussed. The third time everyone thinks they thought of it themselves, and demands credit for it. Alice said it once, said it twice, and the third time she said it into the universities went Gender Studies, women's studies. Soon Equal Opportunities was to make discrimination against the female illegal: the centre gave if the top still held. These days some of the beadiest eyes around the High Table are female. Study of the Humanities is now more or less left to women. Science stays male. No matter. The important thing at the time was to get women trained in feminism, into the teachers' training colleges, and spread the word there. It worked. Soon Rafe and

Roland, to their disgust, were obliged to take cookery classes. And the girls, favoured by their teachers, now predominantly female, got to be better at exams and outshine the boys. Then cookery turned into Food Technology and no one took the subject at all if they could help it. Boring, boring.

But that's another story. All we need to know is that that night Alice made a brilliant speech, and won the hearts and minds of men, and the world shifted a little on its axis and the college cellars ran out of Château Y'Quem.

Alice's father was ill: his lungs were bad. The doctor said he should spend less time with the birds: they were dusty things: they shed showers of mites with every flap of the wings: but her father refused to part with them. Under stress, Doreen turned again to the spirits, went into sudden trances, would put on the expression and voice of a Chinaman and as if from the other side advise Arthur to give up the birds. But Arthur took no notice, and coughed on. Alice consulted her oracles more and more frequently in the desperate hope of hearing good news. They gave her none. Though the *I Ching* once said it was appropriate to 'set forces marching.'

She began to stay away from home more often. She'd be needed in the office and be nowhere to be found. She'd be away staying with friends, or in hotels, or in some writers' retreat somewhere. Nancy felt Alice had handed over the role of daughter to her, that she'd somehow slipped out from under. Doreen left the window open one moonlit night to freshen Alice's by now almost unused room, and an owl flew in, and shat all over the occult paraphernalia before flying out again, hooting. Doreen trembled at the omen. Arthur coughed worse than ever, and shortly after that had a lung out in the hospital. It was

119

Nancy, not Alice, who sat with Doreen by his bedside, while he came out of the anaesthetic, grey white and frightening.

'Darling,' said Layla to Nancy, with real sympathy, 'Alice is out saving the world. She's like Jesus, but female. Jesus said to his mother, 'Knowest ye not I must be about my Father's business?' Alice says, in effect, 'I'm about my Mother's business.' We all make sacrifices. Nothing is achieved without them.'

Though quite what Layla was giving up Nancy could not be sure. She resented being Martha to everyone else's Mary. It worried her to see how easily the eyes of men slipped past her and beyond her, failing to recognise she was female. She was beginning to feel old and invisible. Perhaps she should have stayed with Brian? She'd be a farmer's wife by now, and have kids, and no doubt be a stylish beauty, if only in comparison to everyone else in the locality. Nancy consoled herself with the notion that if you kept company with such exceptionally bright and beautiful women, you were bound to suffer by comparison. And she should not be so trivial — at least she was part of a great revolution. Feminism was heady stuff: it moved at such a pace. Prejudices fell like dominoes. On a good day Nancy knew her personal life was well lost for love of humanity, or at any rate the female half of it. Only on a bad day, after a bad dream, she would find herself pale and trembly over breakfast with a resentment carried out of the dream. On these occasions Doreen would say, 'Oh, expecting Mr Monthly again, are we?' and Nancy would say, 'There is nothing hormonal about this, nothing,' knowing full well she lied through her teeth. Truth can never be too big a price to pay for social change. If you only believe hard enough, what is not true can become true. This is not hormones, this is *me*. Take it or leave it.

Nancy was trusted to talk to the journalists. Medusa held open days to which the media was invited, and often came. The women's magazines, with their vast circulations, were beginning to reduce their knitting pages, their cookery and embroidery columns. These were for little old ladies and young mothers, who had a lot of time but little purchasing power. The ads were what counted, what kept the new glossy formats going: not just circulation, but quality circulation counted. So forget the baby clothes and how to purée the toddlers' dinner, forget the home upholstery, or at any rate marginalise them: woo the new woman out of the home, earning and spending. But how to woo them? What did they want? The old religion of pleasing men had to be unlearned, the new one of pleasing the self understood.

Journalists trooped to Medusa, to find out about the importance of the orgasm, the joys of cunnilingus, to explain there was no such thing as a frigid woman only an inexpert man, to honour the clitoris, to campaign for

121

safer contraception, more humane childbirth, a greater role in the local Council (boring, boring), how to be a person first and a man-pleaser second. How to exist in your own right and not by virtue of role — mother, wife, daughter.

Ideas flowed freely out of Medusa: and freely were adopted.

Men came too, to re-learn their ways, to worship new Gods. How not to be patronising, how not to say 'speaking as a mere man', how not to be the first to stand up at a woman's meeting and declare himself on woman's side; not to claim, 'I am a feminist too.' A man cannot be a feminist: he has not suffered as any woman has. He cannot know, nor claim a victimhood he has no knowledge of. These matters were minefields: Medusa the best mine-detector around. And good PR for Medusa, of course.

Layla and Stephanie, having initiated the open days, would melt away when the journalists actually arrived. They would want to catch a glimpse of the few famous and newsworthy women, but would have to make do with Nancy. Or so it seemed to her. Nevertheless, she got to be a dab hand at the patter. She'd dream it in her sleep; somehow the dreams covered up the sound of Arthur's coughing upstairs.

'Patriarchy is the enemy; what is a wife but a slave, required to provide domestic and sexual services for her master in return for her keep.

What is marriage but legalised prostitution?' And so forth.

'Society is sexist, language is sexist: by sexist we mean the in-built assumption that the male is superior to the female. A set of ingrained and irrational beliefs that condemn women to be second-class citizens, discriminated against under the law, in education, in government policy.' And so on.

Sometimes Nancy wondered if she should simply ask a passing man to father a baby for her. Some women did that. But she couldn't, she just couldn't. She marvelled at her own reluctance. So large a thing in a life — not to have a baby; so little a step, but impossible to set about making one. Fear of rejection could ruin your life.

Let's take a look at Layla walking along Harley Street, London, checking numbers. She walks briskly but she's nervous. She clutches her bag a little too hard. Her small, pretty fingers are bloodless. She wears loose trousers, an easily removable denim shirt. She expects to be examined by an obstetrician. So she needs to wear garments that can be easily removed. She does not want fumbling and awkwardness on her part to put her at a disadvantage.

Doctors own female bodies; they do it by having information about them; information is power. Doctors know what goes on inside there: doctors make you lie on your back, they put on gloves, oil you, tell you to relax, feel inside you, tell you the state of your womb: healthy or otherwise, fertile or not, confirm your pregnancy or shake their heads. Missed a couple of periods, but not pregnant. Thank God, or otherwise. Midwives can get the baby out of you, if it's simple, and they understand the broader processes of labour, but doctors, mostly male, have an arcane, secret knowledge.

There are a few female obstetricians about, but women tend not to trust them. It seems more natural for men to want to put their hands inside you than it does for a woman, unless they're lesbian: and then you might not want that either. People could do real damage in there. But you have to trust, to put these thoughts out of your mind. This is medicine, not sex. Possibly. Men helping; not men with a prurient curiosity and an urge to power. Sadistic? Surely not. In the US the obstetrician looms larger in the woman's life even than over here. Women go for regular check-ups.

'Permission to start sex, sir?' Mothers take daughters along when they look as if they're on the brink of sexual activity. 'Take a look up there, doctor. Is she OK? Is she ready?' What kind of initiation ceremony is this? What's ready, what's not ready? What's OK, not OK? No one knows.

Even after the sixties what's down there is something of a mystery. Women try squatting over mirrors, or holding them for one another, so they can take a look, and tell one another that what they see is beautiful. Actually it's not really. Pinky-red crinkles, and fleshy flaps; the entrance to the squashed soft intricacies of whatever's in there, giving such pleasure, underscoring nearly every human emotion, human activity. The treasure a woman carries between her legs.

Doctor, my periods aren't normal, aren't regular, I get so much pain; they're too heavy, too scanty, too frequent, never happen: what's all this browny granular stuff, why these blood clots: did I have a miscarriage and not know it? Now we wear tights we all get thrush. I'm itching, I'm itching. You can't get the stuff that cures it without a prescription and he's bound to want to take a look. Doctor, I'm so tired. Look inside the rims of my eyes — so pale. I must be anaemic. How can it be natural to bleed like this? Drained, Doctor, drained. Why?

The sisters say there is no pain — just what your mother told you to expect, so you feel it. Deny it. Don't lie down. Don't put your feet up: that accords the male a victory. A practical letting of blood, that's all menstruation is; no mystique, no mystery; get out the mirror, take a look. Stop whining and whinging and clutching your stomach. Be a man, damn you! Hitch on your jeans, undo your bra, ready to go, ready to live!

Get the men into the labour wards; make him hold your hand, see what he did to you. If it takes two to make a baby, by God it's going to take two to get one out. Blood everywhere. Try not to scream, this is *natural*. When there's a father present the male doctors tend to stay away: it's the midwives who show up. That's the upside or the downside, according to taste. They used to put the trainee doctors on to the stitching up after the birth. Out pops baby, up go the legs, into the stirrups, legs apart for the world to see. Here comes young doctor, with needle and thread. And he didn't get taught sewing at school, what's the betting. What a botch up! The stirrups went when the fathers started coming along.

Anyway, it's a minefield. Here comes Layla, up Harley Street, going to visit her obstetrician, Mr Wrightson. She's shown in. He rises from his desk, shakes her hand. He wears a well-cut grey suit and a carnation and as a concession to modern times, a pale pink shirt. His hair is grey, thick and glossy. Obstetricians tend to keep their hair. His face has a grey pallor from the effort of non-affect; if Layla's fingers grow bloodless from grasping her bag too tight, so blood long ago drained from his face; gets so far, no further. The surface of his face is thickly wrinkled; seems made from hide, not skin. Yet how kind he seems: how dignified: how he smiles: why, he's almost jovial. Layla is ashamed of herself, and the unkindness of her thoughts. There are X-rays of her pelvic bones pinned up on the board behind him. Her name plain there to see. His nurse is present: she's in her mid-thirties, wearing a wedding ring; plain, serviceable, competent.

Layla has been able to undress behind a screen. She has been handed, and wears, a gown not too skimpy, which covers her, which has not lost all its tapes in some severe and hygienic laundry. Mind you, she's small.

Stephanie finds medical gowns never wrap round her properly.

Alice is swamped in hers: the fabric neckline comes up to her ears.

Nancy, who, though she tries to keep out of the doctor's way, was once driven by heavy bleeding to consult one, finds such gowns rise up above her knees when she sits. Nancy's doctor examined her and told her he could find nothing wrong; he had to break her hymen to do the examining. She bled all over the paper tablecloth that covered the examining couch, and thought it served him right. But that was Nancy; this is Layla, and Mr Wrightson. How genial he is.

'Why yes, Miss Lavery,' says Mr Wrightson, 'so you found time at last to pop in. How many times have you cancelled, have we got your X-rays out and then filed them again? I understand you're very busy. I keep reading about you in the newspapers. You run that feminist publishing house, don't you? What's it called?'
'Medusa,' says Layla.
'How very cultured of you,' says Mr Wrightson. He is so far above doctor that he has returned to Mister, and if you call him Doctor he corrects you. Physicians stay doctors; consultant surgeons get to be misters, as a reward for their courage in knifing their way into others' bodies, to change and improve what goes on in there: to ease its workings, clear obstructions, remove the source of pain, make hearts and kidneys work, assist the procreative organs. 'Scalpel, Nurse. Saw, Nurse. This is skull we're talking now: hip bone: forceps, Nurse, careful with that head. It's wedged!' Thank you, Doctor, call yourself

Mister and God bless you. You know what the rest of us don't.

'Borrow from the past to enhance the present,' said Mr Wrightson. 'The myths are such a fertile source. The Medusas never existed. There's no evidence for it at all. I'm surprised you didn't call yourself Maenad.'

'We thought of it,' said Layla.

'Bet you did,' said Mr Wrightson. 'Tear the men to bits, that's the way. I hear your company's doing well. You've gone public. Congratulations.'

'Thank you,' says Layla, sitting there in her pale blue, overly laundered gown.

'Gave up the co-operative idea, did you? What a hens' tea-party that must have been!'

Layla realises she faces an enemy, and would leave, if it weren't for the gown. She smiles at him blandly.

'Yes, meetings, appointments, conferences! How busy a young woman like you must be,' goes on Mr Wrightson. 'A pity Mother Nature so likes women to be women and men to be men, and takes it out on them physically if they break the rules. The more women work, the more cases of infertility we see. The more women usurp man's place, the more homosexuals we get.'

'I'm not quite sure that's the reason,' says Layla politely.

'Aren't you?' asks Mr Wrightson. 'Just get up on that couch and I'll examine you. Then we'll get you some more X-rays.'

'Is it necessary?' asks Layla. 'I've only come to be fitted for a coil.'

'Not much *only* about it,' says Mr Wrightson. 'Women interfere with their fertility at their peril. Fitting a coil is a medical process which in your particular case is not advisable.'

'Why not?' asks Layla, alarmed.

'Early X-rays suggest there are some abnormalities present,' he says. Layla allows herself to be examined. The fingers in their plastic gloves are surprisingly swift and adept. He probes and prods in places only lovers are accustomed to go. Layla finds herself pleasured. She can't help it: it is a Pavlovian response, she tells herself: excitement by association. She hopes he doesn't know. Of course he does. The nurse busily clatters dishes, and hums a little.

Mr Wrightson unpeels the gloves.

'Your fallopian tubes are blocked,' he says. 'A history of abortion, no doubt. You have rather a nasty mess in there. I'll book you in for a D and C, which should help the periods. I imagine they've been heavy?'

'D and C?'

'Dilation and curettage. They'll scrape you out. A routine business, you won't need me. It won't solve the fertility problem. I am constantly amazed at the physical risks women will take in order to enjoy their sexual adventures. Abstinence is the only safe contraception, now as ever, but try suggesting that, these liberated days. I just pick up the pieces.'

'You mean you're not going to fit me with a coil? In that case I shall go now.'

'There is no point in fitting you with a coil. Your fallopian tubes are blocked by scar tissue. The neck of the womb — introverted in the first place by pregnancies which have failed to come to term — has thickened. Internal examination reveals a bulky tangle of fibroids. All in all, forget contraception. There is no point in it. It is not required. You will not become pregnant. Well, rejoice, enjoy, as our American friends say. What a lucky girl you are. I daresay such an eventuality suits you very well.'

'Actually,' says Layla, 'no, it doesn't suit me one bit.'

'You have only yourself to blame,' he said. 'You'll have been *on the pill*, as they so blithely say. It has done its work all too well. You can no longer conceive, and your risk of death from cancer or stroke has increased fourfold. You don't refer to that, I daresay, in your various Medusa publications; your books and articles on a woman's right to choose. The right to choose herself and her own fertility: the right to pass on cancer to such daughters as she allows to come to term. Heaven help the coming generations. But don't mention any of that, though you know it well enough. Don't raise the alarm, just have the satisfaction of seeing your name in print.'

'How you hate women,' said Layla, back behind the screen, dressing as fast as she could.

'I am sorry for them,' said Mr Wrightson. 'Why else do I do the work I do. You feminists play with fire. Have your way, get women back to work, and see the children suffer, see the husbands go unemployed. Marriage is the only yoke men understand: do away with that and society will collapse!'

'Mad,' said Layla.

'More importantly,' said Mr Wrightson, 'Nature did not intend the exchange of bodily fluids to be entertainment, recreation, but the means of procreation. She will have her revenge by and by. Wait and see.'

'Like syphilis, you mean?' said Layla. 'How sorry you must be they invented penicillin.'

'Nature is always one step ahead,' said Mr Wrightson. 'I'm glad we were able to have a little chat. I shan't charge you. You may find someone prepared to fit a coil if that makes you feel more in tune with the rest of your generation, but there will be no medical or practical necessity. None. Good day.'

After Layla had gone Mr Wrightson said to his nurse, 'Oh dear, I hope I wasn't too hard on her. But how many times did she miss her appointment?'

'Four,' said Nurse.

132

She was taking off her overall, putting on her coat.

'What are you doing?' asked Mr Wrightson. The working day had another two hours or so to go.
'I don't like you,' was all Nurse said. 'I'm leaving. Don't bother to pay me and I won't work my notice.'

That was in the days of full employment, of course.

Layla, once outside, felt defiled, outraged, humiliated, devastated. She would consult another doctor, who would concur with Mr Wrightson that she was unlikely to get pregnant, but said so nicely. It was a blow. It was not that she exactly wanted a baby, more that she wished to be in a position to have one should she so choose. What woman would not so wish?

What now of Zoe? Remember Zoe, the cast-out sister, whom Layla had condemned for lack of effective sisterhood: the one who chose servitude, not freedom? We are only free, Nietzsche observed, and Layla pointed out, to choose who will influence us.

Zoe chose Bull, her husband. She chose the old wisdom of the past, no matter how little it seemed to apply to the thinking of the present.

Stephanie chose the new, and lived, as did her children, with the consequences.

As for Layla, she had few consequences thrust upon her. She had, as the others observed, a private income, and could slip out from under when required.

Zoe went home with Bull, and had another baby. Well, she would, wouldn't she? This one was a boy; a brother for Saffron: they called him Sampson. Life went on. Bull went out to work. She stayed home. He went away to Africa from time to time: on some new bridge-building venture or other.

Zoe found a love letter in his pocket once, on his return; badly written on lined paper, together with a photograph of an elegant, smiling, black girl in some kind of orange gown. Challenged with this, Bull said Zoe was so caught up in children and domesticity he could hardly be blamed if his fancy strayed: by inference, his dereliction of uxorial duty was Zoe's fault. But he understood her upset: she would do better: it wouldn't happen again. She believed him.

Zoe was writing a book in secret on the fate of the woman graduate: *Lost Women*, she called it. She would go to the public library to do her research, leaving Saffron in charge of Sampson, but always under her eye, playing in the gardens which her table at the library overlooked. And she would write up her notes in the evenings, when the children were in bed, and Bull out, which was often. The book wasn't secret because she was ashamed of it: she just did not rub Bull's nose in her cleverness. He had not been to university, only to technical college. She had a degree: he had qualifications. It didn't do to draw attention to it.

'Such a pity she went off to that college,' said Zoe's father on his deathbed. 'It gave her ideas.'

Zoe would have liked to have taken time off to mourn her father but Sampson had croup and Bull had got promotion and liked to entertain and the house was being redecorated. She needed to keep cheerful for the children. What was the point of giving up your life for them if the life you gave them wasn't worth living?

135

She wasn't exactly unhappy. She just kept her life in two compartments. One was the part of her mind reserved for her book; she had become interested in the level of achievement of not just educated women, but their children; in the changing attitudes to the education of women, over the years. She found it absorbing, exhilarating. In the other compartment was the ordinary day-to-day family life, which included friends, and even parties, but excluded the life of the mind.

Zoe made a friend of Daffy, but that was the nearest she got to the feminists. She'd bring home tales of Stephanie's dereliction of maternal duty to Bull, and he was pleased to hear them. Bull was ambivalent towards Daffy: he approved of her because she made Hamish happy and kept a good house. He disapproved of her because she had not persuaded Hamish to marry her, but times, he conceded, were changing. No harm if Daffy and Zoe went to the sandpit together and sat and chatted on a park bench while overseeing the children's play. If Daffy occasionally took Saffron and Sampson back to her place, so Zoe could spend a couple of hours in the library, he didn't know. Daffy understood the desirability of keeping secrets from men — it went with the territory. Sisterhood thus far, no further. She loved Hamish.

One day Zoe was writing upstairs in the spare bedroom. It was a small eaved room beneath the roof with a window you couldn't open, but the roof tiles around grew grass and a few wild flowers from seeds which passing birds had presumably dropped, so in the summer plants edged the glass, like a kind of bonus from nature. Zoe kept her manuscript under the bed, and her notes in piles of school exercise books. She wrote by hand, on the table, and made a careful fair copy when each page was completed. It had taken her five years to finish two hundred and ten pages. That evening Bull was out at a Masonic gathering: Zoe did what she usually did not do — left Sampson alone in his playpen in the kitchen — he had fallen asleep on his teddy bear — and Saffron watching TV, and had come up to copy out the waiting page. She did not feel guilty. This would not take the thought or attention she should have been giving the children, or what to make for dinner, and what recipe book to consult, or the phone call she was duty-bound to make to Bull's parents — this was just fifteen minutes of routine writing out. Nevertheless she was taken by the idea that the daughters of highly educated women flourished proportionately more than did their sons, when she heard Bull's voice downstairs. Now he was coming up the stairs.

'Zoe,' called Bull. 'Zoe? Where the hell are you?'
'I'm in the spare room,' she called, shoving papers back into a suitcase, shoving the suitcase under the bed with her foot. 'We have to do something about the roof-tiles. We're growing a forest up here.'

Bull pushed the door open.

'But Sampson's in the kitchen alone,' said Bull.

'He's in his playpen and Saffron's watching TV,' said Zoe.

'They can't come to any harm.'

'Saffron isn't watching TV, she's sitting on the stairs,' said Bull.

'I'm sorry,' said Zoe.

'This sort of thing isn't fair on me,' said Bull. 'Isn't work enough of a worry without feeling insecure about the kids as well? Your mind's all over the place these days. Why do you come wandering up here? Well, don't bother to tell lies, you've been writing again.'

'Well, actually I was,' said Zoe. Because when it came to it, perhaps he wouldn't mind so much.

'I've no objection', said Bull, 'to whatever you choose to do in your spare time. Except when it gets in the way of looking after the children. Which, on today's evidence, it seems to.'

'I'm sorry,' said Zoe again, and added hopefully, 'If we go downstairs we can have a drink and I can get on with supper.'

It seemed Bull was home early because of a bomb scare. The Masonic Temple in Holborn had been cordoned off. Bull, as a Master of his local Lodge, was attending a convocation there. Bull would never tell Zoe what went on at the meetings; that had to be kept secret from women. Bull would say it was all very childish but what was good enough for the Royal Family was good enough for him.

'The Prince of Wales refuses to be a Mason,' Zoe had said; but it was the kind of clever-clever remark he didn't like, suggesting she read the papers and he didn't. There had been a terrible row: she had ended up screaming, he had ended up hitting. And all about what? Nothing. When it came to the Masons it seemed easier just to say nothing.

Bull made no move to go downstairs. He looked under the bed, found the suitcase, pulled it out and opened it.

'Untidy,' he said. 'Not a good sign. Most accomplished writers are meticulous in how they keep their papers.'

'I am too,' she was tempted to say, 'unless you come home early and I have to shove it all together and hide it.'

He looked through a few pages.

'Dry stuff,' he said. 'Why do you have to hide things from me? You haven't been seeing the sisters, anything like that?'

'No,' said Zoe. It was true but sounded like a lie.

'Because it can only upset you. Zoe darling, this is a waste of time. All right, so you have a degree, we all know you're a clever girl, but what do you know beyond these four walls? What have you got to say that others will want to read?'

'I know what it's like to be me,' said Zoe.

She had her back to the door. Bull seemed so vast he filled the room. The children were like that too. She'd take Saffron to see friends and be astonished at how little she suddenly was. She loomed so large in the house; how could such a mite fill all available landscapes? Now Bull was doing it too. Filling all the space in front of her eyes.

'It's wonderful to be a wife and a mother,' said Bull, 'but it's hardly electrifying. Housebound is not the stuff of literature. Why should anyone be interested?'

'I'm not writing literature,' said Zoe. 'It's sociology.'

'Even so,' said Bull, reading on, 'I'm afraid this won't do. It's stodgy, constipated stuff. Darling, stop wasting your time. Do what you know about. What you're so good at. You're no great thinker, no great writer, you're our Zoe and we all love you very much.'

He put the papers back in the case, closed it, pushed it under the bed, took Zoe's arm and said, 'Let's forget it. Let's go down and you can make supper. Thank God I have an evening at home, after all. You're a daft brush, Zoe, and I love you for it.'

Zoe ran into the kitchen and snatched Sampson from his pen and hugged him to her.

'Oh Sampson, Sampson, did I leave you alone? I'm so sorry, so sorry. Bad Mummy, naughty Mummy!'

Saffron came in and watched her mother dancing round the room and said, 'Are you laughing or crying, Mummy?' and looked at Bull accusingly.

Zoe calmed down and Bull poured her and him a stiff gin and tonic, and another, and another. Drink made them both feel better, but they kept an eye on it.

Saffron went upstairs to the parental bedroom and came down wearing her mother's high-heel shoes, pouting and grimacing like a grown-up woman.
'Take those off,' said Zoe.
'She's cute,' said Bull. 'Leave her be.'
Saffron looked from one to the other as if making some kind of life choice, and took the shoes off. She was going to be on Zoe's side.

One day when Layla was sitting at her desk at Medusa with her head in her hands, Stephanie came in waving a folder saying, 'Guess what, Zoe's been writing a book. Remember Zoe, who was there at the meeting on the day we'll never forget, but who left early, and missed everything?'

'I remember Zoe. She was a traitor,' said Layla. 'A weak sister. What is the book about? How to keep your husband? How to throw away your life and lose it? Life in three easy stages. Love, marriage, babies, finis. Zoe's way. Or the not so easy stages. My way. No love, no marriage, no babies, finis.'

'My God,' said Stephanie, 'you're in a state.'
'I'm a dead branch on the tree of life,' said Layla. 'I am barren.'
'Well, good heavens,' said Stephanie briskly. She had heard about Layla's brush with the obstetricians. 'There's more to life than passing it on.'
'What, for example?' asked Layla, bleakly.
'There's work,' said Stephanie.
'Boring,' said Layla.
'There's making money,' said Stephanie. 'If you're that sort,' she added, being above mere commercialism herself. They would have laid

down their lives for each other, but not without a one-up remark as each expired.

'Not enough to fucking notice,' said Layla. 'Why is it I never meet an attractive man?'

Stephanie did not deign to answer. Another of Layla's love affairs had publicly bitten the dust. Her lover had married a suitable young woman, and in a church. He had invited Layla to the wedding, and she had gone, though expected to decline. The invitation had come through the post; it had been his way of breaking the news to her. It arrived at the same time as a besieging cluster of pressmen, anxious for a quote and getting none. Layla had worn scarlet to the wedding, and talked animatedly to his parents, whom she had met on many occasions. Nevertheless she was upset. She viewed the prospect of a book from Zoe without enthusiasm.

If this, if that, if only; if only everyone behaved well, how few terrible things would happen. But the chain of wrong choices stretches back so far, so long, it's amazing we get through our lives as well as we do.

'*Lost Women: the Fate of the Graduate Housewife* is a rotten title,' Layla said. 'Trust Zoe to go clump, clump, clump through the tulips. Is it all like that?'

'I think it's brilliant,' said Stephie. 'She's only sent fifty pages but they're readable.'

'It's pop sociology,' said Layla, waving it away.

'You're bound to like it. Whether it's good or not is a different matter.'

'Why don't you read it and find out.'

'I only read novels,' said Layla.

'What do I say to Zoe?' asked Stephanie. 'You're being very annoying.'

'What you always say to everyone,' said Layla. 'Tell her to finish it and get a move on. Tell her we've got another like it in the pipeline, so we have an excuse to turn it down. Tell her anything, but please can we think of something else just at the moment.'

'That is certainly not what I always say to our writers,' said Stephanie, and went away.

Later, Layla went to stand over Stephanie's desk.

'Stephanie,' said Layla, 'all this is getting too incestuous. Friendship is one thing, business is another.'

'That's male talk,' said Stephanie. 'Business is merely an extension of everyday life.'

'Not if it's going to make a profit,' said Layla. 'I think you ought to move out of my house and set up on your own.'

'You want to get rid of me. It's because I see through you.'

'Don't be ridiculous,' said Layla. 'You have no idea where I begin and where I end. You came to my house for a couple of months and have stayed years. This office is getting too crowded. There's no storage space. I want to use your room at home as an overflow.'

'You mean you want total control,' said Stephanie. 'You want everything and everyone under your nose. You're a power freak.'

'I don't want to share my home with someone who keeps telling me the truth,' said Layla. 'I want to fill it with people who admire me and worship me; and that's not you.'

'Feminists don't lie to one another,' said Stephanie. 'Sometimes I wonder if you're a feminist at all.'

'That is not such a terrible accusation as you might fucking think,' said Layla.

Stephanie stared moodily into the middle distance.
'You have a spot on your nose,' said Layla. 'You need more sex.'
'All male sex is an attack,' said Stephanie. 'An exercise of power over women. I don't mean to put up with any of that.'
'Have spots then,' said Layla, and then said, 'I'm sorry. I'm in a bad mood.' It did not occur to her to blame PMT. At that time women did what they could in argument to diminish the difference between the genders, not emphasise it, in the attempt to hoist the status of the female to somewhere near that of the male. A moderate ambition.
'Rejection is the pattern of my life,' said Stephanie. 'My mother won't speak to me, my children hate me, Hamish preferred an idiot to me. Now you too, Layla.'
'Oh shut the fuck up,' said Layla. 'Stay if you like. Stay as long as you like. I took you on now I'm stuck with you.'
'If I'm not wanted,' said Stephanie, 'I'll go. You are so patronising, Layla.'

Layla said how could she be patronising to a mother of two; she, who would never be a mother of even one. She had been brought up in a world which defined a woman as someone who had babies and now she hardly knew what she was or why. Reason told her there must

146

be more to life than simply passing it on, but emotion told her otherwise.

Stephanie said she had been brought up in the same world, obeyed its precepts by having babies, and then found she was less a person for it. The only solution to the continuation of the human race in a way reconcilable with the rights of women was that men should take an equal share in parenting. But give men an inch and they took an ell. Hamish one way and another had deprived her of her children altogether.

They ended up crying in each other's arms. Medusa staff looked the other way.

Layla, as fate would have it, left the office to have a coffee and a breath of less emotional fresh air. From the window of Lentils she watched the customers come and go in the bookshop opposite. And as coincidence decreed who should she see but Hamish passing by. And he saw her and came in to sit beside her.

'Why, Hamish,' said Layla, 'what can you be doing in Carnaby Street? This is the place of the moment, not the past: of psychedelia and feathers, not old oak and Antiquax.' 'I'm getting Rafe a leather jacket for his birthday,' said Hamish. 'The poor motherless boy needs his consolations. Do you mind me joining you?'

He sat rather close on the stool. Their thighs touched.

'Not at all,' said Layla. 'What's the matter? Daffy a disappointment? Not what you hoped? I hear things aren't too well between you.'
'She refuses to move out of the house,' said Hamish. 'Women can be very difficult. So I've had to let her stay, on condition she looks after the boys. We have what you women call an open relationship.'
'You mean she stays home to look after her predecessor's kids while you go out having a

148

good time. Women have other names for that. Oppression, exploitation, that kind of thing.'

'She knew what she was doing,' said Hamish. 'She knew I had kids when she broke up my marriage. The boys are her moral responsibility and I take financial responsibility. I don't see what's wrong with that.'

'At least,' said Layla, 'you are defining a situation with a view to some moral resolution. For a man this is progress.'

'You're looking very good,' said Hamish. His thigh, which over the last few exchanges seemed to have retracted somewhat, pressed close again. 'What are you doing here? Picking up passing strangers?'

'I'm doing market research,' said Layla. 'If someone goes so far as to pick up a book and handle it, eighty per cent of the time they go on to buy it. Had you realised that?'

'If only it were the same in the antique trade,' said Hamish.

'To touch is to buy. I hear Medusa is going well.'

'We manage,' said Layla, cautiously; it is always prudent to deny prosperity, unless attempting to borrow money.

'I reckon Stephie must be earning more than me,' said Hamish, 'considering the number of Medusa books I see on the bookshop shelves. Which being the case, why am I expected to support Stephie's kids and she not?'

'Medusa is a non-profit-making organisation,' said Layla.
'How very convenient for Medusa,' said Hamish.

He smiled at her brightly and she smiled back. Now his hand was on her knee.

'Actually,' said Hamish, 'I'm thinking of giving up the antique trade altogether. People know far too much about the value of their bits and pieces. I blame TV. I shall go and live in the country. If I stay in London I'll only drink myself to death.'
'Why are you more likely to drink yourself to death in the city than in the country?' asked Layla. 'Wouldn't boredom drive you to further excess?'
'In the city,' said Hamish, 'one is so frequently reminded that civilisation has broken down. Now the Arab oil states have stopped quarrelling amongst themselves and united to put up the price of petrol, what future is there for the West? I would rather contemplate the eternal verities of nature, the turn of the seasons and so forth.'
'But you'll leave the children behind in London with Daffy?' enquired Layla.
'Of course,' he said. 'While I prepare a proper home for them. The house I have in mind has no water other than from a well and no electricity, and is not suitable for children.'

'Men go to extraordinary lengths', said Layla, 'to avoid their children, even retreat into nature. As if going to war were not enough.'

'Is that how you see war?' asked Hamish. 'The flight from fatherhood?'

'Of course,' said Layla. 'Traditionally, the families and the generals plot the wholesale death of younger men. Though these days war is more likely to be a male plot to bomb the women and children while the men are safely out of the way.'

'Good Lord,' said Hamish. 'How wonderful it must be to view all human activity in gender terms.'

'How else?' murmured Layla. Distress had hollowed her eyes: she looked haunted as well as seductive. 'It is not nice to be told you are a dead twig on the tree of life, however much you can tell yourself the telling is done by an enemy out to get you. And since Harrods have only two shades of tights in stock — beige and ecru — I can see the delights of civilisation fading. The world as we know it is coming to and end. How shall we spend the last hours?'

His face was near hers, stubbly round the chin, smooth and polished on the cheeks and forehead. His eyes were brown, confiding and intelligent. His hand left hers warm where he touched it. Layla decided she might as well have some fun in life: some affirmative action to take away the taste and flavour of Mr Wrightson the gynaecologist. 'We'll spend it,' said Hamish, 'as people do in the normal end-of-the-world scenario. Your place or mine?'

151

Stephie waited a while for Layla to come back: she wanted to talk to Layla further about Zoe's book, but since Layla wasn't there Stephie decided she'd better make her own decisions, and called Zoe. But Bull answered the phone. Stephanie saw no reason to exercise diplomacy, tact or caution. Women should speak the truth, not be frightened of men, and not dissimulate. To do so was to be seen to act from weakness, not strength. The days of charming, soothing and placating men were surely over.

'Why Bull,' she said, 'it's Stephanie from Medusa. We haven't met for years. I hope we don't seem so much of a threat to you as we once did. Women can take control of their own lives and the world not come to an end. Is Zoe there? No? Can you give her a message? She has sent us some pages of manuscript. Do tell her we'd be delighted to see the rest. It looks really promising and just up our street.'

'I'll tell her that,' said Bull, and if his voice sounded taut and up a pitch Stephie didn't notice. Bull put the receiver down abruptly and Stephie thought how rude men were: had she been a man she would surely have received more courtesy. Men automatically downgraded all female enterprise, in their minds; you didn't need student essays to prove it.

At the other side of the office Alice was conducting an experiment with a wooden frame in the shape of a three-dimensional triangle. This she placed on Nancy's desk. She then put one of two similar apples under the point of the pyramid, and shut the other in Nancy's drawer.

'The one under the pyramid will ripen first,' she said. 'You'll be surprised.'
'Of course it will,' said Nancy. 'It's in the light. There's no surprise.'
'You are so untrusting,' complained Alice.
'That's why I'm an accountant,' said Nancy. She had become sharper — some might say shrewish — of late. 'And I'm too busy for this sort of thing — the Board's coming in tomorrow. I have to be prepared.'

'You can sharpen razors too,' said Alice. 'By putting them under a pyramid. I daresay if I had a pyramidal structure built over my bed my powers of concentration would improve.'
'They're OK as they are,' said Nancy.

Sometimes Nancy worried for Alice. Others claimed that her gullibility in relation to the paranormal left the rest of her mind free for doubt, scepticism and rational assessment in

153

great measure, but the one seemed to be taking over the other. Alice now had a rose crystal on her desk to sop up negative energies, and the books she brought to Medusa for editorial assessment would have titles such as *Healing Chakras of the Mother Goddess* or *Incantations and Levitations — the Female Approach*. Such titles were seldom accepted for publication: it was to be another ten years before the New Age was to dawn so spectacularly. These were just the first twinklings of sickly light that presaged the coming of that deceptive new dawn.

Nancy discovered the apple in her drawer three weeks later; it had withered but not rotted. The one under the pyramid went rotten overnight, and smelt so bad she threw it out without drawing anyone's attention to it, lest they suspect a miracle.

While Alice was setting up her experiment in Soho, Bull was leaping up the stairs to the spare room in Belsize Park. Saffron happend to come out of the bathroom: she had been experimenting with her mother's make-up.

'Take that muck off your face,' said Bull as he went.

'Mummy wears it,' said Saffron. 'Why shouldn't I?'

'Don't answer me back,' said Bull, roaring like his name, but Saffron was accustomed to the noise he made, and drifted up the stairs after him.

'She isn't here, Daddy,' said Saffron. 'She went to the park with Sampson. Why are you home from work?'

'God knows what happens when my back is turned,' said Bull, dragging the suitcase out from under the bed. His mood was such that Saffron thought she should warn her mother of his return, and of a telephone call which seemed to have made him angry, and belted off to the park, though taking care to look to right and left when she came to roads. She was efficient, even as a child; she could prioritise from an early age. Her aim, as ever, was that the household should run smoothly and that parental voices should not be raised in anger, and certainly never fists. To this end she fed information from one to the other, bowdlerising as required.

She came across Zoe sitting next to Daffy on the park bench, while little Sampson played in the sandpit. The dogs were healthier then or perhaps it was that no one knew of the parasites the animals carried which could cause blindness. Ignorance made the times more carefree: no one had even heard of passive smoking and though it was known that cigarettes caused cancer smokers were allowed to go to hell their own way — which Daffy and Zoe now did, sitting companionably together under the trees.

Saffron heard a passing mother look over towards Zoe and Daffy and say, 'It's all right for some,' though goodness knows their plight and hers were pretty much the same. She too could have sat down on a park bench and enjoyed the leisure technology provided. She too, in due course, would open a can of sieved vegetables and beef for the baby's lunch. There was no real hurry in the domestic life: the hunger pangs of children could always be staved off by an iced lolly: your own with a fag and a cup of tea. As the toil grew less, so did the sense of achievement.

'Dad's home early,' said Saffron. 'And he's in a mood.'
'I'd better get back,' said Zoe. It was still expected that a woman should keep her man's loneliness at bay: if he was in the house so was

she expected to be. Daffy gave them a lift as far
as their door, and then zoomed back to meet
the boys out of school and bring them home to
Chalcot Crescent.

Under Daffy's care No. 103 was looking good. There were tubs of flowers on the first-floor balcony, the front door had been repainted and the door knocker, cracked by Bull on the day of Medusa's birth, had been replaced. Hamish favoured the patina of age-old brass, but Daffy had had her way. The knocker was not only new but its newness had been sealed in with gloss polyurethane. Hamish had accused her of having a bourgeois sensibility, which was about the worst he could say of anyone.

The boys went downstairs to the TV room, and Daffy called up the stairs, 'Hi, Hamish. Are you home? It's me,' in the easy tones of those who expect a welcome.
Silence rewarded her. She repeated, though this time more tentatively, 'Hamish? Have you fallen asleep?'

She bounded up the stairs to the bedroom where once she had been discovered by Stephanie, and opened the door. On the bed she there saw entwined who but a naked Hamish and partly naked woman whom Daffy did not at first recognise.

'Hamish?' asked Daffy in a small voice. Hamish obligingly disengaged himself and got off the bed.

'Why are you home early?' asked Hamish. He stood naked and unashamed, his penis pink, moist and still standing, gradually sinking as they spoke until by the end of the conversation it hung docilely and meekly, and as if it were now its owner's possession and not the other way round. It was these sudden switches in ownership which caused confusion to so many; Hamish always seemed helpless before the shifting phenomena of himself.

'I'm not early,' said Daffy. 'I'm exactly the same time as usual.'
'Good heavens,' said Hamish, 'is that the time?'
Layla sat up in bed and said, 'Fuck it, Hamish, at least say you're sorry.'
'What about?' asked Hamish. 'I never told Daffy this bed was exclusively hers, did I, Daffy?'
But Daffy was backing from the room. 'Layla?' she lamented. 'Layla!'

'Anyway,' said Hamish, 'this *you and me* thing has to end. It has got really boring. Don't you think so? Everything has its time.'

But Daffy was running down the stairs crying, Layla was dressing, and Hamish was sitting on the end of the bed drumming his fingers and asking the heavens why he was so surrounded by hysterical women.

'Hysterical' was an adjective frequently applied to women in those days of low female employment: now it is heard rather less, but then women cry and scream rather less, being so focused on the necessities of earning a living. 'Hysteria' as every woman was then told, is Greek for 'womb' — and the early doctors assumed that weeping, wailing and leaping at men with clawing nails was caused by the wandering of the womb through the body, it being an untethered organ. Men on the other hand had all their internal organs fixed and certain, firm and rigid not soft and floppy, and so did not suffer from hysterics: certainly it was not they who ever provoked this exclusively female and distressing phenomenon. Hysterics.

A few streets up the hill, Bull sat beside the anthracite stove which warmed the kitchen and fed sheets of Zoe's manuscript through the narrow bars, pushing them in one by one with the poker.

Before central heating became commonplace, coal was used to heat houses, and very dirty and dusty it was. Zoe had bought this particular stove, a Pither, from Hamish's antique shop. It had cost £15 and dated from the turn of the century: a bargain. It was made of copper and was bow-fronted, stood some three feet high, and had round its rim a metal filigree from which warm and mildly poisonous air escaped. You poured anthracite — small particles of treated coal — into the top of the stove with a funnel: the fire burned at the bottom where a tilted firebrick let the air in, its flow controlled by a nifty brass lever: little by little the fire consumed the stored fuel: the stove itself got hotter and hotter: children soon learned not to touch it. Every day the housewife drove a metal slice between ash and still burning coal and using a hook tilted the grate and emptied out the ash. A cloud of dust and ash would then arise to swirl round the room and settle on shelves, books, fruit bowls, ornaments and polished and non-polished surfaces everywhere.

It was then time to pour more fuel into the Pither. If it was raining and the coal got wet as it was carried into the house in its special bucket, the unburned fuel gave off fumes. Once the Pither stove was as popular as the Aga is today, and induced as much devotion in its owners. 'So much better than an open fire,' people would say. To keep the Pither running required an outside coal stove, coal bucket, funnel, uncracked firebrick, hook and slice. If any of these pieces of equipment went missing the fire would go out and a chilly desolation descend upon the household.

Zoe, returning, watched the pages of her manuscript blacken amongst the burning band of fuel, as Bull stuffed them through the bars. She worried for the fire: charred paper might put it out. The stove was so sensitive.
'The paper only chars, Bull; it won't burn properly; there's not enough oxygen. You'll put the Pither out, and it's such a hassle to get going again. You know it is. Don't *do* this.'

Still he went on ramming in the sheets.

'Bull, really, you have no right to do this. It has taken me years to write this stuff. Please stop. I'll have to start again.'
'You won't start again, you have no stamina,' said Bull. 'I know you.' He worked quite cheerfully. He'd been drinking vodka. Saffron stood by and tried to work out what was going on, whether or

not she had done the right thing in fetching her mother home.

'It's for your sake,' said Bull. 'We have to bring this writing nonsense to an end. You neglect your family and for the sake of what? A bleat of self-pity which takes up all your energy and attention. I don't want a wife of mine made a laughing stock. Your sentences are graceless, the thoughts you express are infantile. You can't write, Zoe, and that's all there is to it.'

'How do you know?'
'I'm a reader, for God's sake. And I don't want to read this twaddle, and nobody else will.'

'You may not be the best judge,' pleaded Zoe. 'You may be the man in the street but you're not the woman in the street.'
'Feminist talk,' said Bull, 'and that's what really gets up my nose. You've been in touch with the harlots from Medusa. One of them had the nerve to phone here.'
'Stephie called? What did she say? Did she like it?'
'No, she did not like it,' said Bull. 'Enemies of society they may be, cigarette-smoking slags with moustaches' — current wisdom had it that career women were more prone to grow moustaches than those content to be wives and mothers — 'but they do at least seem to have some common sense. Your manuscript is unpublishable. There is, your friend the unnatural mother told me, no market any

longer for female self-pity. I'm amazed there ever was.'

Zoe abandoned her feeble attempts to make Bull desist: she sat and watched five years' work burn, in apparent tranquillity.

'Go away Saffron,' she said to her daughter, all the same. 'There is no need for you to witness this.'

Saffron took her mother's advice, and left.

Outside No. 103 Chalcot Crescent, Daffy was trying to get herself, the two boys, and two suitcases out of the house. The boys were on the whole unwilling to leave, being in the middle of their tea and toast and peanut butter — but they liked Daffy and understood the part they were expected to play in the domestic dramas which every now and then erupted around them. They served as Witness to the Life. Hamish seemed taken aback by the suddenness of Daffy's departure. Layla hovered in the background.

'Those are not your children to take,' said Hamish. 'They're mine.'
Alas, he had recently taken Daffy to see Brecht's *Caucasian Chalk Circle*, in one of his attempts to educate her, and she was able to reply, 'Children belong to those who look after them,' to which Hamish responded, 'In boring ideological plays, perhaps, but not in law. Go yourself, but leave the boys.'

'Boys,' said Daffy, 'do you want to stay with your father and his new woman, or do you want to come with me?'
They considered.

'Daffy,' said Layla, 'I have no intention of staying in this house a moment longer than I

165

have to. Hamish told me you were away or I wouldn't have been here in the first place. You and I have never got on, and I think you're a fool and a very weak sister indeed, but I would not deliberately upset you.'

'Like fuck,' said Daffy.

'Actually,' said Layla, 'I don't see what you've really got to complain about. This is only what you did to Stephie.'

'But that was her and this is me, fuck it,' said Daffy.

'Please don't swear in front of my boys,' said Hamish. 'Either of you. Daffy, please leave. Layla, the boys need their tea.' 'Hamish,' said Layla, 'there is not the slightest question of my staying around on any sort of permanent basis. What we did upstairs was act out an end-of-the-world scenario, and alas, the world has not come to an end, so can we all just take up where we left off?'

Hamish took up a paperweight — Victorian, little gold stars embedded in heavy glass — from the rather ugly mahogany coat stand, and hurled it right down the corridor towards the French windows at the back of the house. Glass splintered into a thousand pieces.

'Can we come with you, Daffy?' asked Roland, instantly. 'So long as there's a telly,' added Rafe.

Hamish was hurt and acted accordingly. He stood aside to let his family pass.

'On your own head be it,' said Hamish. 'Remember, this is your responsibility. You are breaking up this family.'

Daffy looked haunted and guilty but went on out of the door, the boys trailing behind her.

'I don't know how you think you're going to live,' said Hamish after her. 'What will you do for money? The boys don't get a penny of support while they're not under my roof.'

'I love those boys,' said Daffy, trailing miserably off into the street, while they trailed after her, looking mutinously and sulkily back at their father. But they did not seem to take the situation too seriously: they knew it would be resolved. Yesterday's children were less easily traumatised than today's. The word 'trauma' had scarcely been invented, let alone 'stress', and in the beginning, as we keep being told, is the word. Without it, what exists?

'Oh dear,' said Layla, 'my name will be fucking mud when this gets round. You are too bad, Hamish. You found me at an impressionable point, a vulnerable time. Nevertheless, I enjoyed the episode very much: I cannot honestly say I regret it. Daffy will come back, won't she?'

'She has nowhere to go,' said Hamish. 'So yes, she will. Which leaves me free to go.'

'I suppose you did warn her when all this began,' said Layla, 'that she was in an open relationship?'
'I didn't have to tell her,' said Hamish. 'Surely it was obvious.' But he had the grace to look guilty.

Back at the Medusa offices Alice was speaking in her quiet and moderated voice to a group of journalists, male and female mixed but mostly female.

'The main movement that is women's liberation,' said Alice, 'has settled down into three separate tendencies. The radical feminists, who see the problem as that of oppression by an entrenched patriarchy. These radical feminists campaign against men's violence towards women, against rape and pornography, and against the military-industrial complex. The socialist feminists — '

She broke off because the door at the end of the room had been thrown open. There stood Daffy, flanked by little Rafe and Roland. Everyone turned to look at them.

Daffy always looked at her best when colour washed over a skin normally so pale it tended to flatten out her features. Whether the flush was due to sexual arousal, or temper, or indignation, or, as now, upset and shock, passion was always to her benefit. This was her good fortune. Other women, upset, would get squinty-eyed, slack-jawed, puffy from water retention and mean-looking: not Daffy. Which did not help her with the Medusa crowd, who in the early days sought to bring justice to the world of looks. If all wore big boots, who would ever know about the prettiness of particular feet? All would have been born equal.

Alice continued. Everyone turned back dutifully to listen. Even Stephie, whose children Rafe and Roland were, paid attention to Alice and not to them. They did not take particular offence, though later on therapists and counsellors were to try to persuade them otherwise.

Children then were grateful to have been born at all; were on the whole uncritical of their upbringing; parents did the best they could in the light of their own natures, it was commonly assumed.

'The socialists feminists see the women problem as that of a male domination linked to class exploitation. The pressure here is to make alliances with other oppressed groups and classes — ethnic minorities, coal miners, gays, for example. We are all not just sisters but brothers too, under the skin. When the State melts away, men and women will find equality.

'Stephie,' said Daffy, 'I've brought your boys back.'

Alice coughed warningly. She never liked being interrupted. 'As for the love of a good man,' said Daffy, 'fuck that for a laugh.'

Alice went on.

'And then we have the liberal feminists: in their eyes the problem is of prejudice combined with custom and practice. Here we find women working for equal rights, equal pay, equal opportunities, and equality under the law. Women work within the civil service, and in voluntary groups to influence the male decision-makers. Their aim is reformation, not revolution. Amongst all strands of feminists you will find those who understand the importance of changing a male-ist language. Chairman becomes Chairperson, or Madam Chairman.'

'And manhole becomes personhole,' said one of the male journalists, and guffawed. 'And what the hell do you do with actress-and bishop jokes if actress becomes actor?'

'All the funnier,' said Alice, but no one laughed. Instead there was a kind of embarrassed silence. Homosexual activity seemed, to everyone except those directly involved, difficuty to contemplate in any detail.

Into the silence first Rafe spoke and then Roland.

'I don't like it here,' said Rafe. 'I want to go back to Daddy.'

'Me too,' said Roland. 'There isn't even a TV.'

'But Radical, Socialists or Liberal,' said Alice. 'Medusa is the point where the strands meet. Our policy here at Medusa is to publish from the whole spectrum of feminist thought. Feminism

171

is a revolution conducted in a female way: by group consensus rather than directive. There are no party headquarters, no policy documents, no book of rules.'

'You must have some sanctions,' said another male journalist. 'We have a policy of constructive self-criticism,' said Stephie. 'Here at Medusa if one of us steps out of line, we will get together and all talk about it. The one great sanction is that no one wants to be declared a weak sister, a poor feminist.' She turned and walked towards her sons, ignoring Daffy.

'I'll take you boys home with me,' she said. 'Now you're here. But you should never have been brought to these offices in the first place.'

'You only ever wanted me to be a girl,' complained Rafe, loud and clear before the assembled journalists.

'Daffy made us come here,' said Roland. 'And I want to go back to Daddy, anyway, not to your horrid place. There's no TV.'

Notebooks were out, pens in action. This was more interesting than Whither Feminism, Whence Medusa.

At which juncture, as luck would have it, Layla walked in, head held high, eyes bright, footsteps clattering into the stilled room.

'That's the woman in Daddy's bed,' said Rafe. 'That's why Daffy walked out,' said Roland.

Layla walked on to her office.

Alice gave her nervous little attention-demanding cough and continued.

'The easiest way for any movement to proselytise is to find a common enemy,' she went on. Journalists flipped pages, and pretended to write, or made indecipherable notes. 'The Marxists have the capitalists, the bourgeois lackeys: ours is ready-made. Ours is man. We are accused of being man-haters, but if we are is it surprising? Is it anything to be ashamed of? It isn't healthy for the exploited and oppressed to love their masters. Women do two-thirds of the world's work, earn one-tenth of the world's wealth. This we mean to change. The shift to equality will be painful, and disruptive to the ways of patriarchal society, but must happen.'

Stephie was staring after Layla. She seemed to have forgotten about her children. Rafe and Roland, their bluff called, broke into tears of grief and rage, and ran from the room. Daffy ran after them.

'Boys, it's OK, it's OK. I'll take you home. I'll make Daddy leave; we'll stay.'

That evening a passer-by on Cheyne Walk would have seen Johnny helping Stephie out with her belongings; stacking them in the back of the Mini.

'You don't have to go, Stephie,' said Johnny. 'We'll miss you. You're just making a drama, as usual.'

'A fine way to put it,' said Stephie, bitterly. 'Look how little I have to show for my life so far. I have sacrificed everything for a cause, for sisterhood with women, and I am left with a bookcase, a lampstand, an old rug, and a teddy bear.'

Stephanie's parents had recently moved to the Canary Islands to enjoy their retirement: the family home had been sold: she felt bereft and alone.

'I shan't stay under Layla's roof a moment longer,' said Stephanie. 'She is unprincipled. Once upon a time I shared a bed with Hamish. I conceived two children in it. I got used to having Daffy in it. But that Layla should then climb into it is unendurable.'

'I think it was only a passing thing,' said Johnny. 'Isn't it rather sour grapes on your part?'

'You'd forgive her anything,' said Stephanie,

trying to wedge a rug between boxes and failing; then throwing the rug into a puddle on the road in her irritation. 'You're in love with her too. Why is it that those who deserve least get most?'

Layla came out of the house at this moment carrying a framed photograph of Rafe and Roland in their very early years, to help Stephanie on her way.
'You forgot this,' she said.
'My children are lost to me anyway,' said Stephie. 'Keep it.'
'Why in fuck's name should I want a photograph of your boys?'
'Because you can't have children yourself,' said Stephie snappily. 'Honorary aunt-hood is the best you can hope for. You'll end up keeping cats.'

Layla curled her upper lip and said, 'Pathetic.' Stephanie banged down the back door of the Mini; the catch failed to engage. She banged it again and again.
'What you need,' said Layla, 'is a good fuck.'

This was practically the worst thing one woman could say to another, being what men were accustomed to say of any woman who annoyed them: part of the male litany of insult and haw-hawing still prevalent at the time. In fact it was so dreadful a remark for a woman to make that it made Layla laugh, at which Stephanie laughed too.

175

'It is time I moved out,' said Stephanie, almost affectionately. 'You won't rest until I've gone. I can see that.'

She had found a little flat in Camden Town, not far from Chalcot Crescent, where the humbleness of her situation, the pureness of her poverty, would not be lost upon the world, or Hamish. It was at this moment, when Stephanie was on the verge of driving off, that a pretty young man in the fashion of the day, blond hair falling over a smooth forehead, full lips in a square jaw, muscled but not broad-shouldered, walked up to Layla's house. He wore flares and a flowered shirt and had a kitbag slung over his shoulders. He was observably gay; you could tell when he opened his mouth. That is to say he was camply spoken.

These days it is much harder to tell a man's sexual orientation, as many a contemporary young woman in search of a partner has found to her cost. Then many men, gay by nature, strove to be heterosexual in looks and behaviour. There came a time when nobody even tried. The tendency to homosexuality in every adolescent — which Freud interpreted as an anticipatory and safe prelude to mature love of someone of the opposite gender — grew to be construed early on as a lifetime's permanent tendency. Bisexuality, a shift in sexual orientation, seemed more than anyone could cope with.

Once a gay always a gay, and gay culture would snap you up before you had a chance to change your mind. Nowadays anyone is anything and honestly, nobody cares, unless they are politicians trying to get votes by wishing the old days back again. Paedophilia is to the current decade as gayness was to a decade thirty years back. But the times they are forever a-changing. There has to be something around in the public mind which deserves castration at worst, death at best.

'Hi there,' said jaunty Richard, defying the world he'd been brought up in, brave, handsome, likeable and perverse. He may have acted from stupidity not principle, but what the hell.

'You're early,' said Johnny, nervously.

'What, no welcome, darling?' said Richard to Johnny.

'Come on now, give us a kiss.'

And he kissed Johnny full on the lips and Stephanie tried not to look aghast.

'Please don't, darling, in public,' said Layla. 'It's not that I don't want scandal, it's just the talk, talk, talk I'll have to do if you two make a phallic meal of it.'

'I've got a few bits and pieces coming in the morning,' said Richard. 'A lamp and a rug or two and my teddy bear.'

'He's moving in?' asked Stephanie. 'You mean I move out and he moves in? What is going on here?'

'At least he'll pay rent,' said Layla, 'which is

more than you ever did.'

'How could I possibly pay rent on what Medusa pays me?' demanded Stephanie. 'You just like to be the one in charge, Layla. You like people to be grateful. You're a power freak.'

'And you're a failed power freak,' said Layla, closing the back door of Stephie's Mini by pressing down lightly rather than slamming. Johnny and Richard went inside, holding hands.

'I never knew,' said Stephie. 'Gay! Poor Nancy.'

'He's only just decided,' said Layla. 'He tried a while with Nancy, because she was the one who looked most like a boy, but in the end why pretend?'

'You make a joke of everything,' said Stephanie, 'and I fall for it. But really this is too bad. You will have to go before the disciplinary committee.'

'What for?' asked Layla.

'For being in Hamish's bed, for spiting me, for filling your house with gays when there are so many sisters in need.'

'There isn't a disciplinary committee,' said Layla.

'Then I'll create one,' said Stephie. 'That man at the media session was right, though I hate to say it. We have to have sanctions of some kind. I want you excommunicated. I want you prevented from describing yourself as a feminist. You bring the whole movement into disrepute.'

'And what's the punishment?' shrieked Layla, hand on hip.

Sometimes she allowed herself a fishwife demeanour. But she had got quite thin lately: she was beginning to look strong and handsome rather than quirky and fetching. Stephanie's face seemed to get more mobile with the years: powerful and conflicting emotions racked her: she had no instinct for self-protection. Her features, once so even, standardly beautiful, had begun to seem all over the place. One fine arched, pale eyebrow now stood noticeably higher than the other. Cartoonists noticed it. These days the Harpies of Medusa, as the press described them, their mythology confused but apt, showed Layla as the blank and stupid beauty, Stephanie as the mad intellectual, Nancy as a dull stodge and Alice as a witch.

'I don't know why you mind,' Alice said once to Nancy. 'People who know you know what you look like. If people who've never met you think you look other than what you do, what can it matter?' But that's by the by.

Now Stephanie shrieked back at Layla.
'You will be struck off,' she cried. 'You will be ostracised by every right-thinking feminist.'
'I am the only right-thinking feminist there is,' said Layla more calmly. 'It's all the others who are out of step.'

Stephanie, snorting, drove off into the night yet again, though this time clothed and on her own. 'Thanks a million, Stephie,' Layla called after her. 'Don't even bother to say thank you for inviting me.'

'Jesus,' said Layla, as she stomped off inside. 'Women!'

Sounds of passion came from Johnny's room as she went through the courtyard, and she wondered what she'd done. There were, she could see, advantages in having celibate tenants. Sex, unconfined by tradition, brought with it the uncertain, strangers, rough trade, energies from the street, all things uncontrollable. You had to be young, brave and strong to take it on board. She hoped she still was. And lucky, too. And ignorant. You might think you were just taking the children to play in the people's sandpit, but someone else's dog might bring in the worm which turned your child blind. She had read a report of such an event in the newspaper. She saw there were many compensations to not having children. You held no hostages to fortune: you need be anxious only for yourself: you could control your circumstances; you were not at the mercy of chance. One of the most frightening things about Stephanie's children was how unappealing they were, thus undermining the power of Stephanie's sacrifice in giving them up.

Women did not, as Layla had often observed, easily give up appealing, pretty and charming children. It was the plain, awkward ones who got abandoned: just as plain, dull, awkward women were the ones who were most often deserted by men. Though that too began to change. Achieving and successful women often found themselves alone.

Layla took a sleeping pill and passed out on her silk and velvet strewn bed. Stephanie had plain, thin, dull, serviceable bed linen. It annoyed Layla that she had shared her washing machine with so much dreariness for so long. Besides, Stephanie had not gone from her life, merely to live under a different roof. Stephanie was angry now, but her angers passed.

News of Richard got through to Nancy. She lay in bed crying in her small room in the outer suburbs. In her hand she clutched a letter from Brian. The fact that Johnny had a male lover, though not by now unexpected, had shaken her. Alice's mother Doreen came in, wearing a quilted dressing gown and with her hair in rollers. Like someone out of a comedy series, Nancy thought briefly through her misery. Misery can make people disagreeable. What had she come to? She pulled herself together. People were not to be mocked for their looks, their accent, their age, their class; this woman had given birth to Alice, had spawned a genius of the age, had encouraged and supported what to her must seem a strange child, and was gloriously kind. What were curlers compared to all this?

'Nancy!' said Doreen, switching on the Mickey Mouse bedside lamp she had bought in Woolworth's as a gift for Nancy, settling herself on the bedside chair. 'I heard you crying. What's the matter? Don't you like living here? Don't we make you happy?'

'Of course I like it,' said Nancy. 'You're very good to me.'

'You had a letter from home,' said Doreen. 'I noticed. Is that the trouble?'

Nancy thought how nice it was to be noticed. Her own mother had done very little noticing. She was a divorced schoolteacher who did a lot of marking, and whenever Nancy had said she was bored said, 'Go and run round the block and you'll soon feel better.'

'It was from my ex-boyfriend, Brian,' said Nancy. 'He was writing to tell me he's getting married to my school friend Beverley. He wants me to be sorry for letting him get away.'
'Men are always so conceited,' said Doreen. 'They want you to be hopelessly in love with them for ever.'
'But part of me *is* sorry for letting him get away,' said Nancy. 'Perhaps I was too picky. Perhaps I did the wrong thing. And now Beverley has got him!' She'd always been in competition with Beverley. This was the weakest moment of all her life. Stolid, reliable, unsexy, handsome Brian. He'd been very young. She'd given him no time to change and develop. He was irritating but who wasn't? He might have grown out of it.
'I'm so tired of being the sensible one,' she moaned. 'I'm not a frump in my heart: I hate the way people see me. Everyone else has someone to share a bed with, never me. I should have married Brian when I had the chance.'
'Dear,' said Doreen, 'everyone does the wrong thing. Do you think it was my life's dream to be married to an ageing pigeon fancier? But that's the way it turned out.'

Nancy wept some more.

'Now what?' asked Doreen.

'My shoes let water,' said Nancy. 'There's a hole worn right through the sole. And I can't afford a new pair.'

'You think that's trouble?' asked Doreen. 'Do you think Alice is ever going to give me a grandchild? Like hell she is. She's right about feminism, of course she is, but she never spares a thought about what goes on inside her own family. Bloody sisterhood.'

'Bloody sisterhood,' said Nancy. Doreen took the rollers out of her own sparse hair and used them to curl Nancy's.

Thereafter Nancy made sure she had curly hair, and the cartoonists, never thwarted, made much of her strong nose, but at least forgot her lanky hair. You can only try.

Picture the scene some three weeks later. Women of energy lose little time. Layla is holding a meeting of the Medusa Advisory Board at her house. She wants Johnny to let the sisters know what they'll be missing should they decide to cast her out of the movement. She will show herself at her most hospitable: she will serve coffee, though not cheese and pineapple on sticks, as was customary at the time, but a whole range of little savouries, and strawberries dipped in chocolate.

Women come up the steps in dribs and drabs, women of all ages and conditions, except there are no hats, no skirts, no nail varnish, no make-up to be seen. God's will, or as is already more commonly said, Nature's will, prevails. God is still held to be masculine — call God 'she' and people fidget and feel uneasy — but Nature is universally held to be 'she'. Layla alone wears a skirt, heels, mascara and lipstick. Any one of those three would be frowned upon; to flaunt them all is odious.

Nancy's in the kitchen with Johnny: they are spooning a mixture of mushroom and chillies into tiny vol-au-vent cases. There is creamed avocado too, but so pungent with garlic they are leaving that till last.

'Layla's crazy,' observes Nancy. 'This mixture is too hot and too fancy! Everyone will hate it.' Though she's developing a taste for it, and occasionally licks the spoon clean. Nancy had catered for many a crowd in her time. She knows you can't go wrong with tomato soup, roast chicken, potatoes and peas, followed by ice-cream, for sit-down lunch and dinners; sandwiches for tea, and coffee and cheese-and-pineapple on sticks for stand up occasions. She was beginning to understand that the at-least-it-can't-go-wrong principle which she applied to so many things, from dress to hair to food, was what was holding her back in life. Other women got away with so much. Layla found by Daffy in Hamish's bed was outrageous, but only Stephanie seemed really angry with Layla on this account. Others seemed to take it in their stride. She said as much to Johnny. Johnny said that since it was Stephanie's bed originally — he understood it was an antique brass bed brought home one day from Hamish's shop — she was surely entitled to be angry.

'Though I don't know why I expect you to understand,' said Nancy. 'You're gay.'
'Don't say that,' said Johnny, alarmed. 'I'll go to prison. Richard's under age. You're not suggesting everyone knows?'
'Of course they know,' said Nancy, irritated. 'You tell everyone.'
'Oh God,' said Johnny, his hand frozen. Richard came along and took over his task, since Johnny was incapable.

186

'They'll need more vol-au-vents than that,' said Richard.

'Knitting makes a girl hungry.'

'Knitting?' enquired Nancy.

'Round the guillotine,' said Richard. 'That's what they're doing. They're planning to chop off Layla's head.'

'They're not out to destroy her,' said Nancy. 'Just to establish a few basic rules of feminist conduct.'

'Lot of Mrs Grundies,' said Richard. 'Women who hate sex and make a virtue of it. But we can't let them go hungry.'

He tasted the mushroom mix and winced.

'Isn't it rather hot?' he asked, but he took some more. 'Personally, I hope Medusa do throw Layla out. Then all the boxes in the hall will go. You women are quite mad.' He pinched Johnny's bottom unexpectedly and Johnny shrieked. 'That brought you back to life,' said Richard, cunningly.

Nancy was pleased to see them so happy, in spite of herself. Friendship with the pair of them was perhaps a better bet than the neurotic love of one of them. She began to feel better. They all had some more of the mushroom mix.

Layla faced a semicircle of her accusers. She listened to their reproaches in silence.

'Anything else?' she enquired, as the volley of stored comment and criticism slowed to a sporadic trickle. 'What, nothing else? Some of you don't like me, some of you object to me swearing, some of you say I ride roughshod over you, that I don't hear you, that I go my own way and take Medusa with me. Well, perhaps so. But that's just me. You can't blame a person for their temperament. So I was found in a man's bed. For how long has that been a crime? If you can't have sex with a man and be a feminist, it's going to be a pretty small movement. Hating men, eschewing sex, separatism, apartheid between the genders was not part of our original aim.'

'We're talking about a particular man,' said Stephie. 'Not just any man. Hamish. My ex-husband.'

'So he's an ex, so fucking what,' said Layla. 'You walked out on him. He's bad news as a husband, but that doesn't rule him out as a lover, doing what he's good at.'

'Daffy's man,' said Stephanie. 'Women should not compete for male sexual favours. They do themselves no good. We have to join together in understanding that all male sex is an attack against women. It is how they bully women into submission: how they exercise their power.'

'And look at you, Layla!' said someone else. 'What you're wearing! Heels, skirt, lipstick! You're determined to make yourself a sex object.'
'If women don't make themselves sex objects,' said Layla, 'the human race is going to have a gloomy time reproducing itself. How do you want it done?'

Someone observed that all men were rapists at heart, and Johnny and Richard entertained themselves by handing round vol-au-vents. Lips puckered and eyes watered, but good manners, a conditioning so strong it was hard to detect in the self, ensured that nothing was spat out.

'Why have we got men in this all-women gathering?' someone else enquired. 'What are you trying to do, Layla?'
'Show men who's in charge,' said Layla. 'That is to say, us. Let men do the coffee and nibbles, for a change. I thought you'd appreciate that.'
'But with great respect,' said Stephanie, 'Johnny and Richard are gay and don't really count as men.'
'Oh thanks!' said Richard. 'Shall I show you my willy?'
'And not only am I wearing a skirt,' said Layla, 'I am wearing frilly knickers underneath.' She stood up and demonstrated. 'And if Johnny and Richard don't count as men why shouldn't they come to a women's meeting?'

189

The general consensus, once the meeting had calmed down, was that Layla had won. Layla pointed out to them that as she saw it the purpose of the meeting was not to bring her to heel as a feminist, but rather as a person. What was important was not her sex life, but Medusa; it was about the power she had, by virtue of being able to accomplish things others couldn't, which made them uneasy. She could make quick commercial decisions, could tell a selling jacket from a bad, could interact with the male world —

'Not half,' interjected Stephie.

'Stephie wants a free hand,' said Layla, 'to get on with publishing her boring sociological tracts. And I try to stop her — that's Stephie's problem. It's nothing to do with me being in her antique brass bed with her one-time antique husband. And Daffy deserves whatever happens, we all know that, in human terms, forget feminist. But I mean to continue in my own way along my own path, because I want Medusa to survive, and it won't without me. Do you want a publishing house which with the decades will become some pathetic fringe survivor, a producer of whining pamphlets more boring even than any Marxist/Leninist tract, because that's the way Medusa will go if you don't have me to contend with. I need to keep you on the straight and narrow, you need me to keep Medusa in business. In your hearts you know this. Come back in ten years' time and you'll have moderated your views; you'll sound less like mad women and more like politicians. I won't be pulling men as I do now, which should suit you. Medusa will be something glossy, wonderful and profitable done by women for women, and little girls will grow up feeling better about themselves. For Medusa's long-term benefit, put your trust in me. By and large I'm OK. The best you've got.'

What chance did they have? Stephie's vote of censure was thrown out. Alice finally spoke.
'It is the fate of the male revolutionary organisation,' she said, 'to factionalise and split. Each faction then devours the other, and the common enemy laughs and carries on. This must not happen here. And on the evidence of today's meeting I do not think it will.'
'OK,' conceded Stephie. 'Layla's not the enemy, but she ought to remember men are.'
'Not individual men,' said Layla. 'Male power, perhaps.'

'I can tell you who's my enemy,' interjected Silvester, who was black and beautiful but who had a grey eye where she'd been hit by her boyfriend, the visiting father of her four children. 'It goes in this order. White men, white women, black men, the system.'
'You can't possibly include women,' protested Stephie, and there was a murmur of agreement.

Silvester got to her feet and said, 'I'm sick to death of the lot of you, with your comfortable lives; I hate the way you patronise me. I put my enemy in any order I choose. What do white women know about black women's lives? You're middle-class, privileged bitches. Long live the Black Feminists!'

The attention of the meeting was thus diverted to the Black Feminists' claims for Wages for Housework. Many professed themselves worried by the lobby: it could foster the notion of women as mothers who did shit work: it suggested that women too, like men, could have a group guilt. Could white women be guilty of the oppression of their black sisters, if only historically? It was impossible. *All* women were victims. But their protests were subdued. No one wanted to be accused of racism. If black women saw themselves as a viable sub-group, how could white women argue? In the race for victimhood, black women at the time were in the lead, and were to increase it over the decades. White women didn't have a hope, not when they were up against the slave markets. Racism took precedence over feminism: that is to say 'racist' was a worse accusation than 'sexist,' and has remained so to this day.

Layla, her interest in the meeting over, went to the kitchen to let off steam to Nancy, Johnny and Richard.

'Who do they think they are?' she demanded. 'The Spanish Inquisition? Why should I put up with them? My house is used like an office, they come in and out as they please, the phone goes all the time, I am obliged to eat, sleep and breathe Medusa, my private life is up for grabs. Nancy, did you buy those coffee mugs?'

'I did,' said Nancy. 'Out of the petty cash especially for this evening.'

'They are fucking hideous,' said Layla, 'and at least two people have admired them. Why is it that ugliness and feminism always go together?'

'We keep telling you,' said Johnny. 'You've fallen amongst Mrs Grundies.'

'If you don't like the coffee mugs,' said Nancy, picking up a couple and throwing them against the wall, so they broke, 'you're welcome to go and buy them yourself. I am sick of being a dogsbody, sick of being the one to make the coffee, sick of being despised and patronised by you, Layla, and being insulted about the coffee mugs is the last straw.'

'I wasn't insulting you, darling,' said Layla. 'Don't get your NZ knickers in a twist. They seem particularly sensitive today.'

'And I'm tired of being got at because I'm a kiwi — '

'Because she's a kiwi,' groaned Johnny and Richard in unison.

'Oh shut up,' Nancy yelled at them, and then said quietly, 'I want a rise, Layla, or else I quit.'

'Poor little Nancy,' said Layla. 'The girl with no proper qualifications and no interest in literature whatsoever, whom we employed on trust, and who used Medusa as a leg-up and is now blackmailing me for a rise.'

'I want one or I go,' said Nancy.

'Oh all right,' said Layla, in a friendly fashion, collapsing as she so often did if anyone outfaced her. 'Bet you lot have been eating the vol-au-vent mixture. There's so much hemp in there I had to add chillies so no one noticed. They didn't. I'm surprised you're still standing. Tell you what, Nancy, instead of a rise, why don't you move in here? You can have my room, rent-free. I'm tired of living above the shop. I want a place I can call my own. I shall buy a nice little place in Notting Hill, with a garden, and leave you lot behind me.' Nancy, although her vision was a little misty, could see the financial advantage of the plan. It would be quicker and cheaper to get to work.

'OK,' Nancy said. 'It's a deal. I'll have to give Doreen a month's notice. That's only polite.'

And she found a dustpan and brush and started sweeping up the broken china.

'Jesus wept,' said Layla, watching her appalled, but Nancy's ears were singing and she did not hear. The meeting spilled itself out into the night.

Three weeks later and it's moving day. Nancy is putting her belongings into the back of the little Medusa car, helped by Doreen and Arthur. And Alice has come back specially from a religious retreat to be of service.

'Don't leave the rose crystal behind,' chides Alice. 'It's for tranquillity.'

Nancy had rather hoped to forget this treasure in the move, since the globule of pure crystal slightly tinged with pink was associated in her mind not with peace but with agitation and tears. Her stay with Alice's parents has been tinged, as the crystal was with pink, with a kind of troublesome sense of obligation. But she utters a polite little cry of horror and runs back in to fetch the rose crystal where she'd left it, kicked under the bed.

'Is there a crystal for assertiveness?' she asks Alice. 'If so, I need it. All that's happened is that I'm getting rent-free accommodation from Layla, and now I'll be obliged to her. If only I'd asked for a rise, I could have had a life outside Medusa.'

Alice laughs and says no such crystal exists: and remarks that it's a matter of pride with Layla never to give Nancy a rise: and Nancy's life *is* Medusa. Nancy would be happier if she didn't struggle against manifest destiny.

Daffy's on the move as well. Hamish has moved back in with the boys. Daffy has chosen to leave, because he will not swear sexual fidelity, or marry her, or put the house in her name. He has seen a house in the country rather better than the ruin he previously had his eyes upon — a substantial farmhouse, in fact — and needs to sell the Chalcot Crescent property. To do this he must get Daffy out of it. To get Daffy out of it he must move back in. This he succeeds in doing. She tried changing the locks but he simply climbed in the window.

Now he cheerfully helps Daffy pack her personal belongings into the back of Stephie's car.
'You came with nothing and leave with a little more,' he says, 'but you have my and the boys' gratitude. It was great while it lasted. And at least you leave with more than Stephie.'

Hamish gives her a glass paperweight from his stock as a memento: a Victorian glass ball with Swiss edelweiss trapped inside, and she feels grateful.

When Stephie says, 'Hamish is such a bastard,' Daffy can hardly remember exactly why he is. She is half upset, half excited by the move. The last year with Hamish has left her stunned and

197

confused, and even she has begun to realise that the boys are both graceless and ungrateful. They are nicer to Stephie now than they are to Daffy. Daffy lost face with them when Layla appeared in the brass bed: she no longer has magic powers over their father, and so not over them. Anyway, they're now expected to go to their mother for the weekends, so they'll see Daffy too, should their allegiance shift again.

Stephie drives Daffy and her belongings to the Camden Town flat and the two women unpack the car. Daffy is moving in with Stephie. It seems sensible. Daffy can earn enough to cover the rent Stephie charges by working for publishers other than Medusa. She will type scripts in the evening. She is good at this, and has found a skill for the detailed work of copy-editing. She looks forward to finding another boyfriend, the thrill of new sex, new love. Her life had closed down and now here it is, opening up again. She does not speak of this to Stephanie. She realises the wisdom of following the see-how-Hamish-has-ruined-my-life approach when in Stephie's company, at least for a little. Accommodation in London is so short any number of lies and fake self-presentations must be spoken in order to attain it and preserve it. It's a marvel anyone has any integrity left at all.

Nancy and Daffy travel light: they go through life acquiring people and things on a very temporary basis. It is obvious when women are young whether they're the kind to acquire things — husbands, children, saucepans, summer houses in the Dordogne or time-shares in Spain, diamonds in the bank or Agas in the kitchen: some do, some don't. Nancy and Daffy tend not to.

Nancy worries about it; Daffy doesn't. Daffy throws away last season's clothes and somehow is always stylish if cheap. Nancy can see nothing wrong in wearing an Aertex shirt a decade after everyone else has stopped: she likes them: they're practical, healthy and easy to wash. She has to chase them to ground in back-street shops: if no one else stocks them she thinks it's inefficiency; if you say 'fashion' to Nancy she looks puzzled. This is something simply not to do with her.

Layla moves out of Cheyne Walk with the help of four biceped removal men and a large van. They move pianos, books, antique furniture, pack up the kitchen — leaving her tenants with the barest necessities — and the bedroom. The van is full. Last thing to go in are a dozen champagne flutes in Venetian glass. Richard brings them out for her, carefully packed in tissue in six shoe boxes — two in each.

'If anyone breaks anything I'll fucking sue,' says Layla. 'And that includes you, Richard.' She expresses gratitude and affection through reprimand. Sometimes she is misunderstood. 'I don't see why our friend uses such bad language,' complains Richard to Johnny loudly.

'Oh, fuck off,' said Layla. 'Thank God I won't have to listen to your double-act any more.' She's really sorry to leave them behind. Rumour has it she needs somewhere more private where her mystery lover can visit, and something more resembling a home than Cheyne Walk became — which was somewhere between a dosshouse, a brothel and an office. As she gets older Layla gets fussier and more pernickety. She even buys art.

Medusa now employs a man. Lennie. Nancy refused to go on as dogsbody, and had actually carried out a threat or so by failing to pack up sale-and-returns for the libraries, on the grounds that she was not employed to break her back. Medusa actually advertised for a male handyman. Since men had muscles, should not women make use of them? There were two hundred applicants, of which five were short-listed: all strong young men, all with 'O'-levels and no 'A's, aged between twenty and twenty-four, fit, and all over five foot ten. Layla, Stephanie, Nancy and Alice interviewed them: did as men did if only to see what it felt like: sat in a row behind a table and asked the applicants in one by one for short interviews, making the others stew. Four were plain and one was handsome.

'How do we choose between them,' asked Stephanie, 'since they all have equal merit?'

It was a rhetorical question. It was obvious what they did. 'We choose the best-looking,' said Layla. And so Lennie came to work for Medusa. He was slender but tough, golden-skinned, blue-eyed, after the main chance, and heterosexual. He drifted round the Medusa offices doing the heavy work, lugging boxes, files, mending fuses, running errands, all the things Nancy had once done. Set free to spend more time with the books, she became almost creative in her accounting, and more likely to say yes to proposed new schemes than no. Medusa grew, and slid into profit, and stayed there easily. Lennie of the golden muscles and square jaw seemed to bring them luck. Stephie's eyes, in particular, tended to follow him, though if she caught herself she quickly looked the other way. She had publicly eschewed sex, and announced herself as a separatist, but that didn't mean she didn't think about sex.

Daffy was startled, a month or so after she moved in with Stephie, to open the unlocked bathroom door one Sunday morning to find Lennie in there, shaving his tender chin. He and Stephanie had been quiet, so as not to wake Daffy, and he had thought to be gone by the morning, but it was October, and while Stephie had remembered to put the clocks forward, Daffy had not. It figured.

They had breakfast together.

'Don't mention this at Medusa,' said Stephie, 'for God's sake.'

One early misty morning in 1976 a small group of people assembled for a nine thirty service at Golders Green Crematorium in North London. It was a beautiful day: sun beginning to break through mist and bounce off golden and russet leaves, shining against the quaint cottage brickwork of the chapel walls, demonstrating architectural detail, bringing even the dull gravel paths to a glittery life. Few were in a mood to notice these benefits of the first funeral of the day. Only Richard, who had taken up photography, moved amongst the crowds, snapping away, seeing shapes, patterns and colours where others looked inwards, and saw nothing but chaos, guilt and grief. The suicide of one undermines the careful constructs of others, which enable them to live cheerfully, forget death, and remain courageous. Life hurls its brickbats: we become adept at fending them off; if someone simply throws in the sponge, says 'that's it, no more life', we wonder why we bother. 'I don't know how to recover from this,' was what Nancy wrote home to her mother, saying all this, mixing metaphors as usual, as her mother was quick to observe in her answering letter. Never mind: Nancy and her mother got on better on airmail paper than they ever had in real life, and Nancy was accustomed to a mother whose first nature was to correct and improve.

Now she and Johnny got through the heavy minutes waiting for the cortège by recording and listing Richard's shots, trailing along behind him. He took pictures of Alice, Stephie, and Daffy; and Rafe and Roland, and most of Medusa's Board: Layla was not there but was expected. Nor was Hamish. There were mothers from the school playground to take pictures of, and teachers and shopkeepers too. The departed had been liked and admired; even her suicide did not keep people away from her funeral. As well as depression and grief, there was an undercurrent of indignation. Whose fault? Whose fault?

The hearse and the cortège were late.

'Where's the fucking hearse?' asked Richard. 'The light's terrific but it's beginning to go.' These days he quite liked swearing.

'Late for her own funeral,' said Johnny.

'It isn't funny,' said Richard.

'You never even knew her,' said Johnny.

'When someone kills themselves,' said Nancy, 'you feel you know them. A part of you gives up as well.'

'Your trouble, Nancy,' said Johnny, 'is that you're a depressive at heart.' Nancy was quite pleased to be found worthy of a category. She felt amorphous, a lot of the time.

Rafe and Roland had found sticks and were slashing at flowers. Their faces were mutinous and troubled. Daffy left Stephanie's side to stop them. 'You mustn't do that,' she said. 'Remember where you are.'

'Only a stupid old chapel,' said Roland.

'I don't believe in God,' said Rafe.

'You are so bad,' cried Daffy, and Stephie came over. They were, after all, her boys.

'Leave them alone, Daffy,' said Stephanie. 'They're boys. They can't help it. Destruction is in their nature.'

A dahlia head collapsed in a pile of bruised petals, and a whole tough hollyhock stalk with splendid flowers upon it flew through the air.

'You could feed them oestrogen,' said Daffy, 'and change their natures. I suppose you'd like to do that.'

'It's nothing to do with hormones,' said Stephie. 'It's culture and conditioning which makes boys behave like boys, and girls like girls. Society trains boys to be aggressive.'

'I just don't believe that,' said Daffy.

'Studies prove it,' said Stephie.

'Hamish says studies prove whatever those who set them up mean them to prove.'

'Quoting Hamish, I see,' remarked Stephie. 'Haven't you got a mind of your own?'

'Little girls flirt with their fathers,' said Daffy, 'and little boys massacre flowers with sticks. That's that.'

'Only because of parental expectation,' said Stephie. 'I expect boys to behave badly, so they do.'

'Don't let's quarrel,' said Daffy. 'We're all upset.'

'I don't see why we should be,' said Stephanie.

205

'Zoe turned her back on us. She saw herself primarily as wife and mother. Let father and children mourn; why should we have the burden, on top of everything else?'

'She was my friend,' said Daffy. 'We'd go to the park together. Now she's dead and the person I want to discuss her death with most is her. There's a hollow in my life and it will never be filled. And I just know her ghost's not going to lie down: it's going to trouble us forever.'

'That's absurd,' said Stephie, but she looked uneasy.

Rafe stopped slashing long enough to ask loudly, 'If it's suicide, why is she being buried in consecrated ground? I thought suicides had to go outside the church wall.'

Roland said, 'It's only ashes, idiot. It's not like a body.'

Daffy said, 'Please behave, boys. It may have been an accident, not suicide at all. I know you don't want to be here, but she was a friend of your father's. He wanted you to come.'

'To let him off the hook,' said Roland.

'Then where is he?' asked Rafe.

And everyone looked round for Layla.

Alice was underneath an oak tree talking to a hard-living, chain-smoking, journalist lesbian of the old school. Her name was Mary. They had gone through into the rose gardens, and now loitered under the arches where flowers were customarily laid. Row after row of wilting floral tributes waited for collection, browning petals indifferent to the focused grief, bewilderment and angst, real or feigned, which had kept them out there, waterless on stone.

'All these male priests dressing up as women,' said Alice. 'I hate cremations. Earth to earth is all right, but ashes to ashes is dire.'

'You're into reincarnation, I suppose,' said Mary, the journalist. She wore a collar and tie and a tweed suit. 'Wheel of life and all that stuff.'

'Nothing else seems to make sense,' said Alice.

'Sense!' complained Mary, a rationalist. 'Who decides, tell me that? Whether you're going to come back as a cow or a horse or a cripple? Which is the more developed form, mud-frog or tree-frog? Is there a committee? Or is it the Prime Mover makes these executive decisions? Or does he have a list to work from? Tell me.'

'You've been drinking,' said Alice, reproachfully.

'It's the only way I can face funerals,' said Mary. 'And why did she do it?'

'I expect she was depressed,' said Alice, and Mary laughed and said, 'Who isn't?' They could see the nose of the hearse appearing the other side of the arches. They stopped gazing at the melancholy flowers and went to join their fellow mourners.

Over in Chalcot Crescent, Primrose Hill, a naked Hamish leant on one elbow above who else but a naked Layla. The house had been sold; it was packed up, waiting for removal men. A fleet of admiring girls had done the sorting, packing, cleaning and stacking, and none of them asked for a penny, because it was Hamish. The bed remained, and its bedding. It felt softer than usual because one of the girls had seen fit to lay six sheets and three blankets beneath the undersheet by way of packing them. Hamish strokes the back of Layla's neck with his finger, pushing his hand between the pillow, one of eight, and her head. She succumbs, in this overkill nest of bedding: the plainer sheets are Stephanie's choice, she supposes, but some are pink satin. These she supposes were brought by Daffy. Layla feels mesmerised. There is no clock obvious anywhere. She can tell she will be late for the funeral.

'I really mustn't be late,' says Layla.
'Who's more important, the living or the dead?'
'The living,' conceded Layla.
'Who else do you love?' he asked.
'You,' she said, and for the moment it seemed true. Love rarely finds a suitable object to hurl itself to grief upon.
'Who do you want?'

'You,' said Layla. There was no doubt as to this.

'What is the proper place for a woman?' queried Hamish, continuing the catechism.

'Underneath a man,' said Layla. 'Only kidding. I crossed my fingers.'

'Don't bother,' said Hamish. 'Owned, controlled, confined. Women will never find their freedom. They like sex too much.'

Sex between them proceeded for once in the missionary position; unfrilled. It seemed enough for both of them; the urgency of time being what it was.

'I don't take any of this seriously, Hamish,' said Layla. 'Don't think I do.'

'I hadn't noticed you staying away,' said Hamish, as her breath came quicker, and her moans lowered a pitch. 'Say oh, oh, oh.'

'Oh, oh, oh,' she said, coincidentally or not.

'What price liberation now?' said Hamish.

Post-orgasmic, Layla remembered her political stance.

'Bloody men,' she said. 'We'll be late for the funeral.'

And she rolled out from under him on to the bare floor — the rug was folded somewhere in the corner — and got dressed.

210

A big black Rolls followed the hearse up to the chapel door. Undertakers, with their steady, practised, servile movements — whether they touch their metaphorical forelocks to the grim reaper, or to the superior status of their living employers, who is ever to say? — eased the coffin on to the waiting trolley. Bull got out of the Rolls, and Saffron and Sampson followed; and Bull's parents and no one else from Zoe's side. She had been the only child of only children. To have had two children herself seemed almost lavish. Zoe's children, Saffron and Sampson, might walk hand in hand in a desert, but at least they walked together. She had seen to that. The other mourners fell in behind.

The duty chaplain took the service. Those who were listening heard the usual chant, or rather snatches of it, for the microphone was not working. The coffin rested on a slab of concrete in front of purple velvet curtains. It did not do to envisage the flesh and blood within. The flesh would be cold, and the blood be hardening in the veins. Without the mind, without the heart, what are we?

Thus spake the preacher, patchily.

'... to mark the passing of our beloved sister Zoe Meadows, dutiful wife to ... ' (a pause while he consulted his notes — one thing to remember the name of the deceased: quite another to recall relatives) 'Bullivant, and mother of Saffron and Sampson ... '

'... Zoe dedicated her life to her family and was a source of comfort to those who knew her ... '

'... kind, generous, bearing her illness, the scourge of depression, with fortitude, comfort and good cheer — '

'Come again?' interjected Mary. 'Hold on a minute there — ' but she was hushed.

'... what can we say of such a woman, an example to all who knew her, who turned her back on the whims and fancies of the new world, but that her price was above rubies — '

At which point Layla and Hamish entered late; Layla's heels clattering on slate floors. Everyone turned. No one was listening anyway. Roland and Rafe waved at their father, who waved back. They were standing in front of their mother, who slapped their hands down. Layla and Hamish took their places just behind Stephie and Daffy, whose jaws were rigid with displeasure.

'You said you'd stopped seeing him,' said Daffy to Layla over her shoulder.

'For God's sake, Daffy,' said Layla, loudly. 'This is a funeral.'

'It's the total lack of judgement,' moaned Stephie to no one in particular.

'It isn't fair on the boys,' said Daffy. 'I don't care about anything else, only them, and I'm not even related.'

Hamish looked smug. The women were fighting over him. All, observing this, subsided, and joined in the hymn. Roland and Rafe moved across to the other aisle, whether because they thought the singing was bad, or by way of separating themselves out from the warring adults, who could tell?

'*Lord of all hopefulness,*' sang the mourners,
'*Lord of all joy,*
Whose trust ever childlike
No care could destroy — '

The curtains were parting, the coffin beginning to slide towards them, or rather to jerk its way along rollers, not all of which were working.

'We are conceived in sin, and born in sin,' moaned the duty chaplain. 'The wonder and the gift is His forgiveness through the miracle of lord Jesus Christ — '

At which point Richard used his flashbulb and the chaplain was offended. The rollers, coincidentally, stopped working altogether. The coffin stayed where it was.

'Out of respect to relatives, flashbulbs are forbidden at this solemn moment,' said the

213

chaplain, 'while the body is being consigned to the flames.'

'Richard's producing a book which Medusa is going to publish,' said Layla loudly from the congregation. 'It's called *The Sorry Ages of Women*, and it's one of Stephie's projects. Everything's OK if you're writing a book. Rule of thumb. The more you upset people and draw attention to yourself, the more likely a book is to succeed.'

She was coming up to join the chaplain at the pulpit. Alarmed, he allowed her to move him over and take his place.

'You, sir,' said Layla to the chaplain, 'are giving our sister Zoe, about to burn to a crisp, a truly rotten send-off. She deserves better than this. Zoe the bright star, Zoe head-in-air, killing herself to prove a point, martyr to our cause.'

Bull was already on his feet, marshalling his parents and his children, to lead them out of the church. But Saffron was lingering.

'Oh, yes,' said Layla, calling after him for all to hear, 'the husband, about to run away from the truth. What, Bull, can't you stand it?'
'You killed her,' said Bull. 'You lot and your ideas. You made her discontented with her lot. You are wicked people, wreckers of happiness. Can't you even let us bury her in peace? You're upsetting my children.'
'Why did you bring them anyway?' asked Layla.

'Funerals are no place for kids.'
Bull was easing a stubborn Saffron out of the chapel.
'I am not so a kid,' she protested as he got her out the door.

Once the deceased's party had left, Layla addressed the startled congregation.
'Of Zoe's friends here assembled: who has anything real and true to say about her death?'

The staider of those in the pews got up and followed the family out, offended and upset. The chaplain once again tried to intervene but Layla stayed firmly planted before the microphone and what is more spoke directly into it, which was more than he had done.

The coffin stayed still, though the curtains were parted. There was sheeting behind, so no flames were observable. Stephie came forward to take the microphone.
'Zoe was depressed,' said Stephie, 'of course she was depressed. She was married to Bull Meadows, and didn't know how to leave him. Women often don't know how to leave, or don't have the means or see their duty to their children as greater than their duty to themselves. She had a husband who undermined her confidence and diminished her. Zoe took an overdose of sleeping pills and alcohol, but it was patriarchy mixed the draught, not Zoe our sister.'

Daffy's turn.

'Zoe died because Medusa turned down her book. Layla didn't like it; but then she didn't like Zoe, so she wouldn't, would she?'

'That is not the case,' said Layla from the pulpit. 'All we ever saw was the first few chapters: we asked to see the finished work. In fact we were very encouraging.'

'That's not what Bull said,' interjected Daffy.

'Well, he wouldn't, would he?' said Layla.

'Bull told me that after a phone call from Medusa, Zoe decided the book was no good and burned it,' said Daffy.

'So I blame Medusa.'

'We'll never know,' said Layla. 'I blame patriarchy.'

'I spoke to Bull myself,' said Stephie, 'and told him how much we liked it.'

'You spoke to *Bull*,' said Layla, aghast. This was the first she'd heard of it. 'Not to *Zoe*?'

'He could surely be trusted to pass a message on,' said Stephie, feebly. The declamatory part of the exchange rang well beneath the vaulted stone ceiling, but when they lapsed into squabbling it sounded the worse. They fell silent. People wondered whether to go.

Then Hamish rose to his feet. 'You all let her down,' he said. 'You were rotten sisters. Bull was right. You put ideas in her head and they festered away and killed her. You meddle with things more powerful than you know.'

216

And Hamish took Rafe and Roland by their shoulders and steered them out of the chapel. 'This is no place for males,' said Hamish to his boys. 'These women are in Maenad mood. They're killers. Let's get out of here.' Daffy told the boys they were to stay. Stephie said they were to go. Since Hamish had them physically by their shoulders they went.

The chaplain managed to get his mouth near the microphone. 'Please,' he said, 'this is a chapel of rest, not a women's liberation meeting.' 'You could have fooled me,' said Layla. 'You are being inconsiderate,' he protested. 'There is another service waiting to come in.'

He was right. Hamish and the boys had to carve their way out through a group of dignified and wealthy mourners, impatient to get the whole sad business over.

'One way or another,' said the chaplain, 'the body has to be consigned to the flames. I would like to do this in a dignified manner.'

He gestured to the organist to set up the music, and looked hopefully towards where hidden functionaries might lurk and somehow start the rollers moving. Nancy had to speak above the funeral march, the microphone to her mouth. 'Zoe died because she was in a hopeless double bind. How could she leave her husband without leaving her children too? She had no money.

Emotional ties are bad enough but any woman with children and unable to earn is helpless. She had a doctorate but who was going to give her a job? Who would look after the children when she was at work? There are state nurseries but take a look at the whey-faced miserable children who're sent there. Why does everything move so slowly? Why do women have to go on giving up their lives for others? This is what Zoe did, until one day she decided to give up her life for her own sake. Sometimes I think we're all going to die before any real change happens: I'm sorry. I'm upset.' She sat down and wept.

'So are we all upset,' said Layla. 'Johnny, your turn.'
'Who me? A mere man? But I can see this much. Zoe was born bright, pretty, happy and female and shouldn't have ended like this. That's the problem you women have to solve. We have enough of our own.'
'Thank you for your condescension, Johnny,' said Layla. 'How fortunate we are to have your support. As a token male, we will give you a single share when Medusa goes public. And one for your friend Richard, too. Two gays make one guy. Alice?'

Alice spoke in her small voice. The organist gave up. Still the coffin did not move. Someone important was knocking on the chapel door.
'Zoe died because she was weak,' said Alice. 'As only women can be weak. She died because by virtue of her gender and her female nature she

was prevented from taking her proper part in society. She wanted to save the world as much as any man but was paralysed. Everywhere men divide us and render us powerless. She was forced to make a choice no woman ought to have to make. We grieve for Zoe. We are angry for Zoe. And let our anger shake the world, as once she felt her husband's did.'

The coffin trembled and began to move. A rather pretty girl no one had seen before stood up at the back and said, 'My name's Janice. I don't know what you're all going on about. I was having an affair with Bull and Zoe found out and now I want to die too. It was nothing to do with writing books, or being a wife and mother. Zoe died of a broken heart, like anyone else. Why do you have to make a martyr of her? Can't you just let her go in peace?'

Janice did her best to walk out of the chapel. When she opened the door, people crowded through spoiling her exit. The coffin disappeared behind the curtains. The organist began to play Bach. Layla smiled politely at the chaplain and said, 'Thank you for your courtesy,' and to those who were still listening, 'Anyone who cares to join us can do so at Medusa-on-Thames,' by which she meant the house on Cheyne Walk, which was still good for a party or so.

Part Three

Part Three

Saffron's Search

OK, it's 1983. Medusa is going great guns. Women have discovered, as they say, their voice, and their history, their literature. The concept of sexism has arrived in the land, as the concept of racism arrived a decade earlier. It doesn't necessarily mean people behave any better, but they have a vague idea of what the new parameters of good and bad behaviour are. The world is not yet female, the gender switch is not yet thrown, God is still the Patriarch, not yet shoved over on his throne by Nature the Matriarch, but we're on our way, for good or bad.

Saffron is fifteen. She has a father but no mother. Her father drinks too much. They live in the same house in Belsize Park as they did when her mother took her overdose in the spare room. The spare room is now Sampson's bedroom. He's ten. Saffron feels, and is, responsible for him. She's a determined and brisk young woman; she has her mother's pale medieval looks and her father's nervous energy. She attends Haverstock Comprehensive at Chalk Farm station, and is well taught in the modern fashion: that is, to think a lot, feel a lot, and know not much at all; which is OK.

The wealthier children here are sacrificed to their parents' liberal principles. Let them mix with the workers, let them leaven the lumpen dough. Let equality rule: leave privilege at home with the stripped pine and the Elizabeth David cookbooks; we shall all be one. These children are feelers into a new world, probes sent ahead to take readings of a strange atmosphere: tender creatures at the sharp end. They tend to get bullied, the lumpen, not without reason, feeling somewhat patronised: but the children of the avocado eaters, the *New Society* readers, understand nobility; they have a feel for social justice: they dumb down and lose their mellifluous accents fast. They do not complain. Saffron as it happens does not get bullied: no one dares. She has a steely eye.

A copy of the manuscript of her mother's completed book remains under the bed in the spare room, what is now Sampson's room. Saffron knowns this but doesn't give the matter much attention. When you are fifteen what is important and what is not is still not necessarily apparent. Sampson never investigates what's in it. It was described to him once as 'your mother's suitcase', and it exists as something you don't open, don't investigate: a vague comfort object.

A Thursday afternoon and school's out; a burst of noise and movement into a sultry street: the pupils mixed boys and girls, black and white, rich and poor: the children of those who aspire and those who despair coming together in a great social experiment. There is as yet no national curriculum: there is no homework: there are occasional exams, which entail some hard work in the run up to them, should you want to pass, otherwise your life is your own. Your teachers are not chided and punished for your failures. A job can always be had, when this purgatory is over. The air you breathe, the water you drink, the bus you ride on, seem freely given: yours by social right. No one notices that the tide is turning, that market forces are sweeping in, as is the notion that the only way to keep inflation down is to keep unemployment up. That for most to be comfortable quite a few must go to the wall, and society is prepared to do it. It is an age of innocence, a flower shrivelling slightly in an increasingly chilly wind.

Saffron leaves her companions and walks briskly down to Compendium Books, the radical bookshop near Camden Town, instead of up the hill and home to her house in the cramped narrow streets behind Belsize Park. She loves looking in the window, to the display therein of global hopes and fears. Books on the Nuclear Threat, CND, Marx, Trotsky, Anarchism, *The Buddhist Path to Serenity*. There's a large section labelled *Wimmin* — the three letters M-A-N in that order seeming to some an insult. Books on the nature of the patriarchy, the particular plight of black women, the male tendency to rape and pillage — though scarcely a one, yet, on incest or child sexual abuse — and a large section given over to Medusa books, which are noticeably glossier and more attractively designed than the rest.

Here find fiction, contemporary and classic, pop-sociology, help-yourself books: how to master the hormones, the feelings, the losses. How not to fall in love. How not to be ruled by your children. How to be well. The book is the key to the female universe. And of course the magazines; though they come and go, rise and fall, penetrate and are spent; in a way more associated with men than women.

For once, Saffron goes inside the shop; she doesn't just look in the window. The bookseller is a woman in her forties; she's wearing combat fatigues, no doubt from Lawrence Corner, the army surplus shop just down the road. She's plain but pleasant. Saffron's leafing through magazines in their special rack. She moves the pages carefully, swiftly and cleanly. This one, thinks the bookseller, may not spend, but at least will do no damage. She's reading *Menstra*, which Madge and Stephanie now edit — Stephanie, at Madge's insistence, is no longer hands-on at Medusa, though she stays on the Board, and in its last share issue was granted a whole nineteen per cent of the company. It was Layla's skill at controlling who got what that finally pissed Stephanie off — or rather Madge, for who could tell them apart.

Saffron put *Menstra* back, with a hapless shudder, and turned to the Medusa display, picked out an Edith Wharton novel, and began to read, standing on first one foot, then the other.

'You're meant to buy, really,' said the bookseller, eventually. She spoke kindly.
'I don't have any money,' said Saffron. 'Books ought to be free.'
She's passionate, rather than rude.
'Then there goes my wages,' says the bookseller. 'Think about it. How nice it would be if money didn't matter. Most 'shoulds' uttered by the young are different ways of saying this. How much money do you have?'

Saffron dived in her pocket and came up with a few coins.
'That'll do,' said the bookseller. 'I'll make up the difference. The hungry till will be satisfied.'
She took what money Saffron had and handed her the book. Saffron looked at the spine.
'My mother once nearly wrote a book for Medusa,' said Saffron.
'Why only nearly?' asked the assistant.

'She died,' said Saffron bleakly, and made for the door. Then she looked back.

'That magazine *Menstra*. Do women really do that? Impregnate themselves with coffee pots?'

'I don't know,' said the assistant. 'They say they do.'

'Yuk,' said Saffron. 'They must really hate men.'

And Saffron left the shop and walked back up the hill, up Chalk Farm Road, alongside the tall blackened brick wall which marked off the old railway land, and the melancholy Round House, where once was housed the horse-driven mechanism of cogs and wheels which pulled the trains up from Camden Town. Decade after decade, groups do their best with the place: enthusiasts try to turn it into a theatre, or a sports centre, or a shopping mall, or a focus for Black Arts, but it never works. The sorrow of the bricks sops up the high spirits: perhaps the horses had a hard time in the sunless building: or their owners: or those who built the place. Some affliction entered in. The road outside, up which Saffron now walked, was the first policed area in the country: it took the rich up from Mayfair to Hampstead Heath for pleasant days in the country, but was the haunt of footpads and highwaymen. The descendants of these villains have taken up their places in Dingwall's Market, now the sixth biggest tourist attraction in London, where the grunge shops are, and all things morbid; you can buy S & M gear and plastic skulls, and studded black leather predominates, and the addicts cluster. The scene spreads out from Lawrence Corner where the overspill from war made a profit for those left behind after the great excitement.

(Hamish had a German officer's coat, long and waisted, made in leather, with a bullet-hole in the centre of the back, which he wore proudly.) Had Saffron walked the other way she might have encountered Stephie's Roland and Rafe, picking their way through piles of old clothes on the second-hand stalls, searching for the latest in cheap fashion. Who is to say how the sorrows of the past seep through into the present? And let us never suppose that the present we live through, and take for granted, and think just about OK, is free of responsibility for the future.

Anyway, here's Saffron, blocking out memory with the printed page, reading as she walks safely up the hill towards Belsize Park, where the air grows brighter, less grungy, and more continental, and home. She finds Sampson on the step. He too is reading a book. It's *The Lord of the Rings*. Like Saffron he too is a reader, as born to it as their mother was to write. Except, weakly, she gave up the struggle. Reading's easier: other people's minds, not your own.

'I'm locked out,' says Sampson, slamming the book shut, leaving Gollum whispering in the Hobbit's ear, halfway up a mountainside, with the glow of pure evil lighting up the sky, and the forces of the Black Lord gathering for their fight against Good.
'Isn't Dad in?' asked Saffron. 'He's meant to be. I haven't got my key either.'
'I rang and rang the bell,' said Sampson, 'and

then I banged, but no one came. Perhaps he's asleep.'

'I expect so,' said Saffron, and with the ease born of practice she stooped so that Sampson could clamber on her back, reach the latch of the window, and effect an entry. Once Sampson had dropped down inside he opened the door to Saffron.

She went in, leaving her book on the step, forgotten, its pages turning in the east wind.

Saffron finds Bull in the kitchen, and he is indeed asleep, in what her literary mind calls a drunken stupor. There is a half-bottle of whisky by his side. There's the very same Pither stove in which he once so inefficiently burned his wife's manuscript. It's gone out. The patch of anthracite which should glow red through the lower bars of the grid is grey and dull. The room's getting cold.

'Dad,' says Saffron, wiping up crumbs, putting on the kettle, driving the metal slice through the grid of the stove, separating ash and half-burned coal from fresh, tipping the slice so it deposits its debris on the tray — a cloud of dust rises, of course, there is no helping it — making tea, putting out mugs, while the dust settles: she is good at priorities, this one: skilled in the logistics of getting things done in half the time anyone else does — then back to the stove: firelighters on the tray, push it back in, light them, remove the slice gently, letting the fresh coal fall: opening the flue wide with the brass lever at the side to aerate the fuel as much as possible — and since the wind is in the east it will probably work — by which time the tea is brewed, she has a mug in her father's hand, and is making tuna sandwiches for Sampson.

She yells up to the spare room.

'Stay up there and do your homework, Sam, I'll bring tea up — ' a yell which also serves to wake her father properly.

'I let you down again,' says Bull, maudlin and tearful. He works for a firm of architects; he is the one who explains why ideas won't work, the mundane engineer, never quite accepted as one of them, a realist in a world of fantasists; drinking too much since Zoe died, trying to bring up his children, wondering how to save himself and them from the same fate, how to postpone death.

Suicide runs in families if you're not careful. Suicide is both catching and a hereditary tendency. Everyone knows it: everyone denies it. Everyone concedes these days to the belief that Zoe's death was the result of an accidental overdose. That she had taken too many pills by mistake; drowsy, she had managed to cram in some thirty-five, inadvertently, and washed them down with gin, carelessly.

Bull had drunk whisky ever since; occasionally vodka, but the clear slow liquid, with the same shiny viscosity as gin, gave him hangovers more to do with memory and despair than alcohol. Really, no one with a family or friends — and few of us have absolutely none — should kill themselves. Let them fake accidental death if completely necessary: but let the fake be truly convincing: otherwise family life is built on a structure of lies, and a casual kick can bring the whole thing toppling down.

'Yes you did let us down,' said Saffron severely. 'Sam had to sit on the step till I got back.'

'Why didn't he remember his key?' He was always good at meeting accusation with counter-accusation.

'Because he needs you to be a father to him and let him in,' said Saffron.

'Just like your mother,' he said, 'too smart for your own good,' but he smiled and she felt an enormous sense of relief. He had never compared her to her mother before: Zoe's name was almost never even mentioned. Perhaps things were getting better. She felt the time had come to set her house in order: and being who she was set about it briskly.

Saffron went up to Sampson's room with his tuna sandwiches. She found Sampson lying on his bed staring at the ceiling.

'You miserable again?' she asked, facing the facts.

'Yes,' said Sampson, and echoing her mood, asked, 'Did our mother kill herself?'

'I think so,' said Saffron.

'You're five years older than me,' said Sampson. 'You ought to know. You weren't there, or anything?'

'No,' said Saffron. 'She wasn't at breakfast, I took you to playgroup and went on to school. I didn't have to cross roads. I came back after school and her body was gone and I never saw her again.'

'We went to the funeral though,' said Sampson. 'I remember.'

'But they took us out at half-time for some reason.'

'Which room did they find her in?' asked Sampson.

'The living-room,' said Saffron, since Zoe's body had been found in the very room they spoke in, and Sampson liked it and called it his own. For some reason moss and leaves grew on the tiles around the skylight and fronded its glass square in an eccentric kind of way. You had to push through foliage to open the skylight, breaking and bruising it, but it always grew back, undaunted. The kitchen everyone used and the living-room was a gloomy room at the best of times. Let the living-room carry the burden. Saffron never had trouble lying.

'It might have been an accident,' said Saffron, kindly.

'Can't you ask someone?'

'Why?' she asked.

'Then I wouldn't think she did it because of me,' said Sampson.

'Eat your sandwiches and get on with your homework,' said Saffron briskly. 'Get on with your own life, forget about hers.'

Sampson obediently got off the bed and did as he was told.

Down the hill and across the way, near enough to the Zoo to hear the lions roar at night, Rafe and Roland, aged sixteen and seventeen, and usually spoken of in that order, youngest first, for Rafe spoke and Roland echoed, wordlessly accepted the cheese on toast Daffy offered for supper.

They wore their pyjamas: their clothes were in the wash. Both were in the school football team. They too went to a comprehensive school but further up the hill than Saffron's. Hamish disapproved of private education, and could not have afforded it anyway.

The bottom had dropped out of the antique trade: as an activity it no longer had much to do with aesthetic judgement. It was not any more a way of turning appreciation into gold. Everyone knew everything: you could not pick up the treasures of the past for next to nothing on account of no one recognising them for what they were but you. Now you had to drive hard bargains; the demolition firms knew what they were doing: the Americans were over shipping out as much of old England as they could by container-load: customers were less interested in the quirky than in the instantly recognisable as 'good'; interiors were becoming less cluttered;

sleeker, along with the economy; house prices were beginning to rise and more was being spent on the fabric of houses than what went into them. Money had once poured into the shop for very little effort: now it was all graft and struggle.

Bookshops felt an underlying chill, as well, though it was not to strike properly for another five years or so. People still bought, but dithered more. There just didn't seem so much to know, any more. Ideas were coming out of the TV and radio, not just the pages of books. Or perhaps there were simply too many titles on the market, so each lost significance. The reading of a new book by a good author, once an all but group activity, was becoming a solitary occupation. Cinemas too were losing audiences, and struggled to survive: special effects were in their infancy. The post-modern age, with its menus of this and that, its bitsy echoes of all things thought of, which would last to the end of the millennium, was moving in from the horizon, and just as the taxi trade is the first to notice the recession, the antique trade is the first to feel the effect of cultural change; our view of the past is the key to what we think now.

Rafe and Roland, oblivious to all this, sat in their pyjamas and watched TV, their muddy clothes churning in the washing machine, while Daffy brought them cheese on toast.
Stephanie had moved in with Madge, cutting all

ties, starting *Menstra*, giving up her flat, and Daffy with it.

Daffy was back at No. 103. Her parents, observing her plight and that of the boys, who did not wish to follow their father to the country, had spent the savings of a lifetime to buy the house from Hamish on their daughter's behalf. Exhausted by the effort, by the sudden shocking understanding of how swiftly one wilful generation could so quickly dissipate the gains of the last, the mother had died within the year, and the father shortly afterwards.
These days Daffy had the sad and serious look of the lonely.

There came a knocking on the door. Daffy went to answer it. Saffron stood upon the step.
'Why Saffron,' said Daffy. 'How you've grown!' Saffron had been thirteen when last Daffy had seen her. 'And how like your mother you are. Does your father know you're here?' 'Of course he doesn't,' said Saffron. 'Never trouble trouble, till trouble troubles you, or something.'
'We parents stick together,' said Daffy. 'I'm not sure I should ask you in.'
'And that's another thing,' said Saffron. 'Why does Dad hate you so? I need to know these things. Can I come in?'

The boys looked up briefly and resumed their TV watching. Saffron declined all offers of food and drink and got to the point. She sat on the edge of the table: it did not occur to her that this might seem unmannerly. Lacking a mother, she behaved in social situations more as a man behaves, with an eye to practicality and convenience, not ritual.

'You were my mother's best friend. Zoe and Daffy. The names go together. You'd go to the park with Sampson and sit on the bench under the oak tree. Sometimes I'd go, but there was a strange woman with a pushchair who'd go by staring at us and saying, 'It's all right for some,' and I'd wonder what she had against us. It wasn't all right for us at all. I came to the park to tell Mum my father was home and in a mood — Why do I remember that day so well?' 'I don't know,' said Daffy. 'But I remember it too.'

In their mind's eye both saw the child Saffron run across green grass, in an ankle-length yellow dress, hair flying: watched Zoe call to Sampson, dressed in a blue knitted suit, that it was time to go home, saw Sampson get up out of the sand and then sit down again.
'No,' said Sampson, years ago. 'Won't.'
'Just like his dad,' said Daffy to Zoe. 'Difficult.'
'Oh no,' said Zoe, 'not really. Bull isn't difficult. He gets tired. He works so hard for us. If anything happened to me he'd look after the chidren.'
Both saw Saffron staring at her mother's face, as children will, searching for understanding, fearing disapproval. Daffy's face was wary too. What did Zoe mean, if something happened? What should happen? Now they watched Zoe

239

manoeuvring Sampson's pushchair up the steps of home, opening the front door and calling 'Bull?' Daffy zoomed away down the street in her little car. The feeling of desolation of that moment stayed with them both.

'What confuses me,' said Saffron, 'is that if you were my mother's friend, why won't my father let me visit you?'

'Your father didn't approve of me then,' said Daffy, 'and he doesn't approve of me now. In his book I'm a feminist and feminism ruined his life.'

'You don't seem much like a feminist to me,' said Saffron. 'Making those boys cheese on toast. It's true I make tea for Sampson but he's still little. You're all cosy kitchens and buttered toast.'

'I'm back in the wrong kitchen,' said Daffy. 'I'm back at a stolen sink. Passions once ran high in this house. This is the birthplace of Medusa, and the birth was cataclysmic. I was a bad girl then, and in Bull's eyes once a bad girl always a bad girl. People don't like to think that others change. So he'd rather you didn't see me. Your father's trying to raise a good girl, a dutiful daughter.'

'My father's an alcoholic,' said Saffron bleakly. 'I saw a programme on TV and he's quite definitely an alcoholic. He doesn't do much looking after us. He uses us as an excuse to stay away from work. He'll get fired one day. Then how will we live? I'm too young to work.

It's a race against time.' Daffy looked as if she was really tired of trouble.

'Nothing's ever over, is it?' she complained, and seemed about to cry, and had Saffron been warmer-hearted she would have changed the subject, let it go. But the children of suicides have half-cold hearts. Given the gift of life by two parents, one then snatches it away. It leaves the child chilly. If both parents die in a suicide pact, forget it; they're iced forever. But mercifully this seldom happens. If both parents decide to go, they normally take the children with them.

'My father disapproving of you is nothing to do with you being a feminist,' Saffron persisted. 'It is more to do with my mother dying, and why, and who was to blame. Don't fob me off, please. I want your opinion.'

And as if the house belonged to her, and not Daffy, Saffron went into the living-room, leaving the boys behind, still staring at TV as if the reality of present and past was nothing to do with them and never had been. She sat on the windowsill, leaning up against the glass through which once the neighbours had stared in to the Maenad dance, and remembered as an adolescent the child's-eye view.

Saffron heard, or thought she heard, Layla's voice, saw Layla's nakedness, and the air danced to the sound of music no one listened to any

241

more, but would again: because where the good tunes are, there the future is.

'Maenad by name,' cried Layla, 'Maenad by nature. 'That's us, the wild and dangerous women, women of the dance, the destroyers not the nurturers — '
'Are you insane?' Stephie's words sung through from a distant time. 'I have said no to Maenad.'
'And I've said yes — '
And the music quietened, as Alice's small hand turned down the volume.
'I think not — ' Now Alice's voice. 'Not Maenad. Rather Artemis, cool goddess of the moon.'
'Oh, Jesus,' said Layla. 'What an uphill struggle this is going to be. OK, a compromise. Medusa. One look, and she turns men's hearts to stone.'
Daffy heard, with little Saffron, the thump, thump, thump upon the door, heard Layla call to Zoe, 'Will you, won't you, will you, won't you, come and join the dance — '

Daffy remembered herself upstairs in bed in coitus interruptus and suddenly cheered up. Some pleasures now are worth any amount of lost future.
'What a day,' said Daffy. 'What a day one way and another: the day Medusa was born.'

'Then Dad came and took me home and Mum home. And she didn't join the dance. If she had she'd be alive today. Dad stopped her. His fault.'

242

'No, no,' cried Daffy. 'It wasn't like that. I looked from the upstairs window and saw the crowd of neighbours and your father coming down the road: how thin and angry he looked. Worried, as if he foretold a future and wanted to stop it. There isn't necessarily a because to everything: you only think so because you're so young.'

'I remember Mum looking out of this very window. She said, 'It's Bull. I told you so,' and Layla said, 'too late,' and they all just went on dancing and I began to cry because I wished they wouldn't. All those women dancing about with no clothes on.'

'*The moment of Praxis*,' Alice said, from out of the past. You don't have to be a ghost to have your past self hovering here and there.

'What were you doing looking out of the upstairs bedroom? You weren't in the room dancing with the others,' observed Saffron. 'But when Dad took us away you were wrapped in a towel in the hall, and someone was talking about a last straw; and I thought that was why I was thirsty, why no one had given me a drink, because the straws were all gone. But I suppose it was you who was the last straw, the one which broke the camel's back, the camel being Hamish and Stephanie's marriage. Hamish and Stephanie go well together. That seems the basic truth of the matter. Hamish and Daffy always had a temporary sound.'

'One up to first wives everywhere,' said Daffy. 'And so it proved to be.'

'You were upstairs with Hamish while Medusa was born downstairs,' said Saffron.

'Some things you can never live down,' said Daffy.

'You drove Stephanie out,' said Saffron. 'No wonder Dad disapproves of you.'

'Hamish drove Stephanie out,' said Daffy. 'I was just there to sop up Hamish's guilt. Hamish is into self-sufficiency now. Back to nature, organic vegetables, ley lines, the refining power of poverty, so long as the beds are soft and the hair shirts are comfortable.'

'You're changing the subject,' said Saffron. 'In the wife's bed while the wife's in the house. That is disgusting.'

'In the husband's bed while the wife wasn't in it, see it that way. Cups are either half-full or half-empty. How respectable the world is getting. Soon every affair will merit a divorce, and what price marriage then? I got landed with the boys. You could see that as a punishment. The nicer you are the more you get landed. You remember that.'

'It oughtn't to be like that,' said Saffron, half aware already that what Daffy said was true.

'There's what there ought to be and what is,' said Daffy, 'and they're different. What is certain is nothing finishes, nothing goes away. Look at you. Little Saffron grown up to be an avenging angel. Who'd have thought it? The crying child in pushchair.'

Saffron's back felt chilly all of a sudden, where the east wind blew against the window pane. She shivered.

'*Nice dancing, Daddy?*' said little Saffron in her head. '*Mummy put your clothes on.*' Anxious from the beginning; always trying to be in charge, lest worse befell.

'*Very naughty Mummy,*' said little Saffron; born judgemental.

'They say a woman ran out of the house,' said Saffron, twelve years later. 'She was naked. She got into a car and drove off. Which one of you was that?'

'That was Stephanie,' said Daffy. 'Stephanie's great day. 'I want nothing of yours,' she said to Hamish, 'nothing.' And it was true for at least a month. And the nothing included her clothes. Normally I'd never leave my clothes. I like a bit of adornment. That's why I could never quite be a feminist. I would always have come back for my suitcase.'

In the kitchen a TV programme ended. Rafe consulted the newspaper and switched channels. The boys were intelligent and perspicacious viewers. They'd had the practice, after all.

'At least Stephanie stayed alive for the boys,' said Saffron. 'Which was more than my mother did for me.'

'Your poor mother was very depressed,' said Daffy. 'Don't blame her.'

'If I can't blame her who can I blame?'

'You could blame Medusa,' said Daffy. 'Your mother was writing a book. It was taking years: she didn't want anyone to say she was neglecting you two. Medusa turned it down. That was your mother's last straw.'

'Kind of easy to blame an institution,' said Saffron, warily. 'I don't quite go along with that. Too off-the-hookish.'

'Go and ask Layla,' said Daffy. 'Go and inquisition her. The past isn't all that easy to talk about. Great chunks of it hurt. People should practice forgetfulness; there's too much remembering going on.'

'You just want me to go away so you can watch TV with the boys.'

'Or you could ask Stephanie,' said Daffy, ignoring Saffron's perfectly true assessment of the situation. 'Though I warn you Stephanie's branched out. She's living with an American named Madge.'

'Stephanie went lesbian? She's a dyke?'

'Don't use that word,' said Daffy, shocked.

'It's what Dad calls them,' Saffron excused herself.

'Well he would, wouldn't he? He's a man, and if women get together sexually, he's out of a job. Madge and Stephanie edit a magazine called *Menstra*. I don't recommend it.'

At that very moment Madge and Stephanie stood inches deep in water in their dank basement flat. The windows were barred. The floors were piled with boxes of files and papers round which the water rose. A pipe which ran across the yellowed wall, and led to the boiler which heated the entire house above, had come apart at the seams. Three women, part of the *Menstra* team, toiled moving boxes, papers, clothes off the floor. *Menstra* communality might of course be a more appropriate word than team; team having a male connotation.

Madge, in a fury, bangs at a rusty flange with a hammer, trying to close the gap in the pipe. Stephie, barefooted in the wet, jumps up and down in agitation, pleading.

'It won't work by brute force. Stop it, Madge.'

'Don't tell me what to do,' snarls Madge.

'Surely we should call a plumber,' pleads Stephanie. 'Please let me call a plumber.'

'Plumbers are men,' says a plump woman called Rosalie Fletcher. Her legs are hairy and each hair is darkened and wet.

'It's only a fucking leak,' said Wendy, who comes from Manchester, and often has to say things twice to be understood. She has freckles, red curly hair and a little rosebud mouth. 'No one got any gaffer tape?'

'That's for films,' says someone else, and the water begins to lap under the front door and soak the door mat. It swills with it cigarette ends, cat hairs, and pieces of cardboard cut to steady spliffs, broken matches, torn snaps of Rizla paper, and stray baked beans. Stephanie averts her eyes. Too much truth is hard to take.

'Sometimes gender is irrelevant,' said Stephie. She did not smoke and never had. Tobacco hurt her throat; marijuana made her giddy and nauseous. The other, stronger, substances available at the time, LSD, speed, were seen as male anyway and anathema. The soupy wooziness engendered by dope was perceived as female.

'Gender is never irrelevant,' snapped Madge. Bang, bang, bang! She was in a frenzy of savage irritation. A chunk of rusted metal broke off, as it was bound to do. Water flooded out at double volume, double pace.

'Doesn't anyone know where the stopcock is?' asked Wendy. Well, who ever does, male or female?

'I knew it,' said Stephanie, tears flooding from her eyes. 'I blame you for this, Madge. You kick and you bang and you hit everything in your path. I can't stand living like this, I can't stand it!'

'Then go, Stephie,' said Madge, who seemed content to leave the pipes alone now maximum damage had been done. Out of the corner of her eye Stephie caught Wendy simpering with her rosebud mouth. 'You are instantly replaceable.'

Wendy's simper turned into a smile which would have been broad only her mouth never seemed to stretch far enough. 'Don't be unkind to Stephie, Madge,' said Wendy. A fine jet of water spurted out between Rosalie's fingers — she had placed her palm over the hole, so that water now went in all directions not only in one — and got Stephanie on the forehead.

Stephie ran from the room and sat on the steps outside, her feet wet and frozen, her hair dripping, and Madge and Wendy damply embraced. Someone from upstairs had already called a plumber. Hardcock and Sons, as luck would have it.

Life at *Menstra* could be hell. Madge and Stephie had a reunion later: tearful on Stephanie's part, grunty on Madge's, but the relationship was never quite the same afterwards. Everything grated: rust ate in.

In the meantime Bull had turned up at Chalcot Crescent to collect his daughter. Instinct led him to where she was, to rescue her a second time. Little girls of three are easy to save, you pick them up, tuck them under your arm, and carry them off to safety. Fifteen-year-olds are a different matter. They look at you sceptically, judge you, dismiss you, and head off wilfully into danger.

'Come on home, Saff,' cajoled Bull. 'I'm on the wagon. Not another drink tonight. Sam needs you. We'll all have supper together in front of TV. OK?'
'OK,' said Saffron, taking the east wind out of everyone's sails. Bull, much relieved, addressed Daffy for the first time in years.

'If I've been unreasonable, Daffy, I'm sorry. Zoe dying really knocked me for six. If Saff wants to come up and talk to you I have no objection. She needs a woman to talk to, I expect, not having a mother. Girls' things. This house is looking really good now all Hamish's junk is out.'
'It's a bit boring, I always think,' said Daffy, modestly. 'I'm all right on clothes but I don't have a flair for houses.'
'Suits me,' said Bull, and Daffy smiled at him, and Saffron noticed.

'Just you and the boys,' said Bull, and by implication 'no man'. 'Don't you get lonely?'

'No,' said Daffy, but Saffron thought she lied.

Bull needn't have thought he'd be so easily let off the hook.

'I have a right to know how and why my mother died,' said Saffron, as he and she walked back home up the hill. 'If you won't tell me I have to ask other people. I'll go on asking, too. Sampson needs to know.'

'This stuff about rights will never end,' said Bull. 'There is no such thing as rights. Only *wouldn't it be nice if*. I've told you how and why your mother died at least a hundred times. I don't like talking about it. It hurts. Understand?'

'What about me?' demanded Saffron. 'Shouldn't you be thinking about me? It's worse to lose a mother than a wife. You can get a new wife but you can't replace a mother.'

'What have I bred?' he lamented. 'What did we breed, your mother and I?' Saffron was pleased because for once he admitted a shared parenthood.

'You must have brought me up wrong. I'm sure I started out with a heart.'

She would not take responsibility for herself. Would not.

Punch, punch, punch went Sampson in the spare room where his mother had died, except he didn't know it. He had a punchball — leather on a fine flexible metal stand — into which he thudded his small, toughening fist.

'Well?' he asked, stopping for a moment to hear what his sister had to report.
'Not much good,' said his sister. 'Same old story. Gentle mother, meek and mild. Kind and loving, wonderful mother, got depressed, accidental overdose. Do they think we're deaf and blind? Do you remember the funeral, Sam? Do you remember what went on?'
Sampson started punching again.
'Oh, forget it, Saff,' said Sampson.
'I can't,' said Saffron, plaintive for once. 'It's too much to have just sitting in my head.'

Sampson had his own view in his head, and memories flitting in and out of everyday life, like streamers, intertwining. Snatches of tune to which the thump of the punchball kept time. '*Lord of all hopefulness, lord of all joy* — ' Layla speaking, '*Zoe the bright star, Zoe head-in-air, killing herself to prove a point.*' The words had been there so long, they scarcely made sense. Someone saying, '*Funerals are no place for children,*' and being half pleased because the

253

attention now focused on him; Saffron denying she was a child; which didn't seem to Sampson to be strictly true.

Now he stopped punching and said to Saffron, 'Can we go to the cemetery please?' and Saffron said yes, OK, tomorrow after school.

So there they were seven years later: up to Golders Green on the Northern line, walk up to Hoop Lane, turn right for the crematorium, the rose gardens, the row upon row of markers for the dead.

It was past five o'clock: the services were over, but mourners came and went, and the people to take the flowers away, and gardeners, and masons to see how slabs were settling. The environs of the dead are always peopled: though few raise their voices, or move swiftly, so the impression is of solitude as the living try not to rouse the envy of the departed.

Saffron pushed open the door of the chapel to the left of the gated entrance. She sniffed the sepulchral air. Inside an old woman in a headscarf scrubbed floors.
'Disinfectant,' Saffron said. 'Do you remember that smell?'
'I'm going to be sick,' said Sampson, so she closed the door, and they went searching for and eventually found their mother's memorial slab.

'Zoe Meadows, 1946 – 1976. In remembrance of a loving mother.'

They stared for a while.

'I don't want to get to more than thirty anyway,' said Saffron.

Sampson looked at her sideways. Women were observably nuts.

'Doesn't say she was a loving wife, just a loving mother,' said Saffron. 'Who decides who puts what on these slabs?' Sampson didn't reply. How could he know if she didn't?

'If she was a loving mother,' said Sampson, 'how could she have killed herself? I bet it was an accident. I wish I could remember her face. She's a sort of idea of a mother, really, isn't she?'

'I reckon so,' said Saffron.

'*The worms crawl in*,' sang Sampson at the top of his voice.

'*The worms crawl out,*
They go in thin,
And they come out stout.
Now don't you think
It's nice to know
The worms are waiting for you below?'

'She wasn't a body, she was ashes,' said Saffron, taking him away, fast before someone heard and took offence.

'I know that, stupid,' said Sampson. 'Otherwise I wouldn't be singing it, would I?'

Having settled Sampson in his head, at least for the time being, Saffron looked up Medusa in the telephone book.

Saffron went to Medusa's offices. She turned up unannounced. Medusa's new headquarters were lavish, as suited the commercial spirit of the times. If you had it you flaunted it: if you didn't no one would be around to see your lack of it. Prosperity was considered catching: bad luck infectious. Women up from the provinces, or with tales of oppression to tell, would be shocked by the apparent opulence of the new headquarters. Layla said a certain amount of flash was necessary if European and US publishers were to take the imprint seriously. And Stephanie was so bound up in Madge and *Menstra*, the bleeding end of the market, as Layla put it, she did not have the energy to moderate Layla's delusions of grandeur. Lavish, lavish Layla.

'I've come to see Layla Lavery,' said Saffron to the receptionist, unaware of how presumptuous this statement must seem. As if Layla saw just anyone. No, she did not have an appointment. She had bunked off a school trip. She had to see Layla and get back before anyone noticed her absence.

'What do you want to see her about?' It was the least any receptionist could do for her employer.

'It's private.'

'Ms Lavery isn't here anyway,' said the receptionist. 'She's at Greenham. So's half the staff, for that matter.'

'Where?' Saffron did not read the newspapers.

'Greenham,' said the receptionist. 'The women are out saving the world. What's the use of a book if there's no one to read it, let alone review it?'

As it happened, while Saffron was in reception, Alice was in Nancy's office cutting and shuffling the Tarot Pack — a flash of the Fool, of the Empress, the Star, the Ace of Spades — 'See how the Major Arcana predominates: great moves are afoot!' — while Nancy spoke to Stephanie on the phone. 'No, Stephanie, no!' said Nancy. 'I cannot lend you money for *Menstra* out of Medusa funds. The Board won't countenance it: you are the wild fringes of the movement: you are out of order in your beliefs.' (The useful phrase politically correct had not yet been coined.) 'You are taking us off in the altogether wrong direction.'

The main thrust of feminist thought at the time was to diminish rather than exaggerate the difference between the genders. Women were urged to take their periods like a man; and here was *Menstra*, not just valuing but almost worshipping every drop of menstrual blood.

'The Board call you the Lavender Menace.'
'You mean they're homophobic.' Stephanie's voice crackled.
'They just don't see political lesbianism as the way forward,' said Nancy cautiously.
'They're running scared,' said Stephanie. 'What a bunch of old women!'
'It's against all policy,' said Nancy.

258

Alice was flicking through the Tarot Pack. She lay down the Queen of Swords.

'This represents Stephanie,' Alice said. 'Stephanie the unwise. Brave, determined, anxious. A maker of enemies.' Nancy tried to ignore her.

'I can't ask Layla because she isn't here to ask, Stephanie,' said Nancy. 'She's at Greenham. But I know what she'd say perfectly well, and so do you. She would not agree ten thousand pounds was peanuts to Medusa and even if she did she would not drop-feed them into *Menstra's* bloody maw.' Nancy was getting angry.

Alice lay the Ace of Swords crosswise over the Queen of Swords.

'This covers her,' murmured Alice. 'Violence, extremism. Pulling asunder. A card of great power.'

She drew another card, the Ten of Pentacles. She was forming a cross. Above, below, behind, in front. 'This rules her. Love of material things, longing, loss, sacrifice.'

Now the Prince of Wands, above.

'This is above her. Duty, obligation, aspiration.'

'You have sold out, Nancy,' said Stephanie. 'You and all Medusa. You play games with important things. You use the women's movement to line your own pockets. You've allowed Layla to have a controlling vote. No one's got the guts to thwart her. I will excommunicate you from the women's movement.'

'How do you mean to do that, Stephanie? From

the columns of *Menstra*?'

'Yes.'

'All the less reason to help you out in your financial predicament,' said Nancy.

Alice meanwhile had drawn the card Death from the pack. 'That is what Stephanie is going toward,' said Alice, casually. 'But then so are we all. Besides, the card's reversed. People like to believe that means re-birth, but I've never found it to be so. If you can't stand the future, don't read the cards.' She drew the Ace of Cups. 'Ultimate success,' said Alice. 'Give Stephanie her money. Isn't it a pretty card? It's my favourite card in the whole pack.'

'Sorry Stephanie,' said Nancy. 'No.'

She put down the phone, and turned to Alice.

'You have finally flipped, Alice,' said Nancy. 'I cannot take you seriously. I will not fund *Menstra* on the strength of a Tarot card. Life is not magic.'

Alice gathered up the pack, offended.

'You'll be sorry,' said Alice. 'I think you made the wrong decision.'

As soon as school was over on the Friday, Saffron went down by train and bus to Greenham Common, some seventy miles west of London, where the US Army had a base, and where it now kept in residence its cruise missiles. These were medium-range nuclear weapons, which could be launched from inside the base, or from the backs of moving trucks.

Saffron's English teacher explained to her that women, in the face of men's destructive frenzy, the desire to protect home and family from the foe gone so strangely wrong, had set up camp on Greenham Common as they were entitled to do under English law, and now by their passive presence, their reproachful chants, the PR that they swirled around them, sought to make the US take their missiles and themselves home. Why should women fear the Russians in particular? They were quite simply a danger. A man was a man whatever his nationality. Let the men stop being a danger to women and children. Women had gathered in scores of thousands from all over the country, all over the world, and linked their hands to form a human chain around the camp as if by force of female magic to neutralise the male power within.

Did Saffron know nothing of this? Saffron, at fifteen, did not. She had seen press pictures of muddy nutty women with wild eyes in woolly caps, juxtaposed with army vehicles, and strong pallid men in uniforms with eyes even wilder than those of the women, but had hardly thought it was anything to do with her.

She and her friends dreamed of nuclear destruction, it was true, and lived in their group unconscious in a sea of post-blast rubble, but that, Saffron had assumed, was family life not national nightmare. The death of a mother, as in her particular case, produces its own rubble: a generation of adults more sexually active than usual, unsobered by thoughts of unwanted pregnancies, creates its own chaos in the minds of the young. Let the cruise missiles fly, those stubbly phallic shapes, once let loose, creating havoc: what else did any young person at the time fear would happen next?

Greenham, then, was the place the demons could be set to rest. And clearly there was a harsh reality here. The swirling discontent between men and women had taken shape, solidified, into penis-shaped tubes of steel and within that the potential fusion of the atom.

Create a new element in a laboratory, pick it apart, and then using these infinitesimal particles of matter, fuse them together again and you could forget birth: you also created death. Saffron's science teacher explained the matter to her. Her history teacher pointed out the perversity of the two major tribes, the Russians and the Americans, so admiring the power of the other they preserved the other from destruction — what fun is there in a dead enemy? — and meant to lay waste the intervening mass of Europe by some lethal firework display.

The range of cruise missiles was so pathetically small that if based on English soil they would never get as far as Russia, and even if, in the worst case, pointed the other way, would simply fall in the Atlantic. The Americans weren't stupid. And the same thing could be said of the Soviet's equivalent based in Eastern European states. World War III, in other words, would be played out in Europe: the home powers would be safe.

A nod and a wink from the teaching staff, and a quick whipround for Saffron's travel, and down she went to Greenham, in search of Layla, and an explanation of her past, though her teachers did not quite understand that part of it.

The bus to Newnham from Reading was full of women with backpacks and expressions of rather mirthless but sisterly joy. They wore layers of clothing: they expected discomfort and persecution: they looked forward to it. Depending on whether you saw an enemy or friend, you saw obsessional self-righteousness, or joyous determination: you saw the Maenads, bent on destruction; you saw the glitter of triumph in female eyes that men had finally proved themselves so hideously, hopelessly, stupefyingly stupid they'd blow up the world rather than give an inch; and you saw the warmth and power of female strength, the power and will of the *wimmin* to save the world.

Wimmin, oblivious to the reasoning of linguistics, so antagonistic to 'man' they wouldn't even let these three letters into the word which described their gender. Any woman who wanted her society preserved, who wanted her children saved from radiation, from the rubble of the world, protested for 'freedom'. What did women, oblivious to the pull of national pride, care about 'free speech', 'democracy'; their oppression was nothing to do with forms of government, with right or left, capitalism or communism, simply to do with this one massive central problem, that of gender now taken to extremes. Men for death, wimmin for life.

To want to take the toys from the boys, to be at Greenham, if only in the mind, with the tanks tumbling, made you at least for the time being an honorary woman. Saffron felt a tingling in her toes, a pricking of the hair on her scalp, as the bus stopped by the high metal mesh fence, to which a myriad straps of wool and little paintings and photographs of children had been tied, and behind which guard dogs snarled and barked, and armed field cars zoomed and tanks patiently trundled, showing the presence, but also the act of charity by which the peace camp was allowed to exist at all.

One whimsical order by some pallid cigar-chewing general, some Mandelsonian *éminence grise* somewhere, and everyone knew the machine guns would rattle, the flame throwers erupt, the doors slide open and the bulldozers emerge to bury the dead, tumbling them over and over in the mud, and that would be the end of the women. Who would really care?

Women may be decent, loving, kindly, soft and emotional creatures, but all men know they are in the end replaceable: there are always more where they came from: they shouldn't have left the safety of their homes in the first place. So the women clustered round their camp fires, trusted in the law, the power of PR, and sang, chanted, did their meditation, voiced their anger, and squabbled. If they were nervous, they were rightly so. And brave, right up there at the edges of nuclear nightmare, dragon's breath felt, as the creature stirred in its hibernation, beginning to toss and turn in its sleep. What restrained it? No one quite knew.

Women had to rely on a male rationality, and how flimsy a thing it was: every wife and daughter knew; and though not everyone is a wife, all women are daughters.

Saffron walked through muddy tracks lined by ill-assorted makeshift tents; little fires burned everywhere she passed; groups of women clustered to prepare food, or sing, or plot strategies. It was a noisy place. The high metal fence, which seemed to go on forever, encircled more land than she had thought possible. It marked one state of reality from another: on the other side of the fence was male power, here, encircling it, was conscience. Here you could smell food cooking and wafts of dope and what she feared was sewage. There on the other side was cleanliness, organisation and all forms of death.

Saffron found she quite wanted to be on the other side. She'd had no idea of the scale of the Greenham camp: her teachers had failed to impress her with it. How to find Layla Lavery in this lot?

Saffron approached a group of women who seemed less unapproachable than others: a cluster of vicar's wives, she thought, staid, pleasant, middle-aged women in wellies and head scarves. Or perhaps they were teachers, or social workers. She felt reassured. Their fire was well made and burned brightly. They sang in tune. A pole, topped by an effectively painted Venus woman symbol, stood firmly rooted in the ground, and stayed upright, which was more than could be said for many around.

Take the toys from the boys
Take their hands off the guns
Take their fingers off the trigger
Take the toys from the boys.

'Excuse me,' said Saffron when the verse came to an end, to the most approachable of the women, who happened to be a doctor's receptionist, by name Evelyn.

'You're new here,' said Evelyn, with certainty. 'There's no mud under your fingernails. Can I help in some way?'

'There's someone I want to find,' said Saffron.

'You'll have a problem, sweetheart,' said Evelyn. 'There are rather a lot of us. You could give up your quest and simply join our group. All women are welcome, and young ones especially so. We do this for your future, not our own. We want to leave a world for you to live in. No special skills required: just your presence and your female power. And your wish for the world to be saved. This is the best thing I have ever done in all my life. I'm never going home.'

Saffron was to find that many women at Greenham spoke at length: once they began there was so much to say they did not stop. All the fleeting thoughts that had come and gone in the past, unattended to on account of the needs of domestic life, arrived in the undomestic, unfamiliar here and now and at last made sense and became coherent at least to the speaker, and even, should they be in sympathy in the first place, to the listener too. Saffron was simply bewildered. Now massive gates were opening too close for comfort. A bevy of uniformed men lingered in the gateway, under blazing lights; each had a couple of dogs on a leash. The women ignored them.

'This is Greenham, honey,' said Evelyn. 'This is where it's all at; the bottom line, the cutting edge, where shell meets flesh, and teeth bite through. This is Greenham. The other side of that fence are the male weapons of destruction. Nuclear weapons. A US arsenal, there by the connivance of our own men. Their aim, to kill, maim and poison women and children, in the name of peace. To kill in order to save. Every now and then the United States likes to take its weapons out and show them to us and trundle them around, like a man exposing himself, going for a walk with his flies undone, his thing sticking up. You must know about all this. Why are you acting so surprised?'

'Well,' said Saffron, 'actually, it's just my half-term. I'm looking for someone called Layla Lavery. I believe she's here somewhere. But there must be thousands of people here. I had no idea.' 'Hundreds of thousands,' said Evelyn. 'Though the press likes to underplay it. Everyone knows Layla. Her tent's near Gate number 8. You can't miss it. Just follow the film crews.'

At the mention of Layla, the friendliness seemed to ooze out of Evelyn. She turned her attention away from Saffron, who felt herself dismissed.

'*Take the toys from the boys,*' the song continued.

'*Gotta make a living.
Take their hands off the guns,*

268

Gotta make a killing.
Get their fingers off the buttons,
Gotta get promotion.
Take the toys from the boys,
Make a bomb, make a bomb.'

Saffron, looking upwards, saw a massive '8' illuminated in the sky, and made her way towards it. Inside the garrison some joker put the 'Star-Spangled Banner' over the loudspeaker system. The women sang louder. Dusk was falling, lights went on inside the fence.

Saffron found Layla by the light of film cameras, as Evelyn had predicted. Layla stood outside a neatly arranged and even ornamental tent; she wore a practical but nifty boiler suit and a headscarf, but managed to look business-like, feminine and attractive. She spoke to camera.

'So what are women meant to do?' Layla enquired of the multitudes who stared at their screens and part rejoiced and part lamented they were not there at Greenham that day. 'Wash dishes while men destroy the world, with their absurdly phallic weapons, in an argument about nothing? Mutually Absurd Destruction? MAD? Europe is where the USA and the Soviet Union mean to fight out their macho quarrel. They're not going to risk their own populations: but we Europeans can be pushed out of existence for all they care. We want these hideous weapons out of this country and we want that now, and we women are not leaving till that happens.'

Saffron thought Layla was wonderful. So did the camera crew, but a tattered group of old handers were assembling, long-term residents of the camp, eyes habitually screwed up against nature and man's villainy. They eased the admirers to the periphery of the group. They scowled at Layla. Saffron was disconcerted. Some sisters

270

were clearly more equal than others. The songs might allow no divisiveness; real life did.

'And by women simply holding hands round the perimeter fence of a US Army base, you really think this can be achieved? Women are going to change the world?' enquired the TV journalist. 'Listen, buster,' said Layla smartly. 'That was the greatest PR stunt of all time and don't you knock it.'

Rita, largest and squarest of Layla's critics, stepped forward between Layla and the lens. 'Actually,' said Rita, 'I'm the group spokesperson round here. Why are you talking to Layla Lavery, and why if she's any sort of feminist, is she talking to you? She knows the rules well enough. Women speak only to women. Where are the women reporters, the women cameramen?' 'Hey look,' said the male reporter, 'I'm on your side.' 'Sorry,' said Rita. 'That can't be. You're a man.' 'That's not fair,' protested the reporter. 'It's hardly my fault.' 'Its called group guilt, sweetheart,' soothed Layla. 'It used to be only the Germans got it, but now it's all men everywhere. Damned you are, even as you leap from the womb. Yuk, it's a boy! All male sex is rape, that kind of thing. Live with it, boyo: it's here.'

'Shut up, Layla,' said Rita. 'Men want war, women want peace. That's all a TV audience needs to know. The women of Greenham say no to war.'

'*Say no to war.*' Women all around took up the chant.

'*Women of Greenham say no to war.*'

'Excuse me,' said Saffron to Layla, pulling her sleeve.

'It's not surprising they point the camera at me,' remarked Layla. 'Since I'm the only woman round here who combs her hair. Do I know you? Your hair seems to be quite recently combed.'

But Saffron had no chance of replying: the reporter also wanted to bend Layla's ear, and he was a professional.

'Jesus,' he said, 'I didn't know I was doing the wrong thing. You're the only one our audience knew. I had to fight with my editor for airtime on this one. He'd only allow it if I got you on screen. What does he care about the survival of the world? If women care about it, it can't be important. That's my boss's thinking. He'd only run it, he said, if I got you on film.'

'My sisters do sometimes have a problem with reality,' Layla apologised, on their behalf. '*Forgive them for they know not what they do*. They only understand their little window on the world, and it is too closely framed by their distrust of men. Or else don't forgive them for they bloody well know what they're doing and don't give a fart. I don't care which you fucking choose: I can never make up my mind myself.'

Layla turned her attention back to Saffron.
'I know you, for God's sake. You're Zoe's little girl. Aged three, in a pushchair. Being rescued by your father. The day Medusa was born. Then at the crematorium, aged what, eight, denying you were a child.'
'You have a good memory,' said Saffron.
'It's terrific,' said Layla. 'Eidetic, too. It can be painful. Never forgetting leaves you with your nerves on the outside of your skin.'
'I have a good memory too,' said Saffron. 'You were speaking from the pulpit when my father took me away. What were you saying? You weren't the preacher. He was furious! I remember that. I thought, at the time, like him, this is no way to conduct a funeral.'

Behind the mesh fence, pooled by alternate patches of brilliant light and dark, moved unexplained shapes: heavy equipment shifting heavy weights; jolting and swaying; massive tyres rolling; fitful, shouting male voices. Layla remembered the chapel of death; shifting light through vaulted windows; rollers on which coffins stuck; heard her own voice.

'*Oh yes, go, Bull,*' Layla was saying. '*Get out before you hear what you don't want to hear. That it's your fault. Why did you bring the kids anyway? Funerals are no place for children.*'

'*I'm not a child,*' Saffron had said, and perhaps she was, perhaps she wasn't; then as now. Some children only play at the role, at the best of times.

'Chickens come home to roost,' said Layla now. 'The bit-part players don't disappear, as you hope they will. They keep coming back for more. So here you are, little chick, once again at the nexus. Hi. What do you want from me?'

'I want the truth about my mother,' said Saffron. Things seemed to have calmed down on the other side of the fence. An ominous silence had fallen. The camp was hushed too, waiting. Lights were extinguished. Fires stamped out. There seemed safety in silence.

'Oh, Lord,' said Layla, looking more frightened by Saffron and the past than she was by the imminent and immanent dangers of the present. 'High drama and all that. Give me a moment. Does judgement day have to be now?'

Rita and her friends were moving tentatively back towards Layla and Saffron: square shapes in the gloom. The camera crew had fled for safety. Layla grabbed Saffron and pulled her round toward the entrance of the tent, and slipped inside it. She did not light the lamp.

'Some sisters,' hissed Layla, 'it's safer not to get up the noses of. Help me pack up, little chick. I think we've got to get out of here, quickly. We'll talk later.'

'Only if you promise,' said Saffron, who has had years of Bull making just such false assurances.

'Promise, promise, promise,' said Layla, and she put her head out of the tent and called to the clustering women 'OK, OK, you win. I shut up. I'm leaving. Have fun.' But the women were dispersing anyway. Gate 8 was opening its steel-mesh doors and a snake of transporters were leaving the base. Women were running up to hammer on windscreens and bonnets, to bare their bosoms, and howl '*Bastards. Murderers. Does your mummy know you're out?*' and suchlike, according to taste.

The men in uniforms seemed pale, abashed but determined; in the eternal fix of men when those behind cry forward, and those in front cry back. But those behind won.

Inside her fringed and fronded tent, Layla packed her suitcases. She worked carefully and methodically. She layered garments with tissue: cosmetics fitted into custom-made cases. Saffron marvelled. Layla talked.

'Darling, I've had my shift at virtue. I've done my bit. They all hate me. I bet Jesus got hated too. They have to admire me, but still they hate me. I've given up my life for women, but does that impress them? No. If this country goes up in nuclear flames they'll be really pleased. 'Told you so,' will be the last word on their lips as their skins shrivel and their gums rot in the land of rubble. They can't decide which they hate most: men, nuclear bombs, or each other. They would tear not only Orpheus limb from limb, but me their sister too. All they know is that to be in the right someone else must be in the wrong. But this is beyond a joke, beyond a demonstration. They stir up fear and we get more fearful. We begin to live in a nightmare. Do you know what children dream of these days? They dream of nuclear holocaust. Bet you do, too.'

'A lake, a beach,' said Saffron, 'trees, people walking, a tower on a hill, everything peaceful. Suddenly, low-flying aircraft, a blinding flash, then nothing but rubble, and the shadow of trees scarred into broken claws: and people, like sticks, looking for those they can't find. Children who went to school, and came back to find nothing.'

'That's the rubble dream,' said Layla. 'All decades have their nightmares and this is ours. That's why I came here. Well, fuck it. They don't want me. I'll go home and save Medusa on the off-chance the world continues. I'll put my head in the sand like everyone else. When the ostriches finally lift their heads, all anyone is going to say is, 'My God, those old things, aren't they ugly.' '

The trucks had gone by, rolling their way through flesh and blood. A couple of legs and a thigh had been broken. Someone screamed. Ambulances, part of the age-old ritual of *first damage, then mend: exercise anger, then forgive*, parted the crowds the sooner to save them. A few women cried, others shouted. Now bulldozers moved out of Gate 9 and plunged in amongst the tents, uprooting them, collapsing them, plunging possessions into mud. The drivers sat behind toughened glass, barely seen, off on their punishment mission. As they went, so the women followed behind, salvaging, piling, sorting, turning even the chaos of wilful destruction into order. There was no winning, no losing in this game. It just went on forever.

Layla's tent, as was to be expected, was not in the path of the bulldozers. Saffron, eyes and ears full of the unexpected, retreated back into it. Layla, she observed, was on the edge of distress. She felt remorse at having contributed to it. It was not an emotion Saffron often felt.

'I'm sure they don't hate you,' said Saffron. 'It's just some of the women here are completely crazy.'

'You're a nice little girl,' said Layla. 'Just like your mother but not so irritating. Why don't you leave it alone? She took an overdose by accident, and it was dreadful. It happens. Face it.'

'That wasn't what you were saying at the funeral,' said Saffron. 'You were trying to blame my father. Or were you just using my mother's death to hold a PR meeting? Perhaps she was just useful as a martyr?'

'*Please, this is a chapel of rest,*' said the chaplain, back in the past. '*A funeral service, not a women's liberation meeting.*'

'I can see all this here at Greenham is important,' said Saffron. 'I can see the world has to change, and if no one changes it nothing happens. But what about my life? What about me? Your case in point was my mother's life.

She and I are real women, not just a theory about what happens next. And what happens next depends on what went before.'

'That's OK,' said Layla. 'I forgive you your many insensitivities.'

Layla and Saffron piled suitcases into Layla's car. Now the problem was the tent itself. Layla was moved to leave it where it stood, simply abandon it, but the very idea shocked Saffron, who took a hammer and started knocking out tent pegs, releasing stays, so the wet canvas collapsed neatly to the ground. The marauding JCB had moved off to more exciting pastures.

'Everyone says my mother was depressed. Why?' said Saffron, pressing her moral advantage home.

'Darling, people are and they aren't,' said Layla. 'There doesn't have to be a cause. And she was married to your father, don't forget that.'

'Why didn't she leave him, if she wasn't happy with him?' asked Saffron.

'It's a mystery, sweetheart,' said Layla. 'Leave it!'

'Or else it was because Medusa turned down her book,' said Saffron, bleakly.

'I can see you'd like to believe that,' said Layla, 'but honestly I don't think that's true. We didn't turn it down. She sent us some pages, and Stephanie rang her and said, 'How exciting, send us the rest.' But she never did.'

'Why didn't she? Didn't she finish it? Perhaps Dad didn't let her?'

'How do I know?' asked Layla. 'Perhaps

Stephanie remembers more about it. Yes, I think you should talk to Stephanie, not me.'
And she hailed a male reporter who just happened to be passing. It was the same lost and lonely man who had earlier introduced Layla to the reluctantly watching world. It is remarkable how little attention the world accords to those who spend their lives trying to save it, as a spoilt and naughty child will take parental care for granted, while trying to undermine it.

'I say, man,' said Layla, 'give us a hand here.' And the man reporter obligingly did; though there was a sudden screeching from inside the mesh fence, as guard systems gave voice, which made his canvas-folding falter.
'Someone's slipped through the perimeter fence,' Layla explained to Saffron. 'They'll end up in prison. Women are very brave, once you get them going.'

Saffron nodded. Agreeing with Layla seemed to be the price she would have to pay for a lift back to London. So much mud and trouble barred the way back to the bus stop she thought Layla's car was a better bet.

'But isn't Hamish the enemy?' Saffron asked as Layla drove west into a moonlit sky. They were, it seemed, returning to London by way of his farmhouse. The mud, noise and turmoil had been left behind. Here was serenity; smooth grass growing by a flat straight easy road. Chaos and order are interdependent, merely placed differently in space and time. Fun and dread here, boredom and safety there.

'No, darling,' said Layla. 'Hamish isn't the enemy. We are all in this together. We have to see it out. It gets dangerous: theory might become practice — we could all die. The cold war switches to hot. Men are people too. No one's frozen in time, in aspic. Just don't try Hamish's home-made wine. It's a nightmare.'
'How well did Hamish know my mother?' asked Saffron, her psychic teeth still searching for the living flesh of those to blame. She'd forget, and drowse, as if Cerberus had been fed tranquillisers, then off she'd go again.
'I don't think your father would have allowed anything like that,' Layla said. 'One rule for men and another for women. MAD. Mutual Assured Destruction. Some men like stealing other men's wives, sure, just as some women like stealing other women's husbands, but Hamish just likes sex. He would not have wanted the full weight

of your mother's emotion, let alone the weight of your father's anger!'

Saffron had a vision, half remembered, half imagined, of her father striding down the road; her mother's frantic complaint.

'I can feel Bull's anger. I can feel it. Male anger shakes the world.'

And Layla remembered it too — the one-time anger of those beasts of men, who had to be charmed, cajoled, soothed, placated, lied to, in case having impaled a woman sexually as was their bounden duty, they then went on to simply tear her to bits.
'These days,' said Layla sadly, 'it's rare to meet a thoroughly potent man: they've lost the knack of it.'

They were crossing Salisbury Plain: dark mechanical shapes drove out of it, towards them, then lumbering by them. Headlights were shielded; just a glimmer of light allowed to distinguish road from verge. The cruise convoy was returning home. Saffron drowsed, exhausted.

The next day Saffron woke to a bright busy rural morning, in Hamish's farmhouse. She'd slept on a broken but valuable sofa in a back room. She found a bathroom and washed; rinsed out her knickers, which she'd been too tired to do the night before, and having found an old hair dryer on a shelf, dried them out and put them back on. She picked other people's hair out of a brush and did her hair. The brush was silver-backed: ornately wrought: more than a hundred years old. The matching mirror was mercury-backed, the glass worn through with age and maltreatment. Looking into it, she thought perhaps she was going to be beautiful. She decided she was. Home made her puffy and anxious, and she understood she would always look better away from it.

She found the kitchen and two roaming dogs, who seemed friendly and had cold noses they dug into her palms hoping for something to eat. A little red hen scuttled around under table and chairs, searching for food. The pans were copper and in need of cleaning: mugs were chipped: kitchen implements rusty and Victorian: every surface cluttered, impossible to clean. The only plastic object she'd seen in the home was the hair dryer, and cobwebs had got into its grill and she'd feared she smelt roasting spider. But at least she had dry, clean knickers. There was no sign of Hamish or Layla. Had they spent the night together? Presumably.

She missed home. She missed her father. She heard, incongruously, the sound of a trumpet playing. Hamish was up and dressed and down the end of the garden amongst the artichokes, playing the St James Infirmary Blues. Saffron peered out at him between latticed window-panes uncleaned for years.

Layla came into the kitchen in what looked like a bathrobe stolen from a hotel years ago and unwashed ever since. In the interests of sex Layla abandoned her role as a packer in tissue, a wearer of fine fabric.

'I hope your father won't be worried about you,' said Layla.

'I told him I was staying with a friend,' said Saffron. 'I didn't think it was wise to mention Hamish.'

'Just like your mother,' complained Layla. 'Put her in a corner and she'd take the wrong way out. Personally, I take care to speak the truth. It saves trouble in the end, though it gets you into a lot of it on the way.'

'How else am I like my mother?' asked Saffron.

'You're not,' said Layla. 'You can't be really. Different decade, different times. You don't care about the world, you care about yourself, you are only interested in who's to take the blame for you. You are solipsistically like all your peers. Well, don't blame the decade, blame the times, don't blame me. Or else face it and blame your father, who is half yourself.'

'I was lying about it being half-term,' said Saffron. 'I should be at school.' She thought she might adopt Layla's habit of speaking the truth.

Hamish came in from the garden. He ground coffee beans in a grinder so old and blunt the noise set the dogs barking and the hen scuttling for cover, crapping as it went. He opened the Aga door, and the smell of baking bread poured out, mellowing all things.

'Look here,' he said, beckoning to Saffron. She looked inside the oven and saw some six bread tins packed inside, and in them crusted brown loaves beautifully risen. 'My triumph,' said Hamish. He eased the tins out of the oven one by one with his bare fingers and hurled them across the room, so they clanged and bounced across the floor and the loaves flew free. Layla retrieved them before the dogs could.

They ate the bread for breakfast. Hamish and Layla sat side by side, leaning into one another. 'Zoe's daughter,' said Hamish. 'Fancy that. I seem to remember you in your pushchair. You grizzled even then. Women are always complaining about something or other. Why can't you just *be*? Have a good time?'

Otherwise he was polite, even sympathetic. He hoped she liked the bread. Saffron said it was a little hot and heavy and personally she liked white sliced bread, hygienically wrapped. They laughed. She thought they liked her and why not? They were all tellers of the truth, members of the club. Most in her experience weren't.

Saffron decided then she didn't really care what people thought of her: it was what she thought of them that mattered. Thus are our characters formed; experiences at certain junctures laid over the pushchair personality. No wonder parents like to keep their growing kids at home: they fear bad company might infect them, and are right to fear it.

'All Saffron ever does is howl,' said Zoe once. *'She's so ungrateful. I'm doing this for her future, not mine. She doesn't realise that. Supposing Bull throws me out?'*
'Bull, Bull, Bull,' Hamish had mimicked, and gone on banging furniture with his chain, metal against wood, flesh unto flesh, Saffron blinking with every blow.

Saffron got back to London and Belsize Park and there in the spare room Sampson was at his punchball, banging flesh into foam rubber and canvas. Bang, bang, bang.

'I wish you'd stop that racket,' said Saffron. 'I'm doing everything I can for you. I've been all the way to Greenham following leads. Why do you leave everything to me?'
'You're older than me,' said Sampson, reasonably.

'It's not that at all,' said Saffron. 'It's because I'm female and you're male, so I have to take all the responsibility.'

Sampson didn't deign to reply. He resumed punching, yet more furiously than before.

'That's right,' said Saffron. 'Develop your muscles. Bloody macho before you even begin. Bloody men!'

'It has nothing to do with muscles,' said Sampson. 'It's hand — eye co-ordination. Supposing I grow up gay? People do.'

And Sampson banged on, unreconciled to his fate, or to the version of the past his sister offered him.

Down by Layla's Chelsea house the Thames ran sweetly by, and the cruise boats plied their wares. *Divorce Reform — Lothario's Charter* read the *Evening Standard* poster. So far so good. Inside the house Medusa posters fought for available space with those for Gay Pride. In the kitchen Johnny and Richard prepared what was meant to be a tranquil and elegant supper for three but Stephanie, the now more-than-likely fourth, was fund-raising for *Menstra*, and having a surprisingly hard time of it.

'Everyone knows the richest people in the world are gays,' she was saying. 'And the poorest are the lesbians. Why won't you help us? We have the same problems; that of the world's opprobrium. Help us and help yourselves.'

'Ask Medusa,' Johnny said snappily. 'Ask the sisters.'
'Medusa are in the straight camp. They won't help.'
'Straight camp!' said Richard appreciatively, but Johnny was not amused.

'Alice was on my side,' said Stephanie, 'but they still wouldn't listen, wouldn't bend. Alice is being marginalised. Sisterhood is a thing of

290

the past. Only ten thousand, Johnny, to keep *Menstra* alive.'

'We need our own money,' said Johnny, bleakly. 'We're beginning to die around you and you haven't even noticed. Go on worshipping your own blood; we've got reason to be fearful of our own.'

'Aids, you mean,' said Stephanie. 'Storm in a teacup. Alarmist nonsense. Sex heals, sex doesn't kill. The doctors are trying to scare you. You're hysterical, Johnny.'

'That's what I keep telling him,' said Richard, and then kindly, since she looked so disappointed, 'Stay to dinner, Stephanie. Share our Beef Wellington. We made it especially for Alice. If Stephanie can't have our money, Johnny, the least she can do is share our food.'

'What's Alice doing here?' asked Stephanie in alarm. 'Why is she consorting with the gays?'

'She's writing her *magnum opus* upstairs,' said Richard, 'and unlike so many does not see our company as polluting.'

Stephanie succumbed to the odour of roasting meat and stayed to dinner.

'Don't tell Madge,' she said.

When over dinner Richard observed that the lesbian alliance itself seemed to be in danger, Stephanie burst into tears. 'Poor Stephanie!' said Alice. 'The fate of the revolutionary is never to see the success of the revolution: the forest is too well hidden by the trees.' It seemed a long time since anyone had offered Stephanie sympathy or understanding. She grizzled, like a child.

'At least you're not Trotsky, Stephanie,' said Alice. 'If this were a man's revolution you'd have an ice pick in your head by now.'

See now Saffron sitting upon her doorstep as evening falls. She's forgotten her door key again. Keeping her company are Rafe and Roland. Now she's met up with these two all have become inseparable. Temperament and gender may separate them: shared experience of a parental generation joins them, and wins. Saffron allows herself, in their company, to feel sorry for herself. It is a great relief. No one ever quite grows up.

'Everyone deserves a mother to let them in when they get home,' remarked Saffron. 'I will not let the loss of mine go unavenged.'
'Everyone ought to remember their front door key,' said Roland, severely. 'I'm sure if your mother were alive she'd be the first to say so.'
'No one should have to have a mother who's a lesbian,' said Rafe. 'Especially not if they're boys. If we were girls we'd be allowed to live with her. Because we're mere males, we are doomed to live with our father's ex-mistress, who is pleasant enough, but no rocket scientist.'

'If we are mentally and emotionally stunted who could be surprised?' asked Roland. 'Our father talks only to vegetables. He pours his heart out to turnips, never to us. But I suppose at least he didn't drive our mother to death, as yours did.'

293

'I've changed my mind about that,' said Saffron. 'Or at any rate I absolve my father from blame. It is too easy to blame men. Everyone does it.' She was more inclined, these days, to lay her mother's death at the door of the sisterhood, though which particular one of them, and through which particular route, she could not be sure.

When Bull came home from work he let all three of them into the house. Tacitly, these days, he accepted some kind of joint responsibility for the next generation. He was courting Daffy, who would never try to write a book. He had a vision of a family rescued: of a life to be lived, not abandoned. He thought he would stop drinking.

Saffron smiles her approval, and bides her time.

Saffron invited Alice to speak to the Sixth Form Feminist Society. Alice accepted. Saffron was there at the gate to meet her.

'I believe you knew my mother,' said Saffron, leading her to the staff-room for the cup of tea which the more sophisticated student groups offered to their lecturers before they began.

'Really?' said Alice politely. 'What was her name?'

'Zoe Meadows,' said Saffron. Alice looked startled.

'That's the one,' said Saffron. 'The one who killed herself because Medusa turned down the book she'd taken five years to write.'

'I don't think that's true,' said Alice, cautiously.

'I heard from Layla you were on the warpath. You don't give up, do you?'

'I see the rewards in not doing so,' said Saffron, bleakly.

'I have very little to do with Medusa any more,' said Alice.

'Try asking Stephanie. She'll know more about it than I do. See if you can entrap her.'

'To tell you the truth,' said Saffron, with unusual candour, '*Menstra* makes me nervous.'

'So it does all of us,' said Alice, and then, 'Is this evening a set-up, so you can challenge me in public about your mother?'

'Yes,' said Saffron, but by that time Alice was at the staffroom, cups of tea were being offered, and it was too late for her to back out. When it came to it, she was merciful, and merely asked ordinary kinds of questions, such as 'Whither Communism' and 'Whence Medusa.' She thought she'd failed.

Saffron could see there was no evading *Menstra* any more. She found their offices in a side street between the British Museum and the Tottenham Court Road, stuck between a shop selling antiquities and another selling ancient maps, sandwiched between Mother Isis and the pilgrims' route to Glastonbury. Once through the blood-red door and up the shabby stairs the place was cheerful enough, and schoolgirlish. Women wore ankle-socks and trainers, jeans stretched over plump buttocks, tatty old sweaters; lesbian chic was yet to come.

Only Madge was stylish, in her thigh boots and frilly shirt. Stephanie seemed harassed. There was a streak of grey in her hair. It had appeared overnight, after a particularly savage row with Madge. She refused to dye it, which angered her friend. What Madge couldn't stand was martyrdom, a trait she felt particularly loathsome and one most prevalent in English women.

On hearing Saffron's business Stephanie seemed merely a notch more harassed than before. Madge's instinct was to get the girl out of the offices. They went, all three, to talk in the health food café Lentils, where the carrot cake with lemon icing was reckoned particularly delicious by those in the know.

'What about me?' asked Saffron. 'You have your movement, your feminism, you have each other. I just have my life. You killed my mother with your theories. The way I see it is that you put ideas into her head, then you wouldn't publish her book.'

'What are you talking about?' asked Stephanie. 'We were going to publish her book. I remember very clearly calling her up to say so, and speaking to your father. It's a long time ago, but all this came up when she died.'

'I don't believe this,' said Madge to Stephanie. 'You mean you trusted a man to pass such a message on? Were you out of your mind? What an amateur you are!'

'My father isn't such a monster as all that,' said Saffron.

'All men are monsters,' said Madge. 'It's perfectly clear what happened. Your mother challenged the patriarchy, threatened the man with an alternative definition of herself, as earner and thinker, not wife and mother. Of course he didn't pass the message on. Stephanie's stupidity. Look no further for the cause of your mother's death.'

'*Menstra*'s folding,' said Stephanie. 'Madge is upset. She spends her time attacking me, physically and verbally. This is the end.'

She stood up; so did Madge. Madge slapped Stephanie's face. Stephanie kicked Madge's ankles. Those munching the famous carrot cake paused mid-munch; sticky strands held upper and lower jaws together.

'Hopelessly English,' yelled Madge. 'Selfish, cold, a terrible cook, and no fun in bed. I'm going home to New York where women are women.'

'The worst years of my life,' yelled Stephanie. 'The worst years — '

Madge pushed a couple of tables and chairs over as she left. Stephanie wept. Saffron left Stephanie to pay the bill, and took the train all the way to the East End, to Canary Wharf, where a group of property developers were pitting the danger of bankruptcy against the erection of the largest office building in the world. In order to build you first had to destroy. In order to reach the sky you first had to dig holes in the ground. Saffron's father's particular skill lay in making sure that vast holes in the ground did not collapse upon and kill those who dug them. In these days of property speculation boom he was fully employed and had little time to drink. He was almost cheerful. Saffron tracked her father down, and found him sitting on the step of a works hut, in a hard hat. He seemed unsurprised to see her, apart from observing mildly that she should be at school. These days his daughter moved with such assurance he assumed she knew what she was about.

'Tell me about the book my mother wrote,' said Saffron.

'Leave it alone, Saff,' said her father. 'Stop thinking about the past. Give me a break.

Here's a hole in the ground that's a new lease of life for London, a new lease of life for your poor old Dad. There's the here and now to get on with. You're going through a morbid phase. I suppose it's better than running round with boys. Pay in this place is performance-related. I can't speak long. It's always good to see you, Saff, but at least your mother never followed me to work. You let me just get on with this and I'll earn enough to pay off our debts.'

'Fuck the debts,' said Saffron. 'I remember you burning something in the Pither stove; sticking pages in through the bars. Was that the book my mother wrote?'
'Yes it was,' said Bull, looking down into the pit. 'And the best thing for it. It was anti-men rubbish. She had everything she wanted from me. Everything a woman could want. Husband, house, kids.' Ah, he was stubborn.

'*Don't act the innocent,*' he said to Zoe once, as Zoe watched the pages burn, and Saffron watched her mother watching. Zoe was passive, and Saffron never would be. So much a child can learn. '*You've been in touch with Medusa. I know you have. Some slag just rang here asking for you.*'
'*That would be Stephie,*' Zoe said. '*Tell me what she said. Please tell me.*'
'*She said no thanks,*' said Bull. '*She said there was no market left for female self-pity. So I am burning this trash to save you the trouble, to save you from embarrassment —* '

'Well,' said Saffron, 'all becomes clear. It's true. You my father drove my mother to her death.'
'I did what I thought was best,' said Bull. 'What more can a man do? And she certainly punished me for it, and you children too. She was the one who swallowed the tablets, raised the bottle to her lips. Why can't you bring yourself to blame her? You know she drank straight from the bottle, didn't even bother to use a glass?'
'I didn't know that,' said Saffron.
'Besides which,' said Bull, 'the burning was a rhetorical gesture on my part, your mother understood that very well. If she'd wanted to go ahead with it, she could have. And she knew me better than to believe what I said about Medusa. Men and women play games, Saffron. Ours just went a little too far. Blame me if you want; I'll throw in this job and go back on the bottle. Why try?'

'OK,' said Saffron. 'OK. You win.' She had the feeling all of a sudden that her father was filling in time before he died too, and was able to join her mother. She felt excluded.
'The children of lovers', she observed later to Rafe, 'are orphans. Tolstoy.'

Someone had said it, once or twice back in the past, and it had stuck.

It was not long after this day of drama, Saffron-induced, that Layla, sitting quietly watching TV in her silk dressing-gown, alone in the evening as she rather liked to be, eschewing parties and hopeful lovers, heard a knock at the front door. It was on its chain. London had become a dangerous place. Women no longer opened a front door without checking who was there. But it was only Stephie.

Stephie came in, and handed Layla a brown envelope, in which was a manuscript.
'Would you believe it?' she said. 'A copy of Zoe's book. Bull called by and gave it to me. It's only seven years late. I daresay everything Zoe said then still applies today. Progress is so patchy. A few things change, most things don't.'

'I heard you've left Madge,' said Layla. 'And *Menstra* folded.'
'She left me,' said Stephanie, carefully. 'I cried for two weeks but now I seem to have forgotten her. It may be that lesbian love makes less of an impact than heterosexual does, what do you think?'
'I have no idea,' said Layla. 'Just please don't ask anyone to write a book about it.'
'I wondered if Medusa would have me back again,' said Stephanie. 'I want work, and mess,

and cheerfulness. I want my boys back. I am so hungry for normality, you have no idea.'

'You want, you want, you want the moon,' said Layla. 'Whatever will ever be ordinary again, and whose fault is that but ours? Come on in, have a glass of wine. We will read Zoe's manuscript page by page. Let's see what we can salvage from the past.'

Part Four

Part Four

Well, I'm Sorry

And that's pretty much how Saffron got to be what she was as an adult, born of a party and some bright ideas, a hope for justice, and too much drink and dope: a trauma or two, and a war surplus store down the road. Sid Vicious on the radio, a monetarist government: teachers pulling one way, society the other: the past a horror, the future a terror, and sex the bringer of death. A child in a pushchair, burning bright, with a will of her own, a steely eye, a method of complaint, an imperfect memory, and the bright child's understanding she'd better be in charge because no one else was fit to be.

Well, we're sorry. Every generation must apologise to the future, and the greater the change that was brought about, the profounder the apology needs to be. Let Galileo apologise for pointing out that the earth goes round the sun, undermining our sense of our place in the universe, let Jethro Tull apologise for agriculture today, and Marconi for TV. Let Jesus apologise for the Inquisition, Mohammed for fundamentalist Islam, and Lenin for what happened in Marxist Africa. The brighter the idea the worse the consequences. Let the feminists apologise for the death of love, lost children, and the diminishing of man. But what was a girl to do? Someone has to reform the world. You can't see what you see and do nothing.

Let's move as quickly as we can into the present. What's done is done. What's yet to be is yet to be. Let's hope we get to Mars and start over. We stand looking up at a vast post-modern building in central London, all steel and glass, its approach a kind of metal drawbridge suspended by a mesh of fine cables. Inside the atrium fountains play, and see, a woolly sheep in a formaldehyde-filled glass tank by way of sponsored art. There must be an air leak in the tank. The formaldehyde is going cloudy. Let us hope that the sheep, who has the sweetest expression, does not go rotten and deliquesce. For the time being it's as pretty as anything dead can be.

It's morning, and people are on their way to work. The building, ComArt House, is dedicated to the Communication Arts. It houses TV and radio stations, a couple of newspapers, complete with weekend and mid-week supplements, some working studios and so forth. It is through this nexus that the nation speaks to itself and to the rest of the world.

A taxi pulls up outside the ComArt building and out of it steps Saffron. We see her now in her late twenties. She wears shoes with spindly heels, her hair is wayward, her skirt very short and her legs very good. Her features are sharp as her father's, her forehead dreamy as her mother's; what she

308

lacks is the melancholy pallor of self-destruct, for which one can be grateful. Her complexion is good. Saffron's grandmother, whom we once glimpsed briefly at Zoe's funeral, but who did not survive the shock of her daughter's untimely and self-inflicted death for more than a year, used to say this — being the assumption of that generation, and who is to say it was in error — that you could tell a troubled child by the colour in its cheeks. Such a child will have too little colour and be altogether too pale, or the colour be wrongly placed, focusing in a spot beneath the cheekbone, not fanning out cheerfully towards the ear.

These days Saffron's colour is pretty good. She looks wonderfully happy, in an efficient kind of way: she cares for nobody, no, not she, and therefore has her happiness in her own grasp. Ah, enviable, if not particularly likeable. But people, unlikeable in their twenties, can improve in their thirties, and vice versa. And we will all go to live on Mars.

Saffron leaves none other than Roland behind in the cab. He leans out of the window — it's a bright warm day — to wish her good luck. 'I don't need luck,' says Saffron. 'I have my judgement.'

309

And in Saffron goes to ComArt House. A couple of newsmen are waiting to snap her, talk to her if they can. Saffron's new job is worth a headline or so mid-paper. She's one of a new female brand of media whizzkids. She brushes the journalists aside — she is not interested in having her face in the papers. She finds anonymity and an undefined personality useful. She goes inside, uses a card to pass security barriers, and goes up to the sixth floor in an elevator which creeps up the side of the building like a space-globe. When the doors open she finds her way barred by a workman standing halfway up a step-ladder. He's elderly and bad-tempered. He's putting up an Art-Deco panel above glass doors. The panel reads *Tiffany*, the lettering in blue on gold. Saffron brushes past, shaking the ladder. What does she care?

'Do you want to bleeding kill me?' demands the shaken old-timer.
'That lettering is meant to be crimson on silver,' is all Saffron responds.
'Blue on gold is what you've got,' said the workman.
'Take it down,' she says.
'Who do you think you are?' he demands.
'The editor,' she says.

And in she goes. The workman's astonishment follows her.

310

Tiffany's reception desk is manned by an elegant black girl called Leonora. She's tall and self-possessed. There's an open-plan office behind her. The clock on the wall says nine o'clock exactly. Saffron glances at the clock, and too many empty desks.

'It's nine o'clock,' says Saffron, without preamble. 'How many in?'

'Eight,' says Leonora. 'It's more than usual, Miss Meadows, in honour of your first day.'

'Saffron will do,' says Saffron. 'More than usual is not enough. Keep a time-check for me, please, Leonora, on all staff for the next two weeks.'

'Senior staff too?' enquires Leonora, shocked. Saffron nods.

'Someone else will have to do evenings,' says Leonora. 'I leave early.'

'Not any more. You do a forty-five hour week here like everyone else.'

'But I have kids in nursery,' says Leonora, who finally after a couple of years has got her childcare sorted.

'Well, I'm sorry,' says Saffron, smiling blandly, as the childless will when confronted by the problems of the childed.

And Saffron walks on, and Leonora, not as easily defeated as Saffron might suppose, picks up the internal phone and dials Personnel. But there's no reply. It's rare for anyone to get in to Personnel before nine thirty or thirty-five.

Roland meanwhile has reached his destination — a ponderous Victorian building in the Strand: like ComArt House it is designed to impress, but by a different age. Roland nods to the driver and is about to walk away when the driver calls him back.

'It's only on account as far as ComArt House, as far as your lady friend went. You pay the extra.'

Roland, somewhat taken aback, and after detailed consultation with the driver, hands over a couple of pound coins. He's grown to be a gentle, good-looking, trusting sort of guy, with his father's smile and his mother's springy hair.

'I'd call the lady stingy,' says the driver, finally satisfied. 'I'd think twice before having her in my life.'

But Roland takes no notice: he adores Saffron, puts up with her quirks, overlooks her occasionally evident desire to be rid of him. She doesn't, in his opinion, know what she's doing all the time. A couple of pounds, a minor humiliation, is a small price to pay for her company, let alone a night spent together. She won't move in, but she does visit: not as regularly as he would like, but often enough for him to think of her as his girl-friend. Partner would be going too far.

313

Once the rooms where Roland and his colleagues worked smacked of dignity and time and space to spare. But now time is money, space is money, and the rooms have been partitioned: corridors narrowed. Now ten work in the space once occupied by one. Roland shares an office with Holly, who's plain, bright, thirtyish, already at her computer. She's pregnant, and married to the wrong person. Really Roland and Holly would be right for each other but both have ambitions above their stations. Thus happiness eludes them. She wants someone richer, he wants someone more exciting. The minute he comes into the office she starts talking. She trusts him to be witness to her aches, pains, hopes and woes, and he is happy to be so.

'I'm getting pains in my fingers,' she says. 'I think it means I'm developing whatever-you-call-it disease. Or syndrome. Everything these days is a syndrome. A whole lot of things get together and produce a set of symptoms, isn't that what happens. I have a headache from staring at this screen and pressure pains running down my thighs. This baby is leaning on the sciatic nerve and also kicking me to hell. I want to lie on my back and stare at the ceiling and instead I have to sit here and try and make two computers talk to one another so mankind need never think again, and all I get paid for it is peanuts. I've used up all my sick days and maternity leave doesn't start for three weeks. I may go into labour any minute now. Do you know how to deliver a baby? No? Thought not.'

Roland says what's on his mind. He too is trying to save mankind from too much thought. Both stare at screens and click mice, going further and further back into the filing system of communal reasoning. If this happened, then that must have, and vice versa. How to make a machine be intuitive? To think like a man, or indeed a woman, and leap from the wrong reason to the right conclusion? Oddly, the task leaves the mind and the mouth free for ordinary, unaspirational communication between one person and another. Holly and Roland ramble on through the days, feeling closer and closer.

'Saff says she's never going to have a baby,' said Roland today. 'She says she does not want to provide hostages to fortune. But I want a child. I want my children to do better than me. I want my genes to continue. I want to be a good father. If I had had a good father myself, what a different person I would be.'

'You seem a good enough person to me,' said Holly, comfortingly, and Roland was indeed comforted.

In the Boardroom of *Tiffany*, once *Weekend Woman*, workmen were busy replacing the new blue and gold signs with yet newer ones in crimson and silver. Their mood was not good. They would work late and not get paid overtime, they had been told, while their bosses worked out whose the error was. Then wage deductions would be fairly allocated. The Personnel Department was to be greatly reduced in size.

Saffron sat on the edge of a table, swinging her perfect legs; part of New Management, the legs are clad in Wolford tights, which are expensive but a pleasure to put on. Saffron never buys anything cheap. To save money takes too much time. Better concentrate on earning more, not spending less. Around her clustered some fourteen newspaper staff, mostly over forty, a few over sixty. All had a dusty look.

'Nothing can last for ever,' said Saffron. 'Face it. It's goodbye to the *Chronicle's Weekend Woman*, with its dreary domestic image, and hi there *Weekly Tiffany*, readership profile under thirty, sensualists, A, B and C, forget C, D, E; and our readers would rather have a boyfriend than a promotion any day, though they deny it. Is that clear?'

'We *will* be keeping the embroidery page?' asked a stolid woman dressed in tweeds and a high-necked shirt with a black ribbon pulling the neck closed, of a kind not seen for thirty years.

'The what?' asked Saffron, apparently baffled.

'Embroidery,' said the tweedy journalist. 'You know, needle, coloured thread, pretty patterns — '

'I hope not,' said Saffron, horrified. 'Our readers don't have time to pick up needles. They're either at work, having face-lifts, or out saving trees.'

'But a lot of women buy simply for that page. They like to read about it even if they never do any. The same way people who never cook like to look at recipes.'

'Not exactly the kind of readers we want to encourage,' said Saffron.

'A lot of young women do embroidery,' the tweedy journalist persisted, unwisely. 'You'd be surprised.'

'No,' said Saffron, 'and that's that,' and the tweedy journalist saw a glint in her eye, and knew the time for her own retirement was just about nigh.

'End of argument. Where's Peter Max? Why isn't he here?'

Ellie's turn to speak. Ellie was thirty-one, and one of Saffron's supporters, a bright conspirator with short straight blonde hair, only minimally dusty. 'He didn't come along,' said Ellie the Treacherous. Peter Max had got her her first job. 'He didn't think the meeting applied to him.'

'I think he'll find it did,' said Saffron.

And minutes later, for it was never Saffron's habit to hang about, other than prudently, Peter Max was looking up from his office chair at Saffron, who stood over him, young, proud and impossible. The meeting waited for her. Peter Max was dandruffy, thin of hair, and splotchy of scalp; an intelligent, ageing, lazy man. Photographs of family pets were pinned up all around him; as worn and tattered as the pets themselves. He was smoking. He was nicotine-stained: even in the short time since he had been transferred, along with *Weekend Woman*, to the new ComArt House he had managed to yellow the walls around and the ceiling above.

'We don't smoke in here,' observed Saffron to Peter Max. 'By the way.'

'I'm the exception,' he said.

'I don't think so,' his new editor replied, amiably enough. 'You weren't at the weekly meeting, now mandatory for all staff. Why not?'

'I'm not a joiner,' he said.

'You remind me of my dad,' said Saffron. 'Never quite one of the boys. But at least he's not a journo.'

'Journo?' He mocked the word. 'Oh, journalist, you mean? Well, that figures. Two syllables being better than three, in the new world. Saves time, saves breath, saves forests, saves thought. Lucky old *Tiffany*.'

Saffron smiled at him in quite a friendly fashion.
'Do you think we can work together?' she asked.
'No,' he said. 'Not really.'
'Well, there we are,' she said. 'Pity. Your mailbag's bigger than anyone's, they say. *Your Pet Problems Answered*. You've been coasting for thirty years, Peter Max. More years at *Weekend Woman* than I've been in the world. Time you grew up, got out into the real world. How about clearing your desk now? And do put out that cigarette.'

Peter Max rose to go. His office drawers were already empty. He'd been preparing for this occasion since news got out that Saffron Meadows was taking over editorship of the new *Tiffany*. She and he would never get along. He stubbed out his cigarette, but then leisurely, took another one from the pack, inhaled, and blew smoke in Saffron's direction.

'Don't worry,' said Saffron, still gentle. 'I have strong lungs. My father smokes.'
'Good for him,' said Peter Max. 'I'll be speaking to my lawyer.'
'Speak away,' she said. 'But remember we are infinitely rich.'

Peter Max left *Tiffany*'s offices with as much dignity as he could muster. But he was not as slim as he once was: his suit was badly cut: he tended to waddle. He was in his exit both tragic and pathetic. Those watching, other than Saffron, were moved. Word got round that men of Saffron's father's age had better look out, they seldom remained employed, for obvious reasons.

Saffron returned to the Boardroom to resume the meeting. Those present had been shocked into both wide-awakeness and acquiescence.

'Pets lover has gone,' said Saffron. 'That's another half-page liberated for the new world, plus one desk, plus insurance and holiday money. Personnel will be going through contracts with a tooth comb and re-writing.'

'We get an awful lot of revenue from the pet-food ads,' murmured someone from Advertising.

'We've also had to put up with the pet-food ads,' said Saffron. 'And they're a pain in the butt. We'd better take a look at all our ads. Get ourselves a buyers' market, not a sellers'. Forget the body copy; it's less than half our total page space: we need to edit our ads. Most of our advertisers have been asleep for thirty years, snoring even louder than Peter Max. We're talking about overall image here. A magazine is the sum of its parts, not a fraction more, not a fraction less. The greater part of *Tiffany*'s whole is to be the ads. That's the ambition. Sure, the body copy matters, but let's use the ads to dictate the body copy, rather than the other way round. We'll run a *Tiffany* award for the best ad of the year.'

'Don't we have some kind of duty to our readers?' asked someone, who had already decided to resign. She would have to get herself fired, or be made redundant, or she'd be seen as wilfully unemployed, and get no benefit, so she spoke tentatively.
'We have a duty to our shareholders,' said Saffron, 'to keep circulation up and profits high. That is the only duty I recognise.'

'Some of us may prefer not to work like this,' said someone brave.
'Yes, some of you may not,' said Saffron cheerfully. 'Let's all do our own thing, our own way. The company is prepared to pay redundancy sums to anyone who feels their way is not my way.'

Down in the country that very morning Hamish waved his dogs goodbye and set out to drive to London. He waved goodbye to Daffy too; Daffy had sold the Chalcot Crescent house at such a profit it seemed only fair for her to move back in with Hamish. Living off the land cost more than could be imagined.

Daffy had worked out that every egg the free-range hens laid cost at least £3.50; if you counted in the man hours spent keeping the fox away it rose to £6.00. It made more sense, now that Hamish was older, and found the long drive tiring, for Daffy to live with him in the country while he visited his mistresses in London, rather than the other way round. Both were happy with the arrangement: old remembered quarrels, old breakings up, the shared feeling of lust lost, added up in the end to a sense of permanence, security, enduring companionship.

'Give my love to the boys!' said Daffy. Hamish would visit his sons for form's sake, even stay the night with one of them if Layla was otherwise occupied.
'That goes without saying,' said Hamish.
'Bet you won't,' said Daffy.
'Argue, argue,' said Hamish.
'Try not to breathe the London air,' said Daffy,

though in fact Hamish's country house sat in a pocket between hills where pollution drifted down from the Northern cities, and the air was as bad as any London offered.

'I've got to breathe something,' said Hamish.

'What you mean is don't go and see Layla.'

'That's what I mean,' agreed Daffy.

'Aren't I past all that now?' he pleaded.

'No,' said Daffy. 'And I'm not either. Don't forget that.'

There was a young folk singer who lived locally and thought Daffy was the best thing ever. She used him to keep Hamish in order. She called the dogs in and Hamish drove off.

Layla sits in her grand office at Medusa Publishing. She has a resentful but good-looking male secretary whom, as ever with her staff, she underpays and overworks. She is managing director, executive manager, executive director, senior literary editor and every other title she can manage. She has, by the skin of her teeth, a majority shareholding in Medusa. She is bored.

Zoe Meadows' posthumous book *Lost Women* had best-sold worldwide and made Medusa a fortune though not for the Meadows family. Bull declined to use an agent, and failed to read the small print of the contract. A Hollywood studio had fictionalised the work, in the modern manner, and turned it into a feature film. The profits went to Medusa.

Twenty or so years had passed since *Lost Women* was written, and though in the centre of cities everywhere the world had changed for women, the further out from the hub of the wheel you got the more relevant to everyday life *Lost Women* seemed. Where the film travelled the book travelled too. But now many had seen the film, and most had seen the video, and everyone who was likely to have read the book had read it. So what next?

Stephanie comes in one day to find Layla with a mirror propped in front of her. She was pulling the flesh back from under her chin, using the skin beneath her ears to do so.

'Layla,' said Stephanie, 'you cannot contemplate a face-lift. It is undignified, dangerous and unsisterly.'

'I know all that,' said Layla. 'What do you think I'd look like?'

'Not yourself,' said Stephanie.

'That is my ambition,' said Layla. 'Why be yourself when you can be another? You left out painful. If I don't do it, it is because I'm afraid of pain, and for no other reason. I have been looking at the pattern of our sales. Just about everyone in the world who wants to read *Lost Women* has read it, or at any rate borrowed it: sales are beginning to drop: soon they will plummet and what do we do for an encore?'

'We carry on as before,' said Stephanie. 'There are enough good feminists out there to sustain the Medusa imprint. We did OK before *Lost Women* came along.'

'Feminism is now mainstream,' said Layla. 'Don't you think we should bear that in mind? Small but virtuous doesn't appeal. Small and bankrupt even less.'

'Small and virtuous is OK by me,' said Stephanie.

'Stephanie,' said Layla, 'Medusa is increasingly large, ponderous and boring. It's because you don't know how to say no, either in your personal or your professional life. Truly nice people, such as you, always create havoc all around. At any rate that is my experience. It now appears that *Tiffany*, which used to be the *Chronicle's Weekend Woman*, and which Saffron Meadows now runs, will not even carry Medusa ads any more. They refuse our money.'

'She doesn't like us,' said Stephanie. 'Because your lawyers drove such a hard bargain with her father, and he was so sharp he cut himself, the family got hardly any return at all from Zoe's book.'
'Since the family drove the poor girl to her death,' said Layla, 'I could never see why they should benefit. That book was written out of a fair degree of personal distress, thanks to Bull. Which of course is why it sells.'

'In your mind the personal has become the commercial,' said Stephanie. 'I don't like it one bit.'
'Give it a rest, Stephanie,' said Layla. 'And there is nothing personal in Saffron's decision. She's a media woman, not a human being. She doesn't like Medusa ads because they haven't changed for fifteen years, because feminism is associated

with all things dreary and non-market-friendly.'
'Of course it's personal,' said Stephanie. 'She's sleeping with my son Roland, on and off. Why? What are her motives?'
'Perhaps she loves him,' said Layla.
'Don't be absurd,' said Stephanie. 'He's not rich, famous or drop-dead gorgeous. She has all London to choose from. Why Roland? Except to get back at us.'

'That is paranoia beyond the dreams of guilt, Stephanie,' said Layla.
'All her generation are monstrous,' said Stephanie. 'What did we spawn? You know she fired poor old Peter Max, for no sin other than being old, male and fond of animals.'
'He did smoke,' said Layla, mildly, 'and we did always want a world which women ran,' at which Stephanie screamed and left the room.

Later Stephanie went round to visit her son Roland in his small bachelor pad in an old-fashioned apartment block behind Goodge Street station. She was tearful. Her large hands seemed larger than ever, and his seemed smaller and neater. These days she was all fulsome flesh — perfectly well appreciated: she was in an actively heterosexual relationship with a lawyer, a recently divorced expert in Third World Development. Roland was taut of body and mind. She represented the macro; he the micro. She looked outward to the world; he inward to its interstices. He was embarrassed, and being difficult.

'But what are you sorry *about*, Mother? I don't understand.'
'I should never have left you boys. It's all my fault.'
'Is there something wrong with me I don't know about?' he enquired.
'I don't mean that, you know I don't.' Dealing with grown sons trying to trip her up, she decided, was worse than dealing with difficult lovers.
'Then what do you mean? Can't we just forget all this emotional stuff? It's self-indulgent. You're not the maternal type. Why should you be, any more than Saffron is. And how could

anyone rational put up with Father for long? He's a pig. A charming pig, but a pig. At least he found us Daffy.'

'That hurts, Roland,' said Stephanie.

'Well Mother,' said Roland. 'That's your problem, not mine. We're friends now: let's just leave it at that. Is that why you came round? To say you were just in general sorry?'

'I want to know why Saffron won't run Medusa ads. Is it personal? Is it because of me? Is it because my phone call to Bull drove Zoe to suicide?'

'If Saffron won't run Medusa ads I imagine it's because they're boring and old-fashioned, your books depress her, you see women as victims, you're so out of touch even your ads bring *Tiffany* down.'

Stephanie went back to Layla and admitted she was in the wrong, which was for her difficult.

'Even our ads bring *Tiffany* down,' said Stephanie, as if she'd thought of it first. 'If Roland says so it must be true. What does she want, the little bitch? Scratch-and-sniff ads? The sweet and fashionable smell of feminism?'
'Scratch me, sniff me,' said Layla. 'The little bitch is right. Why aren't we smelling of roses any more? I haven't been paying attention. I've been leaving too much to you.'

They had been friends for so long, yet now, when each needed the other most, they looked at one another with antagonism. They were growing apart. Stephanie had the settled, righteous look of the woman well suited in bed. Layla was all nerves and sexual aspiration.
'He hates me,' said Stephanie, hoping by a show of desperation to win back Layla's allegiance. 'My own son hates me.'
'At least', said Layla carefully, 'you have a son to hate you. I have none. And you exaggerate. Your Roland sees through you, perhaps: but hate? I doubt it.'

She was on her feet. She gave Stephanie no chance to reply. She stalked into her outer office, startling her partly comatose staff, pretty much as Saffron had done at *Tiffany* earlier in the week.

'I want some action round here,' said Layla to her staff. 'I want a proper breakdown of costs on every book on last year's lists. Why hasn't this been done already? What are you, fucking idiots? Or are you just asleep? And I want comprehensive sales figures, not just the bits and pieces you hand over. What do we have computers for? So you can keep your secrets and empire-build? Not any more. And I want an immediate appraisal of what we advertise, why, whether it's cost effective, and whose idea it was to buy space in *Weekend Woman* in the first place. Why would anyone who bought a rag like that ever want to buy a book? Well? Do I have to think of everything?'

'We were after awareness, as I remember, not just sales,' said Rosalie, who was having chemotherapy, and wore a scarf, since she had no hair for the time being. Her plight did not move Layla.
'You're out of your mind,' said Layla. 'The days of luxury are past. This is the age of survival, not noble feelings.' Which was pretty rich, Rosalie felt, in the circumstances.

Her staff looked at Layla with dislike, affection and admiration mixed, in much the same way as Saffron's staff still regarded her. But it was harder to get a job in publishing than in the magazine world. Imprints amalgamated to capitalise on a rising property market, to cut overheads, to save wages — and in general make one person do the work of, if not two, certainly one and a half. Medusa staff smiled softly at Layla, resented her, and decided that principle would have to take a back seat until times were better. These were, as she said, the days of survival.

Layla now went through to the editorial department, where staff enjoyed a less intensive form of open-plan working: that is to say, they were privileged with the privacy given by glass walls. Layla moved into cubicles and out again, in royal procession, like Jesus cleansing the temple, picking up every Medusa publication she could see from desks, cabinets, shelves, hurling them back behind her the way she came. The room was littered with products now unsaleable.

'Boring, boring, boring,' she cried. 'Hopeless. Repetitive. Futile. Crap. Find me some decent writers. Find me another Zoe Meadows.'
'There isn't one,' said Rosalie, who felt it prudent to accompany Layla as she reaped the doldrums. Rosalie's face was haggard, her eyes enormous. 'So many of our good writers have gone to other houses. We didn't pay them enough. They've gone mainstream.'
'We paid them too fucking much,' said Layla. 'Stephanie insisted. They got ideas in their

heads. They were never as good as they thought they were. As for all this purple and green, it just makes me want to vomit. The suffragettes had no taste at all. How about yellow, white and grey? Something around here has to give.'

At which Rosalie fainted, but probably only coincidentally. The radiation which attacked her cancer cells so successfully attacked healthy cells too. She did not have a great deal of strength to spare.

'You're joking,' said Stephanie, who had caught Rosalie on the fall, and now had her seated, head between knees. 'It goes against all sisterhood tradition.'
'The sisterhood is kaput,' said Layla. 'And you're a fool if you can't see it.' And she stalked back to her office.

Stephanie would not give up. See her after work, pursuing Layla up and down the rows between the stalls of Berwick Street Market. Here displayed were the fruits of the whole world, beautifully presented at a price many, even most these days, could afford to buy. The peachy smell of sweet corruption filled the air.

Layla picked and pressed, sniffed and occasionally bought, and tried to ignore Stephanie.
'We're not making some kind of fashion statement here,' complained Stephanie. 'We're talking principle.'
'Actually,' said Layla, 'I'm talking tropical fruit salad, if anything. Can't you leave it alone?'

But Stephanie couldn't. For all Layla tried to gain her interest in the fact that there was only a day for a paw-paw between perfectly hard and over-ripe, and the fruit had to be eaten at the turn, Stephanie pursued the subject of Medusa, and the enduring plight of the female.

'It is simply stupid to suggest that Medusa's time is over, Layla. Are you blind? Look around you. Women still need their voice. We're still the shit-workers, the part-time jobbers, the victims of male violence, still left alone with the kids then insulted as lone mothers by the state. We're still sluts and slags in the eyes of men; still sex objects. We never reclaimed the night. Rape is more prevalent that it ever was.'

'Stephanie,' begged Layla, 'keep your voice down. This is a street-market, not a public meeting. Melons are such a problem. Galinas are sweetest but go soggy so fast.'

She stuck one under Stephanie's nose, hopefully, but Stephanie brushed it away.

'Did you see today's report on sexual harassment at work?' demanded Stephanie. 'The problem gets worse, not better. It's the backlash.'

'Yesterday's flirtation is today's abuse,' observed Layla.

And then, provoked, Layla said, 'Remember Lennie? Such a lovely tight little butt. Now why was it you fired him, Stephanie?'

Stephanie froze. This was forbidden ground.

'I don't want us to quarrel, Stephie,' apologised Layla. 'You're still my friend; it's just sometimes you drive me to distraction. You may be a woman but you're a human too and I wish you sometimes remembered.'

'Friend?' demanded Stephanie. The apology was clearly not being accepted. 'Then who needs enemies? And why are you wasting your money buying this ridiculous stuff? If you want fruit salad why don't you buy canned, like anyone else? What's happening to you?'

'Because no one buys canned any more, Stephie,' said Layla. 'They like the real thing. The world's moved on and you haven't noticed. Fucking stuffy Stephie. If I want Medusa to change it's only because I want her to survive. We'll be picking over a dead corpse if you're not careful.'

'You personally are the backlash,' said Stephanie, and she snatched the bag of fruits Layla had so carefully selected and flung the contents far and wide. 'And I'll fight you for control of Medusa.'
'Fight away, Ms Moral Highground,' said Layla, retrieving her fruit from here and there. Her bum as she bent was neat and personable. Stallholders whistled in appreciation and she didn't seem to mind one bit, and Stephanie was too agitated to take any notice.

'I have forty-nine per cent of the shares,' said Layla, 'and you have only nineteen. What I say goes.'
Layla raised her hand to summon a taxi, which as Layla's luck would have it, was just passing by. It stopped, obligingly.

'That's what you think,' said Stephie.
'You're just an innocent,' said Layla.
'At least I can keep a man,' said Stephie.
'Or a woman,' said Layla. 'For a time. To win any argument with me over the future of Medusa you will need Alice on your side, with her eleven shares, and Nancy, who has five, and all the other dribs and drabs who have a few up their sleeves, and still you will never make

it, because I'll always have a friend out there. I make a point of asking people to dinner while you write tracts.'

'Are you getting in, madam, because if you don't others will,' said the taxi-driver. 'It's beginning to rain.'
'I'm getting in,' said Layla.
'I hate you,' said Stephie.
'Hate seems to run in your family,' said Layla. 'I expect the boys inherit it from you.'

And so saying she left Stephanie standing in the rain, which indeed began to pour, obliging the stallholders to shroud their wares beneath sheets of ghostly clear plastic.

London these days is ringed by large houses where the rich and mysterious live. Their owners have properties all over the world. They summer here and winter there, finding their own countries too hot to handle. The money comes, presumably, from arms, drugs, the politics of kleptocracy. The houses stand empty for months on end, then the security gates open; in flow the Mercedes and the BMWs; the Russian Mafia with their long-legged ugly-beautiful girlfriends, their stunned and stumpy wives, proud Nigerian delinquents, handsome South Africans, Gulf Arabs with their sulky, sullen sons, their swathed daughters. England is a favourite watering hole: revolution-free, mild-climated, on the whole incurious. Furnishing and fabrics by Harrods, consumer durables by Miele, gardening by Organic and Co. Where the friends come from, God alone knows.

Waterborough Hall, one of the older and more tasteful of such mansions, being genuine Jacobean, and owned by an educated, political family in search of British citizenship by way of cultural foundation, opened up its security gates around that time to let in a certain politician and his entourage from the Indian sub-continent. And Layla just happened to call him on the day of his arrival. She got through to his PA, a suave, dark, handsome young man.

'Miss Lavery,' he cried, in the quiet delight he allowed himself. 'Of course. I'll put you straight through. He's having a lesson, but I know he wouldn't want to miss you.'
'A lesson? Is there anything left for him to learn?'
'He means to be in the Olympic fencing team.'
'Isn't he too old?'
'Experience and wiliness, Miss Lavery, can balance youth in this particular sport. May I say how good it is to hear your voice again?'
How he soothed, pleased, charmed: the grace of far away, of careful kind intent.

'Layla, my dear,' said Jemal, 'how imprudent of you to call and how grateful I am for your imprudence. We are all watched, of course we are, and listened to, but what sort of people are we if we take it into account? My wife stays at home — well, you will have guessed this from the papers — another day, another election. I am here for a week. You are coming to visit me? Of course you are. You will stay tonight. How long since we last saw one another? Two, three years? It is only pride makes me vague. It is two years and five months, and three days and I have counted them.'

Next see Layla at the beautician. She lies on a couch in her slip. Her face is covered with mud. She frets and fidgets.

'Please relax,' says the beautician, who is a tiny, pretty, bossy young thing. 'It's so boring lying here,' said Layla. 'Take this muck off.'
'It's meant to stay on for thirty-five minutes,' says the beautician.
'Ten minutes is more than enough,' says Layla. 'He doesn't love me for my looks alone.'
'That's what all men say,' says the beautician, piqued. 'I'd stay the full time if I were you.'

Layla had been rash. No one likes to hear the tools of their trade, the substance of their expertise, described as 'muck'. This was mud especially imported from the shores of the Dead Sea, mineral rich and difficult to handle.
'Oh, thanks a million,' says Layla. 'Let's put it like this, I don't like trying so hard. It's demeaning.'
'There's no point in taking it off now,' said the beautician. 'Your hairdresser isn't free yet, and the manicurist's at tea.'

Layla tried to settle; she had to. The girl had gone.

'Do you like this job?' she asks the girl when finally she consented to return.

'If you're unhappy you get wrinkles,' says the girl, 'so I make sure I like it. And if you're married you have to put up with a man. I'd rather put up with a job.'

'Don't you want babies?' asks Layla.

'They're so bad for the figure,' says the girl. 'And so expensive. How could I afford a baby? I'd have to have a man to go with it. No, thanks.'

'Some women quite like men,' said Layla.

'None I know,' said the girl. 'Men are all wankers. What I don't understand is why all the women who come in here are so scared of losing them. Mind you, they're mostly the older crowd.'

When Layla finally managed to get out of the beauty salon, resolved to go home at one and comb the spray out of her hair, wipe off the rouge and soften the hard line of lipstick and mascara, she encountered Hamish, up in London for the day; he came out of the elevator which she hoped to enter.

'What are you doing here, Hamish?' she enquired. 'This is no place for a man with mud on his boots.' All around was pink and gold, the colours of little girls never grown up.
'They told me at Medusa I'd find you here,' he said. He was in a helpless, hopeless, dependent mood: the one he used nowadays to get her attention. The older he got the easier he found it to revert to little boy mode. His hair had thinned on top but not around the edges: his smile was as sweet as ever. He looked as if he was still prepared to enjoy whatever the world had to offer. Others grew bitter from age and experience, bored from knowing too well what was going to happen next: not Hamish.

'Bet they sneered,' said Layla. They sat on the little mauve and grey lacquer chairs which the Beauty Salon still provided for just such conversations.

343

'Yes, they did,' he said. 'Will you come out for lunch with me?'

'No,' said Layla.

'They told me you were free.'

'You're with Daffy again,' she said. 'Leave it at that. Time to grow up, Hamish.'

'I'm not happy with Daffy,' he said. But he smiled as he said it: it was so evidently not true.

'Too bad,' said Layla.

'Your secret lover's in town,' said Hamish. 'I read it in the paper. That's why you won't have lunch with me.'

'What secret lover?' she asked.

'The one with the money, married to the Head of State.'

'How can you know about him?'

'Pillow talk,' he said. 'You told me once.'

'I must have had a lot to drink. Those were the days.'

It was all Perrier water these days, and no-cholesterol eggs, and live for ever, filtering the past through therapists, examining the self, seeking non-experience.

'The lover who funds Medusa, who owns thirty per cent of the shares, whose proxy you have, whose existence you never admit to the sisters.'

'Hamish!' said Layla. 'This is terrible. Knowledge is power and you have too much of it. Besides, he isn't a lover. He's an uncle. Family.'

'Liar. And you still can't have lunch with me?'

'No lunch,' said Layla. Behind the little boy lay the *enfant terrible*. Sometimes Hamish's eyes revealed him. They did now. But Layla did not take too much notice. If she had lunch with Hamish she would not have time for the pleasure of preparing for an assignation, and spending the night with him was out of the question.

They went down together in the ornate lift. 'Give my love to Daffy,' said Layla. 'Do what you should, go and see your boys. You've got a family; try for once to act as if you had. Be grateful for it. You should have stayed with Stephanie. You could have stopped her from changing the world. As it is, you drove her to it.'
'Everyone these days blames everyone else,' he complained. 'A decade ago they looked for their roots. Now they spend their energy allocating blame. It's too bad. Are you trying to finish with me, Layla?'
'Yes,' she said. Though she hadn't known it till that minute.
'You are such a hypocrite, Layla,' said Hamish. 'And all you women misremember so much. I did not leave Stephanie, she left me. What's more, it was you who egged her on. Your fault, Layla. All of it.'

When the doors opened he walked on into the crowd and disappeared amongst them. He was limping slightly. The countryside is damp and arthritis had got into his left knee.

Hamish's limp was exaggerated as he walked round Safeways, at lunch-time, with his son Rafe, who had baby Gabrielle strapped to his back in a kind of yellow and green cocoon. Gabrielle was nine months old, and had a beaming, solid presence. Rafe used a scanner to record his purchases. Hamish every now and then would take an article from the shelf and drop it into the trolley, thus undermining his son's attempts to save time at the checkout.

'Why does the cocoon have to be such a terrible colour?' asked Hamish.
'It's bright and cheerful,' said Rafe. He bent down to reach marmalade from a bottom shelf.
'Won't the baby fall out?' asked Hamish.
'No,' said Rafe, shortly.
'You had a pram when you were a baby,' said Hamish. 'I'm sure you did. And I'm sure as hell I never went out shopping pushing it. In fact the only shop I ever went into was my own. No, I tell a lie. I once went with your mother to buy some light-bulbs because she failed to understand about wattage, quite deliberately. We left you parked outside. Couldn't do that now, could you? It would get stolen.'
'The baby's a she, not an it.'
'You take offence so easily,' complained Hamish.

346

Rafe sighed heavily, and made for the disposable nappy section. Hamish followed after.

'I never buy marmalade,' said Hamish. 'They put in the rind, and everyone knows the rind is drenched in chemicals of one kind or another.'

Rafe looked startled and put the marmalade back and sought to negate the purchase with the scanner, and decided the system was finally screwed. He would have to queue up at the checkout with the other non-technicals.

Together they stared at row upon row of disposable nappies.

'There's a new range of nappies out, gender specific,' said Rafe. 'Can you see them?'

'Hardly ecologically sound,' said his father. 'Aren't you ashamed of yourself? Surely you should be washing cloth nappies and re-using? Your mother used to do yours by hand. I wouldn't have a washing machine in the house. I couldn't stand the sound of domestic machinery. Never could.'

'What you're trying to say is that single-handed you were the cause of feminism?'

'You're like your mother. No sense of humour. Layla was the only one of all those women who ever made me laugh. Even Layla seems to have gone off me; perhaps it's just because her secret lover's in town. Did you realise that Medusa is funded by a man? That the so-called feminist publishing house is kept going by male money, and always has been?'

Rafe seemed more interested in calculating the exact kind of nappies Gabrielle required. If you got the right brand, the right shape, you would still end up with the wrong age and gender. They were out of nine-month-old girls' altogether.

'Did you know that?' Hamish insisted.
'Most money's male money,' Rafe remarked. 'That's what Marly keeps saying. Men hold on to financial power. But even that's going. Under forty and women are beginning to overtake men in the promotion stakes.'
'And you speak as if you're pleased!' complained Hamish. 'Traitor to your gender! Vicar of Bray! Auntie Tom! New man!'
'Don't speak so loudly,' begged Rafe. 'Really, I wish you'd stayed home.'

'It isn't natural,' said Hamish. 'Men with babies on their backs doing the shopping.'
'It is perfectly natural,' snapped Rafe. 'And sensible. Marly earns and I look after the home. It works just fine. You're a dinosaur, Dad.'
'And you're married to a feminist and a therapist,' lamented Hamish, 'and she's sucked the will out of you.'
'Oh, for God's sake,' protested Rafe. 'We're partners, not man and wife.'

And so the two men squabbled, united by genes, divided by a generation, and not a single thing one could offer the other by way of understanding or advice.

Later that day find Hamish persecuting his younger son Roland. Pizza has been ordered. Saffron sits on the floor going through the contents of her briefcase, which she spreads around her long bare legs. It's hot and she's wearing shorts. Hamish tries not to look at her legs too much, but she doesn't mind where she puts them, or how. The flat is small, poky and untidy, but no one cares. They live in their heads and in the bed. Saffron takes out a pocket recorder and makes a verbal note or so. In the morning her assistants will transcribe it. Hamish wants to be entertained by wit and gossip but no one bothers.

The doorbell goes. It's the pizza delivery. Roland extracts Hamish's share of the cost from his father, not without difficulty. It is left to Hamish to open the box and stare with evident disbelief at the contents.
'That's supper?'
No one replies. Roland consents to search for paper napkins. They will tear the pie to bits, eat with their hands.

'Do we women want our men beautiful?' asks Saffron of her recorder. 'Yes, we do! Liposuck the beer belly. Ellie, commission someone. But be careful. We're getting a male readership, but my feeling is if we address them directly they'll run a mile. This is over the shoulder stuff.'

'Not even knives and forks?' complains Hamish. 'And what are those bits?'
'It's Hawaiian,' says Roland. 'They're pineapple.'
'Revolting,' says Hamish.
'You don't have to eat with us,' says Roland.
'Nobody cooks any more,' observes Saffron.
'I do,' says Hamish.
'I remember,' says Saffron, 'loaves bouncing around the kitchen floor in the dog dirt. And a little red hen. I'm surprised you're still alive.'

Hamish takes out a cigarette.
'This is a non-smoking household,' says Saffron.
'Hang on a moment, Saff,' says Hamish. 'This is my son's flat, not yours. What is more, I seem to remember paying the deposit.'
'They're my lungs,' says Saffron. 'I don't choose to passively smoke.'

Hamish put his cigarette away. The child in the pushchair finally won.

'She's a monster,' observed Hamish to his son. 'Blame your mother. She created the world in which your girlfriend flourishes. Layla helped. What hypocrites they are. You know it was male money got Medusa started? And still does. Layla's secret lover.'
'Tell me more,' said Saffron, and switched her recorder on. At last he had his audience.

'She tells me he's an uncle but I don't believe it. She tells everyone she has forty-nine per cent of the shares, but I know for a fact she has only nineteen. The other thirty per cent are proxies from the lover. Perhaps the lover isn't as ardent as he was: Layla's not the young hopeful she used to be: who's to say what goes on? Just that Layla might not be as powerful as she thinks. One united push from everyone and she'd be off the Board. That would certainly suit my ex-wife.'

'Do you know the lover's name?' asked Saffron.
'My dear,' said Hamish, 'that is the question that has haunted the decades. No. I don't. But I believe in his existence. It's why in all these years I never got a decent emotion out of Layla. She cheated me.'

Roland began to laugh. It was a rare sound.
'I mean it,' said Hamish. 'There was always another man looking at you out of her eyes. Strange, isn't it, the collapse of Western civilisation because Layla Lavery falls in love with a married man.'
'It collapsed?' enquired Saffron, politely. 'It looks OK to me.'
'You're young, pretty and female,' said Hamish, 'and earning well. Of course it does. But look at the breakdown of family life. Look what's happening to the young men. Forty per cent of all children are diagnosably psychopathic. I read that somewhere.'

'And none of it's anything to do with you?' asked Roland.

'No,' said Hamish. 'People go to hell their own way.'

It was a jumbo-size pizza. Hamish consented to eat it, but tore the filling off with his teeth and chewed it and left the crust.

Hamish drove home that night singing along to his radio as he crossed Salisbury Plain. The moon shone down, brightening his life. Layla hadn't lunched with him but he had paid her out. When he got home Daffy was already in bed.

'How was it?' she asked.
'OK,' said Hamish. 'Saw the boys. I don't have much in common with them, but I suppose it's my duty.'
'Did you see Layla?'
'No,' he said.
'I didn't think so,' she said, 'or you'd be in a better temper.'
'I'm just fine,' he said, getting into bed beside her. 'All that's over now.'
'I'm pregnant,' she said. 'I went to the doctor today. Three months pregnant. I thought I was just getting old, but no.'

There was a silence from Hamish. Eventually he said, 'Aren't you too old?'
'I can't be,' she said. 'Since it happened and it's holding.'
'Is it safe for you?' he asked.
'What, to go through with it?' she asked, surprised. 'I thought you'd have hysterics and I'd have a termination.'

353

'Do you want to?'

'No,' said Daffy.

'Then don't,' he said. 'I'd like to have another go. We'll get married. Get it right this time. God, those boys are boring. I messed them up. My fault.'

'Don't blame yourself,' said Daffy. 'Blame the genes. We'll do better.'

They held each other under the full moon. As time went by it proved them right in their initial instinct to be together. When he undid her boiler-suit buttons all those years ago, and she let him, they both knew what they were doing.

Layla arrived at Waterborough Hall as night fell. Jemal sent his chauffeur for her. They drove past the main gates, down a back lane, and approached the house from a side entrance. Who the watchers were, Layla was never quite sure. Perhaps they were merely domestic; a man could fear his wife even more than political assassins. Perhaps he was paranoiac. Perhaps the practice of secrecy fuelled his self-esteem. Perhaps all of these things. Reasons seldom come in ones: becauses cluster, and are often paradoxical.

She was met at the side door by the sleekly polite PA: the car disappeared blackly under silent garage doors. The corridor into which she stepped was dark. She made no sort of target. Light and luxury increased as she was led further into the house, along corridors first painted, then panelled, first centrally lit and shadowed: then glowing from shaded wall lights. No sound but the rustle of her dress: which was old blue taffeta, full-skirted. Finally, the library, book-lined, the fire, the silk rugs, and Jemal, hawk-faced, patrician, coming forward to see her; the same lurch of the heart, the catch in the throat: the timeless eroticism of the secret, the forbidden: the melting of the body, the abandoning of separateness.

'Jemal,' she said. 'Do we have to do this cloak and daggery stuff? What's it for?'

'It's the press, my dear,' he said. 'They're interested in you, as much as me. I love the dress. You look beautiful. You haven't changed. Can you stay the night?'

'If I had any sense I wouldn't,' said Layla, cheerfully. 'You ruined my life. Look at me; an old maid, childless, all for the love of a married man.'

'You look all right to me,' he said. 'You suit the new world; and it suits you. If you gave your life for anyone it certainly wasn't me. It was for Medusa. And your life is in no way finished yet.'

Soon enough they lay together in a four-poster bed. 'If I'd been a peasant,' he said, 'and not husband to a Head of State, and if you'd been some goose-girl, not a revolutionary, we could have lived happily ever after.'

'A revolutionary? I'm glad that's how you see it. Feminism, the bloodless revolution. The casualty rate was high. Suicides, the collapse of relationships; so many of us alone, because who would put up with us, and how could we put up with them? When every casual word is examined for implication, assessed for correctness, life gets exhausting. Easier to get up in the morning to a silent house, and listen to the radio in peace, and do all the chores yourself, not first consult the chore list in the wall. Or I find it so. Lovers come and go. If they stay too long I argue.'

'I don't want to hear about them,' he said.

'They're only by the by,' she said. 'Not important. The revolution was the thing, and we brought it about so successfully no one even noticed. Today's radical idea becomes tomorrow's conventional wisdom. No one can even remember what the fuss was about. And Medusa? I want to get out of Medusa. I want to get it on the right road, and then forget it, and give up this forlorn love of ours, and begin again. I want your shares as a parting gift.'

He sat up in the bed, startled. 'You want to be paid off? My money was never conditional on your sleeping with me.'

'Self-interest is always the best excuse. Everyone believes it. It's so difficult these days to believe in love. OK? I'm here because I want to be, but this is the end of it. Never again, Jemal.'

'You forget; we have a child between us: Medusa. Supposing I fight for custody? I might well. I might not want this divorce you've suddenly thrust upon me. I might not agree with you what the best road is to set our child upon. You want her to be profitable, you say. But what's money? It's a tool, not a goal.'

'Easy to say that,' said Layla, 'when you have so much of it.'

'Why, why?' he lamented. 'I don't understand this.'

'I'm growing old and you will want a younger woman,' she said. 'I want to get out before that happens.'

'Insane!' he marvelled.

357

Back in London Roland and Saffron lay entwined upon his hard bed in the moonlight.

'I wish I understood more about stocks and shares,' said Saffron. She always declared her ignorance, at the first opportunity. It disarmed others, and also impressed them.

'See control of Medusa in the form of a pie-chart,' said Roland, happy to be able to instruct, for once, 'as round as this evening's pizza. She who has the biggest slice of pie controls the rest. According to my father, the she turns out to be a he, Layla's mystery love. He has thirty per cent, but is a sleeper, customarily giving his proxy to Layla, who has nineteen per cent of her own, as has Stephanie. Alice has eleven, Nancy has five, Johnny and Richard have two between them, and bits and pieces own the remaining fourteen in single shares. Everyone customarily votes with Layla, anyway: she controls forty-nine percent and someone's always round to agree with her, so what's the point of arguing. Though my mother would love to.'

'Someone needs to prod the sleeper awake,' said Saffron. 'Pie-charts! What a genius you are.'

'I'm glad that's how you see me,' said Roland, a little surprised, but she seemed to mean it.

At any rate her arms crept closer round him. He meant to call his mother in the morning and report what his father had told him, but he forgot. Whenever he called her she tended to say, 'Oh, such a long time since I heard from you,' and things like that, so he'd put it off, and then it really *was* a long time, and he'd put it off more. Impossible.

Stephie, contrary to Roland's belief, was not brooding about her sons but was on the road from London to Glastonbury. Out of London, past Stonehenge, and into the wild west beyond, into UFO country around Westbury, cut left before Shepton Mallet and the Babycham factory, avoiding the road which the plastic baby deer straddles, past the charred remains of Alexandra Ludd's house on the by-pass, past the site of the Glastonbury Festival, with its great pyramid stage and the slung-low power lines, and the giant floodlit cross put up by the Christians to subvert evil pagan energies; and there, black against a moon-pale sky, was the Tor in the distance, that sudden hummocky hill rising out of flat lands, crowned by a stone tower, round which (according to some) baby flying saucers forever wheeled and spun like fireflies, winking in and out.

Stephanie stopped for fuel at the haunted petrol station at the foot of the ruined abbey. Some say the poor startled spirit of the Abbot, beheaded by Henry VIII, still lingers by the petrol pumps, this being the spot his head rolled down to, and stopped. Others say it's a more recent arrival: they hold Black Masses weekly up the hill. Now past the Chalice Well, with its overflow of sacred water pouring ceaselessly from a rusty pipe which juts out of a stone wall, where the wise driver stops to fill up his windscreen washers; up the narrowing lane which circles the Tor itself, past the astrologer's houses, and down the other side to the levels, and the dykes, and the field in the middle of which lives Alice, in a caravan. Alice, who owns eleven per cent of Medusa. A narrow slice of pie, but important.

Alice came out to greet her, dressed in a long hippy gown and beads. She carried a flashlight. The caravan was lit by hissing gas lamps. She prepared herbal tea.

'I suppose you are Stephanie?' asked Alice. 'You're not a walk-in?'
'I don't know what you mean,' said Stephanie.
'Sometimes walk-ins are visual. Mostly the presence is felt in the head, but they can take bodily form. You might just look like Stephanie to me.'
'Fuck it, Alice, of course I'm Stephanie.'
'Sounds more like Layla to me,' said Alice, and laughed. 'OK, you're Stephanie, not a walk-in. A walk-in, for your information, is a highly evolved being who turns up to take over a lesser personality.'
'You mean like when you're mad?' asked Stephanie.
'Occasionally,' said Alice. 'It's true that when people do something quite out of their normal character it can be because of a walk-in. And the phenomenon can get construed as insanity. But

361

mostly the walk-in acts as a refining, peaceful influence.'

'Like when you've taken a lot of dope?' Stephanie enquired.

'Oh no,' said Alice. 'It's not like that at all. We don't need chemicals to alter our mood states.'

'We?' asked Stephanie. Poor Alice. Finally flipped. She felt to blame. They had all indulged Alice, allowed her her gullibilities. Now see. Once unreason crept in, it could overwhelm the mind altogether.

'Just a group I happen to run,' said Alice. A black cat jumped on to her knee, startling Stephanie. The cat seemed to come out of nowhere, but then Stephanie was tired. She'd been on the road for three hours, and there was nowhere here for her to sleep. The day wasn't yet finished.

'You're working on a new book, I hear,' said Stephanie, politely.

'*Rites of the Mother Goddess*,' said Alice. 'It's nearly finished. It's just that time seems to move so fast around me. Do you feel that?'

'We're getting older,' said Stephanie. 'That's what happens.'

'Oh no,' said Alice. 'It's Glastonbury. We're at the hub of all things here, so naturally one has the perception of the rim moving faster. We're at the heart chakra of Planet Earth. Planet Earth is the heart chakra of the universe, so obviously whatever's going to happen is going to happen

362

here first. We are so privileged.'

'Uh-uh,' said Stephanie.

'I know it's hard for you to understand,' said Alice. 'You're still bound up in the false reality. You haven't yet outgrown it. When you've read my book you'll know more. You think I've really flipped, don't you?'

'Well, yes, actually,' said Stephanie.

'I haven't. I'm caught up with the war on Sirius, that's all. It can get to a girl.'

'The war in Syria?' Stephanie was baffled. Was there one?

'Sirius the dog-star,' said Alice. 'It's a binary. There's Sirius A and Sirius B. The organic and silicon life forms are battling it out.'

'Whose side are we on?' asked Stephanie. Alice looked cross. 'The fucking organic, you silly bitch. Sirius A. Why should we be on the side of stone? Those Mars landings were a secret intelligence mission set up by Sirius A, helped by us here on Planet Earth. If I talk about these things round Glastonbury it sounds perfectly reasonable. If I talk to you about it I can see it sounds totally bananas.'

'It is,' said Stephanie. 'I don't think Medusa in its present state will want to publish *Rites of the Mother Goddess*. Of course if it was up to me I'd publish like a shot. But you know what Layla's like.'

'I do,' said Alice. 'Layla was always the weak link. Worldly and slippery. Feminism has lost its way. We should be all striving for unification under the Mother Goddess.'

363

Then she looked at Stephanie as if all at once responding to her actual presence, not just some idea of her. Some mist over her eyes seemed to clear.

'Stephanie? What are you doing here? Why didn't you write or phone? I could have been away.'

'You don't answer letters, Alice, and you haven't got a phone. I had to come. I want you at the next Medusa shareholders' meeting.'

'They're so boring, Stephie. It's really nice down here.'

'It's next Monday.'

'But next Monday's a solstice. I'm convening a celebration on the Tor. I'll send my proxy to Layla as usual. I don't want to get involved in any bad feeling. Is there any?'

'I'd rather you came,' said Stephie. 'You might prefer, for once, to vote with me. Layla has no principles any more. All she does is talk about face-lifts and go to beauty parlours.'

'Good for her,' said Alice.

Stephanie perceived Alice was not going to be a pushover, for all her eccentricities.

'One should pay the body the compliment of looking after it,' said Alice. 'The Mother Goddess loves adornment. She is so glorious, Stephanie. Did you know I'd actually seen her? She revealed herself to me in all her glory.'

'No, I hadn't heard that,' said Stephanie. 'But I'm sure when you send your finished MSS to Medusa, and if we publish, and I'll certainly press for it, everyone will get to know about it. You will have so many converts!'

'I'll come to the meeting,' said Alice.

'If the entrails are right?' asked Stephanie.

'I'll come anyway,' said Alice. 'You always were a blackmailer, Stephie. I like that. Everyone down here's so sweet. Sometimes I can't stand it.'

The next day Roland happened to say to Saff, 'You know all this stuff I tell you about Medusa and my mother, you do realise it's all restricted? You won't use it in any way? Holly says I shouldn't tell a soul, not even you, but I daresay she's jealous. Sometimes I think she likes me quite a lot.'

'Of course I won't tell a soul,' said Saffron. 'Do stop quoting Holly at me.'

'Sorry,' said Roland.

The day after that, had you been sitting in The Ivy at lunchtime, you would have seen Saffron being led, through its dark grandeur, to the table of one Marcus Liebling, who was elderly, small, quick and grey, and who owned a handful of newspapers, including *Tiffany*, and who controlled a satellite or so. Saffron was in froth-of-chiffon mode, which was rare for her. She had to shrug her shoulders back from time to time to keep the dress from falling too low across her bosom. She was not accustomed to either dresses or vamping. Marcus Liebling, as it happened, was as little interested in either as she was, but she hadn't met him before. You never knew.

Saffron did not wait for the menu, but once seated briskly cleared cutlery, napkins and glasses to one side, the better to be able to spread out her papers. He was, as it also happened, not particularly hungry and preferred sales sheets to food. This she had anticipated. The powerful prefer business to dinner, any day.

'Under my editorship,' Saffron was saying, 'subscriptions are already up fourteen per cent. The reps are enthusiastic; new advertisers are clamouring for our business, as the older readers sign off the young ones sign on, and that's after

367

only a couple of months in the new format. We're picking up on the general *Chronicle* turnaround, that's true, but things are looking proportionately good.'

'It's not fourteen per cent' he said, glancing at the column. 'It's thirteen point four. You exaggerate. Be exact. More important than any amount of rounding up. People believe you if you tell the truth to a decimal point.'

A waiter hovered.
'I'm not hungry, don't bother about it,' said Saffron to the waiter. And then remembering her manners said, 'or do you want to eat?'
'It's what I usually do when I come to restaurants,' he said.

He asked the waiter to bring him some soup in a cup, since his guest wouldn't allow him room for a bowl.
'Same here,' said Saffron.
The waiter went.

'We have to find some way of paying the restaurant for its time and work,' observed Sir Marcus Liebling. 'It's usually done by eating the food. Every time you go out the door you have to contrive some way of benefiting others. Remember that. Who on earth brought you up?'
'I brought myself up,' she said.
'You didn't do too bad a job of it,' he conceded, and actually smiled. The waiter brought chicken noodle soup.

'So you're pleased with me,' she asked.

'Not really,' he said. 'What I expected to happen, happened.'

'Jesus,' complained Saffron.

'You have the guts to fire people,' he said. 'That's all it takes to succeed. You have to be a good pruner. The women have got it, the men have lost it. Women understand you have to be cruel to be kind. I'm putting in women everywhere. I liked the old *Chronicle* myself. I liked the pets' page in *Weekend Woman*. I always read it. But it had to go. You were quite right.'

'Couldn't you cheer up a bit?' she asked. 'I'm making you millions.'

'You've saved a few losses, that's all,' he grumbled. '*Weekend Woman* was a useful tax-deductible. Now where am I going to look? Do you only ever eat soup?'

'I eat pizza,' she said.

'That's what it looks like,' said Sir Marcus Liebling. 'Skinny. It isn't good for you. Women should have hips. I don't want to look at your sheets of paper. I take your word for it. What do you want from me? Anything I can do?'

'You could buy me Medusa,' said Saffron.

The now steady in, out, in, out of his soup spoon paused.

'Put in an offer, quick,' said Saffron. 'They're in financial trouble but could be swung around. Buy it now, do nothing for a year, put me in as general manager, then asset-strip. I can turn it around if anyone can. I'll be bored with *Tiffany* by then. I get restless.'

'You fired poor old Peter Max,' said Sir Marcus. 'Don't know how you had the heart. I was a cub reporter with him on *The Argus*, in the old days. He told me how to get rid of fleas in my dog.'

'How?'

'You use a Hoover. Doesn't work on cats. They think of snakes and run for it. But dogs love it.'

'I'm sure you're grateful,' said Saffron. 'But Peter Max ended up with *Pets' Problems* and you own half the communication world, plus the ComArt building.'

'I married the right woman,' said Sir Marcus. 'That's all it takes. The right size capital at the right time. He should have married for money, like I did. Do you think he'll do himself in?'

'I hope not.' She was alarmed.

'So you *are* human,' he said. 'I was beginning to wonder. You're very young to take on Medusa.'

'It's not that I'm so young,' she said. 'It's that they're so old.'

Remember Brian? Whom Nancy ditched when she first came to London, on the grounds that he was boring, insensitive, and probably sexually dysfunctional? Who later married her best friend Beverley, whom he'd made pregnant. Nancy is back with Brian. What a turn up for the books. Beverley discovered she was a lesbian and Brian eventually divorced her. Around the same time, Brian discovered he was a sailor at heart, and since Beverley made some difficulties about access to his little daughter, even to the extent of alleging, quite fantastically, child abuse, he had sold the farm, bought a yacht with the proceeds and taken to seafaring.

Brian looked up Nancy when at Chichester, found her to be sane beyond belief in comparison to Beverley, and she found him, so many years older, wiser, full of sexual affection, and far less certain that he was right. In fact he was positively insecure. They re-fell in love. Brian with his boat and his debts. Nancy with her five per cent slice of the Medusa pizza, a twenty-hour week, which she had finally contrived for herself at a lower salary than any other Publishing Finance expert in town. But enough to pay for a lick of paint and some new saltspar or whatever for Brian's boat. She was vague about nautical terminology.

For Brian's sake, she put up with the sea and those who went down to it in boats. She liked lying on decks in the sun listening to the slip slop of water against a hull. She seldom read a book, or passed a moral judgment. She was happy. One day when the law suits were over she would be step-mother to Brian's daughter.

Beverley, who attributed her conversion to lesbianism to one of Medusa's publications, which she had picked up on the day of Zoe's wake, was calmed rather than aggravated by Brian's getting together with Nancy. It made her feel less guilty. One day, Nancy could see, they would all be back in New Zealand, back home, and friends again. And she would have made good.

And here was Stephanie clumping up the gangplank, talking about publishing, shares, Board meetings, dividends, Layla's delinquency.

'It now turns out,' says Stephie to Nancy, 'that the sponsor, the mystery sponsor, the presumed female sympathetic relative, is no female but a man. What is more, is Layla's lover. I feel so totally betrayed and insulted.'

'He must have put up with a lot,' remarks Nancy. 'What with your ex and all the others.'

'Don't be trivial, Nancy,' said Stephie. 'Years of our lives, all that work and effort, based on a falsehood.'

'It's such a glorious day,' said Nancy. 'Don't worry about it.'

'You've changed,' said Stephanie, reproachfully. 'You're relaxed.'

At which point Brian, bearded and greyly-blond, put his head up from the galley and offered them food — pork and baked beans — and beer. Stephanie pointed out that she was now a vegetarian; but presently relented. She wanted a closer look at Brian, this man whom Nancy had suddenly pulled out of her spinstery hat, to surprise everyone. Women kept on doing it. First there'd be no one, then there'd be someone.

Women in their twenties thought they could do without men altogether, if only it wasn't for sex. In their thirties they thought they could do without men if it wasn't that they needed fathers for their children. In their forties and thereafter they knew they could do without men perfectly well, if it wasn't for companionship and someone to go out with, and someone around so you didn't have to sleep forever in an empty bed: someone just to share a past with, and to look forward to a future with. And as so often what you said you didn't want was what you wanted most, and what you had didn't matter, and what you didn't have mattered most.

The world of the personal, Stephanie thought, was not just political but so complicated it could exhaust you. But what you didn't want, you knew. And what Stephanie didn't want was Medusa betrayed, like Sampson by Delilah; Medusa's tangled, gory locks cleaned up and

373

shorn, so weakened and prettified a man could gaze and gaze and not be turned to stone.

Nancy said she couldn't be bothered to come to the shareholder's meeting. She wanted to do the cross-channel Cherbourg race with Brian. She'd give her proxy to Layla as usual.

Stephanie stamped her foot. A squelch of sea water welled up between the floorboards. The hull was due for caulking. Brian trusted too much to luck, Nancy thought.

'Nancy,' begged Stephanie. 'Please! I'm not asking for your proxy. I'm just asking you to come up for the meeting and just listen to what's going on, and vote.'
'Oh well,' said Nancy. 'OK. I reckon the Cherbourg race is out, Bri, until this boat is properly seaworthy.'
'She crossed the Pacific and then the Atlantic OK,' said Brian. 'What harm can the Channel do?' He still hated wasting money. Some things in a man can never be cured.

Stephanie went next to St Stephen's Hospital, an old and dreary institution in the Fulham Road, to see Johnny. Johnny had AIDS, and was hospitalised. Richard was HIV, but showed no sign of crumbling yet. Johnny refused to let Richard visit. He did not want his dissolution witnessed by those he loved. He let Stephanie visit because he had never been sure he liked her, and he certainly didn't love her. Let her see what there was to be seen. It would do her good. As it happened, she scarcely seemed to notice his physical state. Even in this his extremis, she refused to acknowledge the facts of AIDS. Some people were like that. Flat-earthers, UFO watchers, Marxists — all determined to believe what they wanted to believe, not what was observably true. Truth, like reality, is what doesn't go away when you stop believing in it, but try telling Stephanie that.

One of the problems with dying of AIDS was that your mind stayed clear. Unless of course it affected the brain and you died raving or half-witted, but this had not happened to Johnny. People came along and told him he'd had a good life and young men half his age were dying, though the epidemic seemed to be waning, and all kinds of things he didn't want to hear and didn't particularly help. Stephanie would think only about Medusa, and she was speechifying. Well, he was a captive audience and she'd always loved those.

'The price of female freedom', said Stephanie, 'is eternal vigilance. Women have got so complacent it's dangerous. Look what happened in Afghanistan. One minute women are free, educated, working, earning, rebuilding a society, nurses, lawyers, engineers — the next day the Taliban sweep in, and women aren't allowed to earn, have to stay home, have no way of feeding their children; if they leave the house at all it has to be in a shroud, and not a patch of flesh showing or they get beaten to death by young male militants. Can you imagine what it must be like, looking out at the world from behind a veil? Everything dim, blurrred?'

'My eyesight hasn't been too good lately,' said Johnny.

'Medusa has to continue,' went on Stephanie, 'and in the old tradition. It has to continue the struggle. Any movement survives on the integrity of its writers, its teachers, its leaders. Layla is still my friend, but she is no longer Medusa's friend. She doesn't care about principle, only about profit and her own image.'

'I don't know about that,' said Johnny. 'She sold the Chelsea house so she could pay for my treatment here, and didn't tell a soul. Not even you knew that. The money will just about see me out.'
'Surely the State pays?' said Stephanie. 'I don't approve of private medicine. Typical of Layla. Generous to a fault but always the wrong money at the wrong time, and completely whimsical. Playing into the hands of the enemy!'
'What enemy are we talking about, Stephanie?' His voice was feeble, his face all skin stretched across bones, his eyelids seemed scarcely able to cover his eyes. She stayed oblivious. Most people winced at the sight of him and tried not to let him see. He was almost grateful to her.
'The Great Universal Enemy, Johnny,' said Stephanie. 'Blindness to what is going on. Like

the Great Universal Theory, knowing everything in one swoop. The one great basic explanation of all things. Will you be well enough to come to the shareholders' meeting on Monday?'

'I may be dead by Monday, they say. The Great Universal Death, everything gone in one swoop.'

'Don't be so silly,' said Stephanie. 'If you're not feeling up to it I'll have your vote by proxy. Every vote will count on Monday. Even yours and Richard's. Especially your two, actually.'
'You're too late, Stephie,' said Johnny, not without satisfaction. 'Richard signed his share over to me, to assuage his guilt. And then some girl came along with a lawyer and offered me two thousand pounds for them. I signed some form or other — I can still just about write if someone holds my hand. My Medusa shares are gone, finished, kaput. Nothing to do with me. Your two token half-male shares. Two gays making one token male.'
'Why did you do a thing like that? I don't believe this!'
'There's a new drug out. It costs five hundred a week for a four week course.'
'Who was it who came?'
'You remember the woman who killed herself? Richard took some brilliant photographs at the funeral. One got into the Photography Year Book. Zoe, was her name. One of you lot, I think it was Layla, started making speeches and I left. It was her daughter came to visit. That was

nice of her. Pretty girl. She didn't stay long.'
'Saffron,' said Stephanie, dismayed. 'Saffron!'

Johnny closed his eyes as well as he could
and slept.

Move now to a grand party for grand people
in a London hotel. The Mercedes and BMWs
fill the driveway faster than the valets can
park them, or the chauffeurs get out to circle
the Park. It's mayhem. Security men cluster
and gossip and stare, and judge, and indulge
every form of grim paranoia. Taxis draw up
and pretty girls with long legs alight, and are
nodded through. There are politicians here, and
the gay diplomatic set, and stars and captains of
industry and a few carefully selected journalists.
And Jemal is there, and Saffron, wearing black,
as are all the women, and showing a lot of
translucent limb. She comes in on Sir Marcus
Liebling's arm. She is not having an affair with
him, but neither are averse to the rumour that
she is. They just get on together. He instructs.
She listens.

'My dear boy,' says Sir Marcus to Jemal. 'Dear
lad, how goes your Empire? Does it survive
Islam?'
'How goes yours, sir? Does it survive the
computer?' Jemal is polite, but edgy.
'Horrible things, computers,' says Sir Marcus,
genially. 'Ruin the eyes. But if people want to
use them they have to learn to read first. Which
benefits me and mine, and the whole print
empire. Computers lead to more of everything,

not less of some things. How rich in paper is the paperless office. This young woman here on my arm is not what you think. She is what they call a bright cookie.'

Jemal turns his eyes upon Saffron, whom hitherto he had ignored, supposing her to be in the general run of denatured female so often apparent at these occasions. She had clear, bright, intelligent eyes, and reminded him of Layla. He smiled. There was a slight pause before she smiled back. He liked that.

'And the young will rule the world,' said Jemal.

'She has a proposition to make,' said Sir Marcus. 'But not of the kind you might at first glance suppose. It concerns the publishing house Medusa. You know Medusa?'

'I know Medusa,' said Jemal. 'My child.'

The next morning Roland was on Bull's doorstep at half past seven hammering on the door, as once Bull had hammered on Roland's father's door. These things are catching. After some five minutes' sleep, Saffron, nightgowned, opened the door. Roland lunged at her.

'You didn't come home last night! Where were you? Who were you with?'
He tried to shake her. She wriggled free.
'What's the matter with you, Roland? I wasn't with anyone. I'm not answerable to you anyway. I go where I like.'
'We're together.'
'We're not,' she said. 'Not any longer. You don't own me. Go away. I've got to get a couple of hours' sleep in before work.'

A young man appeared behind Saffron: he was good-looking, fleshy, body-pierced, vague-eyed, shaven-headed.

'Who the fuck are you?' he asked. 'Leave my sister alone. Get the hell out of this house.'
'You know who I am,' said Roland. 'Or are you too ecstasied out to remember? I sat on this doorstep with you often enough. What happened to you?'
'But you're a suit,' Sampson said, dejected: and

then turning to his sister Saffron said, 'What are you doing with a suit?'

Sampson was a mixture of non-comprehension and nervous energy: it felt dangerous to Roland. Bull appeared, dressing-gowned, behind his children: he was sulky and hungover.

'I'll call the police if you don't go away,' he said. 'I'm not having my daughter persecuted like this.'

'Saffron,' begged Roland, 'don't do this to me.'

'I'm sorry,' she said, in helpless mode, which he didn't believe one bit. 'I can't get tangled up in this kind of emotional thing. I've got this lot to look after. Look at them: the moment I turn my back they're unemployable. I've got no time for anything else.'

And Sampson pushed him out and Saffron slammed the door in Roland's face. Roland stood on the step and wept a little and then went round to his brother's house for breakfast.

Rafe and Marly live in a little Georgian house
stuck between housing blocks for the desperate at
the back of Mornington Crescent. It is furnished
in the minimalist style, fast littering up with the
necessities and comforts of domestic life. Marly
is frizzy-haired, academic-looking, earnest, kind.
She is training to be a psychoanalyst. They are
having breakfast and comforting the distraught
Roland. Gabrielle sits in her high-chair and stares
in friendship at her uncle. She has the look of
her grandfather Hamish about her: she bangs
the back of her spoon into her cereal from time
to time to celebrate her contentment. Patiently,
her parents clear up after her.

'I'm glad you want to share this with us,
Roland,' says Marly. 'It brings us more together.
We need to be more of a family. What you
had with Saffron wasn't love, it was neurotic
dependency. All you had to look forward to
was a whole set of negative emotions. Be glad
you're out of it.'

'I see it rather differently,' says Rafe. 'Why was
she with you in the first place? She could have
had anyone.'
'Well, thanks,' says Roland, bitterly.
'That's what brothers are *for*,' says Rafe. 'Saffron
wanted information about Medusa. Once she'd

got it, that was the end of it. She lost interest.'

'I can't believe that,' said Roland, but he was beginning to.

Gabrielle gurgled and beamed, and made them all feel better.

They were all there at the Board Meeting on the Monday morning. The Furies, as some called them: Layla, Stephanie, Nancy, Alice. And Saffron, of course, who parked her car in a Director's parking space without so much as a by your leave. Rosalie and Wendy were there, and everyone else who ever spoke up, and women whose names no one could ever remember, all of whose lives had been changed, one way or another, by the pursuit of feminism. They made a lively, intelligent, attractive, undisappointed lot. Age had been kind to them. They had lived by mind and principle, not by their looks, and it showed. You could imagine that the best of their lives was in front of them, not behind them.

They had got things wrong, personally and politically, but who ever got everything right? They had wept, screamed, shouted, protested, loved and laughed more than most. If the separatists had won over the socialists and the radicals, if young women everywhere assumed men were an optional extra, a decoration not a necessity, not essential to their well-being, or survival, that too in time would shift and change, and become more merciful. Men are people too. Gender, like the state in Marxist aspiration, might in the end wither away, and

385

be relevant only in bed and the approach to it, and the aftermath. There is no harm in living in hope.

On shelves and in showcases all around stood Zoe's book *Lost Women*. She had lost her life but saved Medusa, at least for a time. She had also created Saffron. Saffron took her time and entered the meeting last, and late. Faces turned as the door opened. She wore white jeans, a yellow shirt and a grey baseball cap. She came in a flood of light.

Layla was already on to item two of the Agenda.

'In view of the lack of profitability shown in the accounts and our inability to pay a dividend or redeem preference shares, there are certain proposals I must put to the shareholders. Saffron, what are you doing at this meeting?'

'I'm a shareholder too,' Saffron said.

Stephanie got to her feet.

'If Saffron Meadows is a shareholder it's only because she bullied poor Johnny on his deathbed, until he sold his miserable two shares to her for two thousand pounds. I vote she be expelled from this meeting. We do not operate within some kind of calculating male subterfuge, but according to a meaningful female consensus.'

'Johnny was a man,' said Saffron, unperturbed. 'If you are all so principled, why give a man a vote in the first place? At least I'm female. Look at it like that and be glad. I have a legal right to stay and vote and that's what I'm doing.'

'Johnny wasn't exactly all that male anyway,' said Layla. 'And at the time it seemed OK to let him have his shares. Everything always seems OK at the time. No one thought anyone would ever be unreasonable or press a legal point home. But this is the age of lawyers, contract, and enforcement. Caring and sharing, forget it. Saffron stays.'

'Get to the point, Layla,' said Stephanie.

'I'm resigning,' said Layla. 'That's the point. I don't want to be Chairperson any more. Not only that, I'm tired of being Managing Director. This leaves Medusa with two options. We find someone as good as me, or better than me, to take Medusa forward into the new century. Or we sell out. Personally I favour the second option. This way at least we get out, all of us, with some money.'

'You really believe you are irreplaceable, Layla?' Stephanie was quite pink with indignation, on her feet, and showing no signs of sitting down.

'I am irreplaceable,' said Layla flatly. 'You're all good women but hopeless at business. But as I understand the major shareholders intend to make a fuss I will do you the courtesy of examining the first option. Who are the front-runners for Chairperson from within our ranks? Stephanie, Nancy, Alice? Any one of them, Managing Director? Of Medusa? You're joking! Let me take the least likely, last. Alice as Managing Director. Alice is more interested in life forms on Sirius than in the philosophy of feminism, or in feminist publishing. She'd rather consult the *I Ching* than the sales figures. I don't deny what Alice did for us in the beginning. She gave us our language, our spirit, our integrity. She was our mother. She swung the whole educational system of this country in our direction. But then the Mother Goddess took her away and claimed her as High Priestess and swallowed her up.'

'You are too bad, Layla,' said Alice. 'I only came here to vote, and under protest at that. Today is the summer solstice.'
'So I take it you won't be voting for me, but for Stephanie,' said Layla. 'Eleven per cent down the drain. Now how about Nancy? She's steady, rational, and brilliant at the books. She can tell you where your next ten thousand pounds is coming from, or not coming from, but she never had the gift of bringing it in. Frankly, boring. Impossible to envisage as Managing Director. And she's found her man, and I wish her well, but honestly, she can hardly wait to get back to catch the tide. Sorry, Nancy, but that's about it, isn't it'

'Well thank you very much, Layla,' said Nancy. 'After all that, I'm going now. Stephanie can have my proxy.'
She stalked out, but changed her mind at the door, and stayed.
'Another five per cent down the drain,' said Layla. 'And another friend lost. But that, alas,

388

is what I'm here to do; to lose friends. It's the price I have to pay if Medusa is to be saved. Now, Stephie. Fucking stuffy Stephie. Whatever changed? I've left a lot to Stephanie of late and where's that got us? Down the PC drain. No one wants to know about women as victims. These days it's girls on top. Medusa has to be in the forefront, she can't afford to lag behind. Our readers can't live by gender alone; and women mustn't end up as unpleasant to men as they ever were to us.'

'You're joking,' said Stephanie. 'You're out of your mind.'
'You made the most sacrifices, Stephie,' said Layla. 'I can see it's hard for you to move on. But to suffer and be good is not necessarily to acquire wisdom. Another nineteen per cent gone. Add Alice's eleven, plus Nancy's five. Stephie, my erstwhile friend. We set great store by friendship, but sometimes friendships fail, as marriages do. We should have thought of that, we who gave up family life as a matter of principle.'

'Or for love,' said Saffron, from the back. 'That old thing.'

'That young woman always has to be drawing attention to herself,' complained Rosalie, but no one paid any attention.

'Layla,' said Wendy, 'this is tough stuff you're giving us. No one's ever going to forgive you.

You can't expect any of us to actually vote for you after this.'

Stephanie was sitting again, her head in her hands.

'People don't get forgiven for telling the truth,' observed Saffron, 'but on the other hand they often get what they want.' Hostile faces turned to look at her.
'Without Stephanie, Alice and Nancy,' Layla went on, 'who is there? No one. Small publishing houses live and breathe by the vision, passion and commitment of a driving force. We found it in feminism; feminism found it in us. We were swept along with the tidal wave of a great cause, on the crest of anger. The wave did its work, receded, passed on elsewhere, and has left us floundering in the shallows. Stephanie, Nancy and Alice, all three of you, you need to bow out of Medusa now. Resign, along with me. New brooms sweep cleaner if the old rubbish is gone. Alice, will you resign?'
'No,' said Alice.
'Nancy?' enquired Layla.
'No,' said Nancy.
'Stephanie?' asked Layla.
'You're out of your fucking mind,' said Stephanie.
'This being the case,' said Layla, 'I have no choice but to ask the meeting to vote on the following proposal; that Medusa allows itself to be bought. We have two offers. Marcus Liebling

is an interested party. ComArt is diversifying into the world of books.'

'Liebling!' shrieked Rosalie. 'Medusa sell out to the gutter press! Never — '
'Or there's Chapter Books,' said Layla, 'one of the few small publishing houses left, with a good list and capacity for growth. I understand they're prepared to make us an offer. Not such a good one. Mingy in fact. And honestly, the future of publishing is not with the small presses, however much emotional attachment we have to them. Medusa is dreary enough already. So dreary and full of self-pity the magazines won't even accept our ads.'

'You mean Zoe's daughter Saffron wouldn't take them,' interceded Wendy. 'Everyone knows she has a grudge.'
'You'll need Saffron's votes to swing it, Layla,' said Nancy, who'd been doing sums.
'I will,' said Layla. 'And I don't know which way she'll jump.'
'You'll need more than that, Layla,' said Stephanie. 'You are the only person in this room who wants to sell, and it's who's in the room that counts.'

And in triumph Stephanie produced the printed booklet which had been on everyone's chair when they came in, and demanded those assembled turn to page three, section four.
'You will see here,' she said, 'that under Rule 16A of our constitution proxy votes are

391

disallowed on a majority vote of a quorate meeting.'

'What have we come to!' lamented Layla. 'Stephanie appealing to an agenda technicality! How very male. I told you this was the age of lawyers, and Stephanie's living with one. As it happens, Stephanie, I'm not using proxies. Saffron now owns the votes I used to hold by proxy. She was sold them by our mystery backer, only yesterday. Saffron is now a thirty-two per cent shareholder, counting the two from Johnny. Shall we take a vote? That we sell Medusa? For the proposition?'

No hands rose other than Layla's and Saffron's. 'I win,' said Layla. 'And thank you, Johnny, wherever you are. Johnny died early this morning, in St Stephen's. He was our great friend.' She allowed them only the briefest of pauses, to take the news in. 'OK, we sell Medusa. Do we sell to Chapter Books?'

All hands rose save Layla and Saffron's. 'To Liebling?' asked Layla. All hands stayed down except Layla's and Saffron's.

'Medusa sells to Liebling,' said Layla.

There was silence in the room. Some were taken up with grief for Johnny, others for the loss of Medusa, others for friendship shattered: all with the suddenness of events.

'See it as a new beginning,' said Saffron. 'Not an end,' but even she could see her words fell on stony ground.

'No one wants to strip and dance, I suppose?' said Layla.
'As a kind of closing ceremony?' But not one of them did. The Goddess had deserted them.

'Oh well,' said Layla, 'that's that,' and she walked out, followed by Saffron, out of Medusa and into the street.

People cannot bear too much reality. Medusa's hair will in the end get washed and shorn: there's no help in it. It falls now in a silky cloud, no longer in a wreath of twisting snakes. How pretty Medusa looks, how unravaged her face, like Saffron's. Medusa turns no one to stone; her power is gone; she is thoroughly approved of, upsets nobody and could be any gender at all. Layla gets marvelled at, Saffron gets admired. So it goes.

Only Stephanie can't forgive: fucking stuffy Stephie. This time the rift can't be healed: it went too deep. It hurts them both; they miss each other dreadfully. They may go to each other's funeral but don't bet on it. In the meantime they scour the press-cuttings for mention of each other.

Alice gave up the Goddess, quite suddenly, one day, as people will give up smoking. Decide and do it. Perhaps she felt the Mother in the Highest was turning her brain to porridge and got alarmed, as once beloved Zoe was alarmed by the consequences of child-bearing. Not enough to *be*, a woman has to *do*, as well.

Alice stares into space a lot. Ask her what she's thinking of and she says 'A book I'm writing in my head.' Ask her what it's about and she says 'If I knew, I wouldn't have to write it.'

Nancy sailed off into the sunset with Brian, but in a new boat which didn't leak. All four women made a million or so each out of the sale of Medusa, so really now they can do as they please. Four women who changed the world, because it seemed simpler than changing themselves. Big women, not little women, that was the point, and still flourishing.

THE END

Other titles in the Charnwood Library Series:

LEGACIES
Janet Dailey

The sequel to THE PROUD AND THE FREE. It is twenty years since the feud within his family began, but Lije Stuart, son of the Cherokee chief The Blade, had never forgotten the killing of his grandfather. Now, a promising legal career beckons, and also the love of his childhood sweetheart, Diane Parmalee, the daughter of a US Army officer. Yet as it reawakens, their love is beset by the beginning of civil war.

'L' IS FOR LAWLESS
Sue Grafton

World War II fighter pilot Johnny Lee had died and his grandson was trying to claim military funeral benefits, but none of the authorities have any record of Fighter J. Lee. Was the old man once a US spy? When PI Kinsey Millhone is asked to straighten things out, she finds herself pursued by a psychopath bearing a forty-year-old grudge . . .

BLOOD LINES
Ruth Rendell

This is a collection of long and short stories by Ruth Rendell that will linger in the mind.

THE SUN IN GLORY
Harriet Hudson

When industrialist William Potts sets himself to build a flying machine, his adopted daughter, Rosie, works through the years as his mechanic. In 1906 Pegasus is almost ready, and onto the scene comes Jake Smith, a man who has as deep a love of the air as Rosie herself. But Jake sparks off a deadly rivalry, and the triumph of flight twists into tragedy.

A WOMAN SCORNED
M. R. O'Donnell

Five years after the tragedy that ruined her fifteenth birthday, Judith Carty returns to Castle Moore and resumes her flirtation with its heir, Rick Bellingham. The tragic events of the past forge a special bond between the young couple, but there are those who have a vested interest in the failure of the romance.

PLAINER STILL
Catherine Cookson

Following the success of her previous collection of essays and poems, LET ME MAKE MYSELF PLAIN, Catherine Cookson has compiled a further selection of thoughts, recollections, and observations on life — and death — together with another collection of the poems she prefers to describe as 'prose on short lines'.

THE LOST WORLD
Michael Crichton

The successor to JURASSIC PARK.
It is now six years since the secret disaster of Jurassic Park, when that extraordinary dream of science and imagination came to a crashing end — the dinosaurs destroyed, and the park dismantled. There are rumours that something has survived . . .

MORNING, NOON & NIGHT
Sidney Sheldon

When Harry Stanford, one of the wealthiest men in the world, mysteriously drowns, it sets off a chain of events that reverberates around the globe. At the family gathering following the funeral, a beautiful young woman appears, claiming to be Harry's daughter. Is she genuine, or is she an impostor?

FACING THE MUSIC
Jayne Torvill and Christopher Dean

The world's most successful and popular skating couple tell their own story, from their working-class childhoods in Nottingham to world stardom. Finally, they describe how they created their own show, FACE THE MUSIC, with a superb corps of international ice dancers.

ORANGES AND LEMONS
Jeanne Whitmee

When Shirley Rayner is evacuated from London's East End, she finds herself billeted with the theatre's most romantic couple, Tony and Leonie Darrent. She becomes firm friends with their daughter, Imogen, and the two girls dream of making their names on the stage. But they have forgotten the very different backgrounds from which they come.

HALF HIDDEN
Emma Blair

Holly Morgan, a nurse in a hospital on Nazi-occupied Jersey, falls in love with a young German doctor, Peter Schmidt, and is racked by guilt. Can their love survive the future together or will the war destroy all their hopes and dreams?

THE GREAT TRAIN ROBBERY
Michael Crichton

In Victorian London, where lavish wealth and appalling poverty exist side by side, one man navigates both worlds with ease. Rich, handsome and ingenious, Edward Pierce preys on the most prominent of the well-to-do as he cunningly orchestrates the crime of his century.

THIS CHILD IS MINE
Henry Denker

Lori Adams, a young, unmarried actress, gives up her baby boy for adoption with great reluctance. She feels that she and the baby's father, Brett, are not in a position to provide their child with all he deserves. But when, two years later, life has improved dramatically for Lori and Brett, they want their child returned . . .

THE LOST DAUGHTERS
Jeanne Whitmee

At school, Cathy and Rosalind have one thing in common: each is the child of a single parent. For them both, the transition to adulthood is far from easy — until their unexpected reunion. Working together, the two friends take a bold step that will help them to become independent women.

THE DEVIL YOU KNOW
Josephine Cox

When Sonny Fareham overhears a private conversation between her lover and his wife, she realises she is in great danger. Shocked and afraid, she flees to the north of England to make a new life — but never far away is the one person who wants to destroy everything that she now holds dear.

A LETHAL INVOLVEMENT
Clive Egleton

When Captain Simon Oakham of the Royal Army pay Corps goes A.W.O.L. immediately after a suspicious interview with the security service, Peter Ashton is asked to track him down. The key to it all is an embittered woman whose unsuspecting knowledge of a lethal involvement makes her especially vulnerable.

THE WAY WE WERE
Marie Joseph

This is a collection of some of Marie Joseph's most outstanding short stories, and is the companion volume to WHEN LOVE WAS LIKE THAT. With compassion, insight and humour, these stories explore the themes of love — its hopes, joys, disappointments and reconciliations.

EXTREME DENIAL
David Morrell

When CIA agent Stephen Decker is sent on a sensitive mission to Italy, his partner is Brian McKittrick, the incompetent and embittered son of the former chairman of the National Security Council. Disobeying orders throughout the mission, McKittrick makes one final mistake: sleeping with the enemy.

THE WOOD BEYOND
Reginald Hill

Seeing the wood for the trees is a problem shared by Andy Dalziel and Edgar Wield, the latter in his investigations into bones found at a pharmaceutical research centre, and the former in his dangerous involvement with animal rights activist Amanda Marvell.

RAGE OF THE INNOCENT
Frederick E. Smith

The first of a trilogy.

Young Harry Miles clashes with Michael Chadwick, son of a wealthy landowner, and sows the seeds of a lifetime's conflict. When the 1914 – 18 war breaks out, Harry is driven into volunteering and finds himself under Chadwick's command. Taking his revenge, Chadwick makes Harry a machine gunner . . .

MOTHER OF GOD
David Ambrose

Tessa Lambert has just created the first viable artificial intelligence programme — a discovery so controversial that she must keep it a secret even from her colleagues at Oxford University. But soon there is to be a hacker stalking her on the Internet: a serial killer who is about to give her invention its own terrifying and completely malevolent life . . .

THE ANDROMEDA STRAIN
Michael Crichton

When *Project Scoop* sends satellites into outerspace to 'collect organisms and dust for study', one of them crashes into the town of Piedmont, Arizona. Soon after, all but two of the inhabitants are found dead from a strange disease. The scientists must trace what is causing the horrifying virus before it spreads . . .

TO WAR WITH WHITAKER
Countess of Ranfurly

When World War II broke out, Dan Ranfurly was dispatched to the Middle East with his faithful valet, Whitaker. These are the diaries of his young wife, Hermione, who, defying the War Office, raced off in hot pursuit of her husband. When Dan was taken prisoner, Hermione vowed never to return home until they were reunited.

IN PRESENCE OF MY FOES
Frederick E. Smith

Sequel to RAGE OF THE INNOCENT.
Harry Miles is now recovered from his war wounds, but a mysterious and compelling urge drives him back to the Front. He faces the menace of Michael Chadwick, his commanding officer and life-long rival, and the fearsome German offensive of March 1918.

YEARS OF THE FURY
Frederick E. Smith

The third volume of the trilogy which began with RAGE OF THE INNOCENT and continued with IN PRESENCE OF MY FOES.

The First World War has ended and, with Harry Miles back from France, he and Mary are hoping to settle down to their married life at last. But they have not taken account of their two unrelenting enemies.

FAMILY TREES
Kate Alexander

Catherine Carew fills her life with good works and is a pillar of the community. But in her distant university days she was a very different person. One night's indiscretion leaves her with a burden of guilt and regret that overshadows her later years — until a stranger appears on her doorstep . . .

INDIAN SUMMER
James Mitchell

Mixed blood courses through Veronica Higgins' veins, resulting in an exotic beauty. But to the expatriates in India at the height of the British Raj she is just another 'bloody chee-chee'. When her Aunt Poppy falls in love with an English industrialist, the three set off for his homeland. The arrival of one of England's richest men with two exquisitely beautiful women causes a flurry of excitement . . .

VANISHING POINT
Morris West

When Carl Strassberger, the son of an old
New York banking family, renounces his
position in the business to become an
artist, his place is taken by his brother-in-law,
Larry Lucas. But when Larry disappears, Carl
must put himself at risk as he investigates
those who live 'on the dangerous edge of
things'.

THE RUNAWAY
John Grisham

In Biloxi, Mississippi, a landmark trial
begins routinely, then swerves mysteriously
off course. The jury is behaving strangely,
and at least one juror is convinced that
he is being watched. Is the jury somehow
being manipulated or even controlled? If so,
by whom? And, more importantly, why?

SHADOWS OF THE PAST
Palma Harcourt

When Christopher Grayson, a young Oxford
don, decides to trace his family history, he
learns that during the Second World War
the de Mourvilles were condemned as Nazi
sympathisers. Even worse, his grandfather
was accused of crimes against humanity.
But someone is on Christopher's trail,
willing to kill in order to keep a tragic
secret.

YEAR OF THE TIGER
Jack Higgins

When Paul Chavasse looks out of his window on a November evening, he is unaware that the figure standing opposite knows a great deal about his past. Back in 1961, Chavasse — now chief of a little-known section of British Intelligence — had been captured by the Chinese. When he had at last escaped he knew that he could be taking with him the means of his betrayal.

THAT CAMDEN SUMMER
LaVyrle Spencer

It is 1916 and Roberta Jewett has returned to the town where she was raised. But in Camden, Maine, a woman divorced is a woman shunned. Only Gabriel Farley treats her with respect. Although the chemistry between them is undeniable, they fight it. Then, a brutal act of violence forces them to aknowledge the powerful feelings that have grown between them.

PASSIONATE TIMES
Emma Blair

When Corporal Reith Douglas was injured during the Second World War, he lost his memory. But once he returns to his wife, Irene, in Glasgow, he gradually recalls the joy of his early married life, and the pain he suffered when Irene declared her love for a renowned villain. Little does he realise that he could well recapture the passionate times of his past.

NOT JUST A SOLDIER'S WAR
Betty Burton

For Lu Wilmott, the call to Spain is irresistible. Signing up as a driver, she breaks the last link with her past and becomes Eve. Her work takes her close to figures of many nationalities, but it is the country and its people in the struggle against Franco that have the greatest effect on her.

THE WITCH OF EXMOOR
Margaret Drabble

The Palmer family and their children are coming to the end of an enjoyable meal. As usual, their conversation is brought back to their eccentric mother, Frieda, who has abandoned them and gone off to live alone on Exmoor. She has always been a monster mother with a mysterious past. What is she plotting against them now?

LEWIN'S MEAD
E. V. Thompson

The sequel to the bestselling novel BECKY
When artist Fergus Vincent forsakes the Bristol slums of Lewin's Mead he leaves behind him Becky, the street urchin whom he loved and married. After Becky is struck down in a cholera epidemic, she is cared for by Simon McAllister, a blind musician. But she never gives up hope that one day Fergus will return.

ENDPEACE
Jon Cleary

When Detective Inspector Scobie Malone's host, the wealthy Sydney newspaper magnate Sir Harry Huxwood, is shot dead in his own bed, it is Malone's job to name the killer. He uncovers the stuff of headlines, including a family dogfight over millions of dollars.

TO THE HILT
Dick Francis

Artist Alexander Kinloch's peaceful existence on a remote Scottish mountain is shattered when he returns home one day to find a group of strangers waiting for him. The days that follow contain more danger than he could ever have imagined.

WISH LIST
Fern Michaels

Hollywood actress Ariel Hart has become tired of the empty glamour, so she returns to the place where she was once truly happy — where she was plain Aggie Bixby, in love with a dark-eyed boy named Felix. Then she comes across wealthy rancher Lex Sanders, and there is something familiar about those smouldering eyes . . .